14

Praise for *The Fallen*

A great sequel to the second installment in The Light Bringer trilogy, this book takes the story to a whole new level as it depicts good and evil in the world.

—**Dr. Tom Hill**, coauthor of *Chicken Soup for the Entrepreneur's Soul*

The team that brought you *The Light Bringer* returns with an even more engrossing tale of good vs. evil. Combining elements of police procedural and supernatural, *The Fallen* will grab readers and take them on a wild ride.

—**Vicki Erwin**, owner of Main Street Books

Better than the first—*The Fallen* starts off where *The Light Bringer* left off and refuses to blur into grays, tackling mortality and death with compassion and care. Drawing together a story that feels personal and sincere, readers can draw hope from this supernatural thriller, even though it doesn't shy away from dark themes. Fast-paced and easy to read, it is a standout novel and great addition to a series. I'd love to see turned into a televised show!

—**Pat Hrebec**, owner of Paperbacks Etc.

The Fallen is a worthy successor to *The Light Bringer*! Amazing analogies, compelling conclusions, and crime fighting at its otherworldly best!

—**Robin Tidwell**, author of *Reduced* and
owner of All on the Same Page Bookstore

Magic happened when authors Chris DiGiuseppi and Mike Force penned *The Fallen*. Gripping and thought provoking, this second installment of *The Light Bringer* takes readers on a heart-pounding supernatural journey into the afterlife.

—**Janet Bettag**, author of *Normal* and
contributing writer for *Barter Magazine*

The Fallen had me at the prologue! It is a fast-paced adventure that takes you on a ride through the realms of good and evil. It's a thought provoking read that will leave you thinking about *The Fallen* long after you put it down.

—**Kim Reese**, administrative assistant

THE FALLEN

The Light Bringer: Book Two

CHRIS DIGIUSEPPI
AND
MIKE FORCE

Health Communications, Inc.
Deerfield Beach, Florida

www.hcibooks.com

The Library of Congress Cataloging-in-Publication Data
is available through the Library of Congress.

ISBN-13: 978-0-7573-1713-2
ISBN-10: 0-7573-1713-8
ISBN-13: 978-0-7573-1714-9 (e-book)
ISBN-10: 0-7573-1714-6 (e-book)

Publisher: Health Communications, Inc.
        3201 S.W. 15th Street
        Deerfield Beach, FL 33442–8190

Cover design by Larissa Hise Henoch
Interior design and formatting by Lawna Patterson Oldfield

*To Patty and Nicole, along with
Ryan, Michael, Ashley, Kevin, Samantha,
Jacob, Emma, and Christopher.
Light flows from the love of a family
pushing out the darkness.*

PROLOGUE

LIEUTENANT ALAN CRANE PEERED DOWN THE center aisle of the church to where two uniformed police officers stood.

As he approached, one of them said, "She's right here, Lieutenant," pointing to something down on the floor. Alan nodded and made his way past them to stare at a tiny old woman lying facedown between the pews. A large pool of blood formed around her head, then spread out like tiny rivers cutting pathways through the grout of the gray tile floor.

Alan began counting the stab wounds on her back out loud pointing to each so he could remember how many there were: "eight, nine, ten . . . "

He was soon distracted by something that caught his attention.

"Patrolman," he yelled to one of the officers standing nearby.

The officer made his way closer to where Alan was studying the body. "Yes, sir?"

"Who found the body?"

The officer pointed to the other side of the church at a tall thin man. "A priest, Father Sedrick Burke."

"Have him join me over here. I need to ask him some questions."

The officer nodded and walked away to retrieve the priest. Moments later an older man dressed in black pants and a dark shirt, which displayed a white tab collar distinguishing him as clergy, approached Alan and gazed at the body. His face was pale white, and Alan thought that he looked as though he were going to vomit. Alan walked behind him, and the priest turned his gaze so he could no longer see the bloody scene.

"Father, I understand you were the one who found her."

"That's correct," said the priest, as tiny droplets of sweat formed on his forehead. He wiped them onto his sleeve and took a deep breath, obviously shaken by the murder.

"Who is she?"

"Her name is Sister Lucille Franconi," the priest answered, with a quiver in his voice.

"Who could have done this, Father?" asked Alan, as he watched the priest's expressions closely.

Father Burke shook his head, and his gaze returned to the body. Alan placed his hand on the priest's shoulder. "Father, don't look over there; concentrate on me. I know this is a shock, but I need your help. Who could have done this to her?"

The priest looked at Alan. His eyes filled up with tears as he whispered, "Nobody wanted to hurt her. She had no enemies. She was a missionary and has helped hundreds of people. Everyone loved her."

Alan nodded. "Tell me how you found her."

The priest drew forth a wadded-up tissue from his pocket and dabbed his eyes. "I arrived early this morning to prepare for Mass. I noticed something in the center aisle as I entered from the back and thought that a banner had fallen from the ceiling." He paused for a moment and pointed upward. Several large purple-and-white banners hung motionless. His gaze refocused on Alan. "I flipped on the lights and found her. I notified the police at once."

"You walked back out and called the police, or did you approach Sister Lucille's body?" asked Alan.

"I walked out and called from the office phone, which is located off the vestibule," replied the priest, pointing toward the back of the church.

Alan turned and looked in the direction of the body, as did the priest. "So none of those footprints are yours?"

As the priest looked at the shoe prints around the body, he shook his head again. "No, but it looks like there are more than one set."

Alan confirmed, in a concerned tone, "Yes—there are, in fact, twelve."

CHAPTER 1

Fear the Wind

CURTIS NORMAN LIVED WITH HIS MOTHER in a run-down shack that sat in the middle of their land, located on the outskirts of a small rural town called Mossy Grove. He was twenty years old and helped his mother run the family farm, or what was left of it. Since his father had died three years ago, the farm had slowly deteriorated, and portions had had to be sold off in order for him and his mother to survive. He felt lost and alone in life, with no real sense of direction, since he had nothing to look forward to.

Despite his depression, he had an upbeat demeanor today because he had been invited to attend a meeting with some local boys who had started a club. He knew very little about the club other than the fact that it was led by Johnny Bartel, who was a few years older than he and the person who had invited him to attend. Everyone was supposed to meet at the old barn on the McCallister farm at 10:00 PM.

He glanced down to his wrist at the tattered cheap silver watch that had once belonged to his father. His mind wandered back to the day of his father's funeral and the cold dark feeling of emptiness that had consumed him. A vivid picture of the grave site appeared in his mind as he recalled looking at his father's cheaply made wooden casket, which had cost his mother so much money that they had had to go without food for three days after the ceremony. His stomach twitched as he recalled how horrible those three long days had been. He and his mother would have gone longer without eating had it not been for Old Man Burnstein, who owned the small grocery store in town and had brought food over on the third day. After a few months, his mother had tried to pay him back for the groceries, but the old man wouldn't take it. Curtis could still recall the conversation as though it had just happened.

"When that bad storm hit," Mr. Burnstein had said, "and the entire roof of my store had been torn off, your husband helped me repair it and paid for the materials himself. He never asked for anything in return. He saved my livelihood and my family." Mr. Burnstein had half smiled and looked extremely appreciative.

Curtis remembered working on the roof of the store with his father. While they were replacing some of the shingles, he had asked, "Why are we doing this, Pop?"

His father had finished hammering and wiped his forehead. "Because Mr. Burnstein needs help. He can't afford to fix this himself, nor is he young enough to climb up here on this roof." His father had paused and taken a long drink of water from a thermos tied to his belt, then pointed his finger at Curtis and continued, "I want you to remember one thing, son. When people are in need, you help them—even if it looks like there's nothing in it for you. You do it because it's the right thing to do. You got that?"

Curtis had nodded and said, "Yeah, Pop."

A tear began to well up in Curtis's eye as he remembered how much he missed his father. Just then a loud horn and the sound of screeching brakes caused Curtis to jump and nearly lose his balance. As he came to his senses, he realized that he must have wandered out into the street— he was standing inches away from a car that had nearly struck him.

Looking back down at his watch, he noticed that it was 9:55 PM, and a sense of urgency overtook him as he remembered that it was a fifteen-minute walk to the McCallister farm. He sprinted off down the street.

As Curtis ran up the winding dirt drive that ended at the old brick farmhouse, he looked across the large bean field to see the old barn still standing erect. He jumped the fence and made his way along the side of the field until he reached the clearing where the huge wooden barn stood. Looking around, he noticed that there were several cars parked near the roadway that ran along the north side of the bean field. Pausing for a moment, he stopped in front of the barn door to catch his breath; he didn't want to be embarrassed in front of everyone by having to admit that he didn't have a car and had to walk.

As he opened the old tattered door, it creaked, and Curtis thought that it might fall off its hinges. Peering inside, he could see ten people milling around. All were boys about his age, either sitting on the nearby hay bales or standing. As Curtis made his way farther inside the barn, a voice behind him said, "Curtis. How are you? I didn't know you were coming. Do you want a beer?"

Curtis turned to see a short boy with brown hair that hung down to the top of his collar. Jeremy Albert was his name, and Curtis recognized him from school. From what Curtis remembered, Jeremy was always somewhat of a follower who did whatever it took to fit in with the crowd. He lived with his mother and father on a farm just to the south of Curtis's property.

"Uh, no, I'm good, Jeremy, but I appreciate it—maybe later." His father had detested drinking because Curtis's brother had been killed in a drunken driving accident. In the center of the barn was Johnny Bartel, a tall, burly young man with a scraggly short beard.

"Hey, glad you made it," said Johnny, as he turned to look at Curtis.

"Well, I'm glad you invited me."

"No problem, we need more people," Johnny replied, as he stepped up onto a small wooden table that was placed in the center of the barn.

"Now that everyone is here, we can get started," Johnny announced. "This meeting of the Hammer of God will now commence."

A skeptical look came over Curtis's face as he heard the official name of the club for the first time. He thought it was rather stupid.

Johnny continued, "Our first order of business is to deal with this problem we have in town. That Jew store owner we have won't take a hint. We trashed his place and left him a note to get out of town, but he refuses to listen. He reopened today, and one Jew in town is too many, so we need to take matters into our own hands. Tonight we will break in and wait until he arrives to open the store. I know he gets there about four-thirty in the morning, and nobody will be around. All of us will be waiting inside, and once he enters, we rid this world of another worthless Jew. All of us will carry out the will of God by killing this bastard, and nobody will be left out."

Johnny whispered something to Jeremy, who was standing next to him. Jeremy nodded and produced a pillowcase that he opened to allow Johnny to see inside, then he closed it and began walking toward the others gathered in the barn. Whatever was in the pillowcase clattered and clanged like horseshoes.

Johnny's face broke into a large smile, and Curtis could see a look of sincere hatred in his eyes as he spoke. "Okay, Brother Jeremy will be handing out the tools that we need to fulfill God's will."

Jeremy walked toward two boys who were seated on a nearby hay bale. Reaching into the pillowcase, he withdrew a couple of wooden-handled steak knives and handed one to each of the boys. Curtis watched as he continued around the barn handing out the knives. Finally, Jeremy stopped in front of Curtis, drew out a knife, and presented it. Curtis took hold of the wooden handle and noticed that the knife had been recently sharpened. To his horror, he saw that the handle was stained with a dark brownish-red hue.

Blood, he thought, and fear began to grip his throat. *They must have stabbed somebody else with these.* His breathing began to quicken, then his fear turned to disgust and finally anger as he clenched his teeth.

"We will all participate, as I have said," Johnny stated. "All of you will get a chance to fulfill what we are destined to do."

Curtis dropped the knife, and at once all eyes were upon him. "No," he said.

Everyone seemed frozen for a moment, then Johnny spoke, "No?" he demanded in a threatening tone. "You would tell God *no*?"

"You're not God." Curtis was defiant and stern. "And I won't hurt Mr. Burnstein. He saved my life and my mother's. I won't do this!"

Johnny slowly walked toward Curtis with a knife in his right hand. "So then, what will you do?" he asked accusingly as his wild eyes narrowed.

Curtis took a step back and placed his hand behind his back to feel for the doorway. "I'll do what's right! That's what my pop taught me. No matter what happens, I'll do what's right."

"We're going to kill that Jew—Burnstein—and if you're not with us, then you're against us," Johnny hissed in an evil whisper.

The door was now right behind Curtis. He turned quickly in an attempt to flee, but Jeremy caught hold of his leg and tripped him. As Curtis's body struck the ground, the dry powdery dirt of the barn floor flew inside his mouth and became like paste. Coughing, he spat it out as three of the boys closest to him hoisted him up and held him by the arms.

Jeremy pressed the blade of the steak knife to Curtis's throat and asked, "Should I cut him, Johnny?"

Johnny replied, "No, that's for the Jew. He's a Jew lover—let's string him up."

One of the other boys brought out a rope that they flung up and over one of the barn rafters. Another boy quickly made a noose and walked toward Curtis. As he approached, Curtis kicked him in the knee, and the boy fell to the ground, writhing in pain. Curtis was able to free his right arm and struck another boy under the chin, causing him to fall to the ground also. The struggle continued as the remaining boys closed in to gain control.

Curtis reached down and grabbed the steak knife that he had dropped. He swung it wildly, which caused several boys to back off. After planting his feet firmly, he brought the knife down hard into the shoulder of the boy who was holding him on the left side, which freed him from the boy's grasp and sent a fountain of blood spraying all over the front of his clothes and down his right arm. Breaking free, he dropped the knife and made it to the barn door again.

Suddenly, a sharp pain shot through his back as his muscles seemed to seize up, causing him to fall to the ground. Looking up, he saw Johnny standing over him with a cattle prod. Another boy ran over and slid the noose around Curtis's neck, then tightened the knot. Two others hoisted him to his feet, and the remaining boys began to pull on the rope. Curtis looked over to see the boy he had stabbed still rolling in pain on the ground with a large pool of blood beneath his body. As all the slack was taken up, the rope began to dig into his neck, and he found himself gasping for air. Reaching up, he grabbed the rope just above the knot in an attempt to relieve the pressure. As he did, the others grabbed onto his legs to drag him back down.

Curtis felt his neck straining, to the point that he thought it might snap and he would die; then suddenly the tension was released, hurling him downward onto the floor of the barn. He could hear a sense of panic in the others' voices. It took a few seconds to regain his senses, but as he did, he heard something strange. It sounded like a large rumbling sound that shook the ground. He could see people running by him toward the barn entrance as the sound grew louder. It was now like thunder that never ended, and Curtis noticed the old wooden barn wall rattling violently.

As he stumbled to his feet, he saw the last of the boys scramble out the door, except for the one who had been stabbed. On shaky legs, Curtis plowed forward, and as he made it to the front door, he felt something tug at his pants leg. Looking down, he saw the blood-soaked hand of the wounded boy, who pleaded with him, "Please, don't leave me. I'm sorry, please help me."

Curtis kicked his hand away and pushed the barn door hard. The rusted hinges screeched, and a cool breeze kicked up a small whirlwind of dust that danced around the barn. He paused for a moment as his father's voice echoed in his mind, "Always do what's right." Then reluctantly, he bent down to where the boy was lying, picked up the steak knife, and cut off the arm of the boy's shirt completely, exposing the wound. Quickly, he tied the material around the boy's shoulder and pulled it tight to stanch the bleeding. With one arm, he hoisted the boy to his feet and placed his uninjured arm over his shoulder.

As Curtis focused his gaze through the open door, he could see what was causing the sound. A storm must have blown in, and as the two boys distanced themselves from the barn, Curtis could see a huge vortex whirling across the sky beyond the field. The wounded boy yelled, "Twister! We need to get to a cellar! Run for the house!"

Curtis plowed forward as fast as he could toward the old brick house, with the weight of the injured boy dragging him down. The tornado was at the barn now, and Curtis looked across the field to see the other boys scattering in all directions. Shaking his head as he tried to maintain his balance, he wondered how the storm had blown in so quickly. It had been clear and sunny when he entered the barn.

The edge of the field was very near, and the fence was only a few feet in front of them. Heaving the wounded boy over, Curtis watched him topple to the ground on the other side. Curtis jumped the fence and once again lifted up his maimed counterpart, then braced him against his shoulder. They ran by the parked cars, and as they approached the opposite side of the roadway, a sudden jerk caused Curtis's feet to fall out from beneath him. The rope that was still tied around his neck had tangled around a fence post. The wounded boy's body flung forward and landed on the grassy area near the driveway that led to the house.

"Keep going!" Curtis screamed at the boy. The wind was now unbearable. Running back to the fence, he began tugging at the rope to free himself. Despite his desperate attempts, the rope would not budge, and he could see the vortex closing in. Giving up on breaking free, he decided that the only chance he might have would be to lie down in the ditch next to the fence.

As he did, he watched the path of the whirling mass of air coming across the field, and he noticed something odd. He'd seen many twisters before in his lifetime, since the small area that he lived in was known as Tornado Alley, but never before had he seen a tornado behave as this one did. It seemed to move and change directions frequently. It weaved through the field and quickly shifted to the left, then back to the right.

Refocusing his attention to the horizon, Curtis could make out the distant image of the other boys running across the field. To his disbelief, it seemed as though this tornado was following them. Watching more intently, he saw one of the boys get sucked upward into the wind. The twister changed direction once again and seemed to be tracking another boy; it quickly was upon him and scooped him from the ground, like an enormous cat pouncing on a mouse.

Once it had consumed that victim, it backtracked into the field again, and Curtis could see it closing in on Johnny, who was running in the opposite direction from the others. It enveloped him quickly, and Curtis saw Johnny spinning upward, flailing his arms and screaming.

Looking toward the house, Curtis saw that the wounded boy was nearly up to the small trap door that led to the old cellar. The twister plowed through the center of the field and into the front yard of the farmhouse. As the wounded boy opened the cellar door, the tornado moved directly overhead, and he clung to the handle with his body waving in the wind like a kite caught in an updraft. The force of the wind was too much, and Curtis watched as the wounded boy was sucked upward.

Fear began to grip Curtis, and he sank low into the ditch. The swirling air reversed its course once again and came back across the road directly toward him. His heartbeat quickened as he tried to find the lowest spot possible to hide in. The twister was now on the other side of the parked cars, and as Curtis looked up into it, a feeling of sheer horror overtook him. As the vortex grew closer, he lowered his head to wipe the dust and debris from his eyes. When he looked up again, the twister was directly in front of him, and he stared into the center. His fear peaked as he continued to gaze at it in horror. Something hovered in the middle of the massive tornado, and although Curtis could not make out its exact outline, he was definite about one thing. It was laughing.

CHAPTER 2

Bodies in the Trees

LIEUTENANT ALAN CRANE AWOKE from the monotonous tone of his pager sounding on the nightstand. His wife, Alison, said in a groggy voice, "Oh no, it's three in the morning! What now?"

He grabbed his cell phone and called the number displayed on his pager. A voice on the other end answered, "Captain Lee."

Alan attempted to speak in a clear voice, as though he had been awake. "Yes, it's Lieutenant Crane."

The voice replied, "Lieutenant Crane, this is Captain Lee from the Major Case Squad. We've been activated on a case in Mossy Grove. You and several others are needed to respond to the scene. You'll get a full briefing upon arrival. Grab a pen, and I will relay the directions to the location of the incident."

Alan thumbed through the nightstand drawer and finally found a pen and paper. He jotted the directions down and stumbled out of bed. Dressing quickly, he kissed his wife good-bye and shook his head in an attempt to revive himself from the dreary state he was in.

As he wandered out to his car, he wondered if his new position was worth the bother. He'd recently been promoted to lieutenant in the investigations division of the Riverston Police Department, and with the promotion came a mandatory assignment to the Major Case Squad, which was composed of the top detectives throughout a five-county area. His county, called Abersteen, contained three cities: Riverston, a moderate sized city of approximately 15,000 people; Evansville, a much larger city located to the west; and a small rural city to the north named Mossy Grove, which contained a small downtown district and numerous farms.

As Alan drove, he turned on the radio and caught a short spot on the news. The news reporter said, in a deep monotone, "A deadly tornado struck the small town of Mossy Grove over night, leaving nine people dead." Alan thought that this must not be coincidental, but he could not understand why the Major Case Squad would be investigating a natural disaster; after all, there's no crime in that.

As his car rambled down the narrow dirt road, he noticed several unmarked police cars and an ambulance parked in both the driveway and the front yard of a small farmhouse. He pulled in behind the ambulance and got out. As he began approaching the house, he noticed a strange-looking object on the roof. Squinting his eyes in an attempt to focus more clearly on the object, he was interrupted by a voice he recognized.

"Alan, glad you're here," said a tall slender man. The voice was that of Detective Sergeant Rich Blane of the Evansville Police Department. Rich was a polygraph examiner who conducted examinations for the Major Case Squad.

"Rich, who am I paired up with?"

"That would be me, my friend," replied Rich, with a quick smile.

"Good, and what is that thing on the roof?" he inquired, pointing to the object that was draped across the top peak next to the chimney.

"Well," said Rich, as he pointed to the roof, "that would be victim number three. We've been numbering them in the order that we find them up to this point; however, that may change if we can determine the order of death."

Alan's eyes grew wide. "I see, and where is victim number one?"

Rich pointed to a small plastic inverted V-shaped placard with the number 1 in the middle. The placard was only a few feet in front of them, at the bottom of a huge oak tree.

Alan's face contorted in confusion as he squinted hard at the tiny sign, then asked, "He's buried in the ground?"

Rich shook his head. "Oh no," he said sarcastically. "It's way better than that." He grinned and pointed up at the tree.

Alan's face registered an expression of shock as his gaze continued to scan up the great trunk and over numerous branches, where he saw what appeared to be a body intertwined in the topmost limbs.

He continued to study the body as he tried to estimate how high it really was. "I heard something on the radio that said there was a tornado that struck here in Mossy Grove and that nine people were killed. Are we sure this is a homicide and not a natural disaster?"

"We told the press that we thought it was a tornado," Rich admitted, "and now we need to buy some time to see what we have. I'm sure the reporters are on their way, and our story isn't going to hold water once they get here. Captain Lee is organizing people to block off the roadways to establish somewhat of a perimeter; of course, this won't help once they get the news helicopter here. Follow me up this way," Rich added, as he continued walking toward the house.

"Do we have any indication that someone killed any of our victims?"

Rich nodded and stopped on the side of the farmhouse, where the body of a young man was lying on the ground. Several crime scene technicians were starting the initial processing. Alan noticed a great deal of blood around a makeshift tourniquet that was tied near his left shoulder.

"Knife wound is our initial guess—looks like he was stabbed. Lee actually has a medical examiner on the way to the scene. He wants autopsies to begin immediately. His office wasn't exactly happy, but they said they'd do it, given the . . . "—Rich paused for a moment, trying to find the right word—" . . . uh, strange circumstances. We also found a pool of blood in the old barn down beyond the bean field. We're having it collected now."

Alan shook his head, confused. "That makes no sense to me. This guy gets stabbed and is able to do a tourniquet with one hand, or perhaps the person who stabbed him did it. And how did he get out here? And what about the guy in the tree? Who's our suspect—a gorilla?"

Rich let out a small laugh to ease the tension, but it didn't seem to help. They walked from the farmhouse and back out to the roadway.

"Let's think about this tornado theory," said Alan. "You said it won't hold water. What's the problem with it?"

Rich pointed to the area straight in front of them. "We found nine bodies, total. Some in trees and some on the ground. The one on the farmhouse roof and even one on the far side of the barn roof, and yet we have no structural damage. That tattered barn would have blown down in a second. We have no trees uprooted." He pointed around to the many trees that surrounded the field to corroborate his point. "If it was a tornado, it only destroyed one specific thing." Rich stopped, looked Alan in the face, and lowered his voice: "People."

A sick sensation began to build slowly in Alan's gut as he surveyed the surrounding bean field and the old rickety barn. *He's right*, Alan thought. *Nothing was touched. Even the rows of beans are unblemished.*

Rich motioned for Alan to follow him again. "Come on, we need to talk to the couple who owns the house, Mr. and Mrs. McCallister."

The two made their way back up to the front of the house, where an elderly couple was standing. Alan extended his hand to the man as he said, "Good evening, I'm Lieutenant Crane from the Major Case Squad, and this is Detective Sergeant Blane. I was wondering if you could answer some questions."

The old man nodded, and Alan continued. "Were both of you home all evening?"

Both of them nodded, and Mr. McCallister replied, "Yes, we were here all afternoon. We were sleeping, and a storm blew up. The wind was blowing around like crazy, and I could hear it hitting the trees. After a few minutes, I heard someone screaming. It sounded like it was far off in the distance. I woke up my wife and told her that we needed to get to someplace safe, so we ran outside and made our way down into the cellar."

"What did you see when you came outside?" asked Rich.

"Nothing," replied Mr. McCallister. "I couldn't see a thing. The wind was too bad; it was hard to even open my eyes. I had to feel my way over to the cellar door with my wife holding on to my shoulders. I was afraid we were going to blow away."

"You said that you heard screaming," Alan interjected. "Did you hear anything else or ever see who was making the noise?"

The old man nodded. "Once we got into the cellar, we ran to the back. The cellar door opened, and I heard the screaming once again. I ran to the front of the cellar and saw a young man who was trying to come in, but the wind had lifted his body into the air. He hung onto the cellar door for a few seconds, and I ran up the stairs to try to grab his hand, but the wind started dragging me upward before I could get close enough. The cellar door gave way, and the young man disappeared, and . . ." The old man stopped as a disturbed look came over his face.

"Yes?" Alan prompted, as he placed a hand on Mr. McCallister's shoulder to encourage him to continue. "What happened?"

"It stopped," replied Mr. McCallister. He had difficulty getting the words out. "The wind . . . as soon as the boy was gone . . . it stopped. I ran outside, and everything was clear. I've seen a number of twisters in my time and been through a good deal of storms. One time I had my tractor blown into the next county, but I've never seen anything like this."

Alan nodded. "Mr. McCallister, was anyone in your barn this evening?"

The old man thought for a moment, then shook his head. "Not that I know of."

Mrs. McCallister finally spoke up. "I caught one of the local boys poking around the barn the other day. The door was slightly ajar, and I thought I had forgotten to close it. So I went over and looked inside, and a young man I know from town was walking around, moving hay bales. I asked him what he was doing, and he ran past me, then disappeared through the bean field. He nearly knocked me down."

"Do you know this young man's name?" asked Rich.

Mrs. McCallister thought for a moment, then replied, "Yes, it's Johnny Bartel."

Rich jotted down the name on a small notepad he produced from his pocket, and Alan informed the couple, "It seems that several people were killed here on your property by this storm."

Mr. and Mrs. McCallister looked shocked but remained silent. Alan continued, "It would help us very much if you could try to identify some of these boys. Perhaps one of them is Mr. Bartel. Would you follow me, please?"

Mr. and Mrs. McCallister nodded, then followed Alan up to the closest body, the young man with the stab wound. As Mr. McCallister saw the face of the boy, he winced, then said, "That's the one who tried to get into the cellar, but it's not Johnny."

Alan and Rich walked the McCallisters to the areas where the other bodies were located. The process took awhile, since some of the victims had to be carefully extracted from high tree branches. Captain Lee had called several branches of the fire department to assist with their ladder trucks. As the last body was taken down, Alan felt the rustling of the trees overhead, and at one point a slight sense of anxiety overtook him. He thought the tornado had come back, but as he listened, he could hear the thumping mechanical sounds of a rotating blade cutting the air and realized that it was the sound of a helicopter.

"There's the press," said Rich.

Mr. and Mrs. McCallister confirmed that none of the deceased were Johnny Bartel.

The McCallisters weren't exactly suspects at this point, but Alan wasn't ruling anything out. He asked, "Mr. McCallister, I hate to ask this of you, but it's routine procedure for us to look into all leads, and given these circumstances in which nine people have died, I would like to get your consent to look through your home."

Mr. McCallister replied, "No problem, Officer—anything we can do to help."

Mrs. McCallister nodded, and as she spoke, tears began to well up in her eyes. "I can't believe all of these boys died. I knew some of them and their parents. This is awful."

Alan put his arm around her and said, "We'll do everything we can to find out what happened. I promise."

Alan and Rich made their way up to the front door of the house, and as Alan was about to enter, a dark-colored Ford Crown Victoria with tinted windows pulled up onto the roadway and parked. A man in a dark-colored suit got out of the car, and Alan recognized him immediately: Special Agent Michael Simmons.

"Feds are here," Rich noted.

"Yeah," replied Alan. "I wonder what took them so long."

The man was walking toward them, and as he drew within earshot, he said, "Hello, Alan."

"Hello, Michael. I was wondering what took you so long. The McCallisters have consented to let us look through their house."

"Ah, I see," said Special Agent Simmons. "I wouldn't waste too much time in there."

Alan nodded. "Guess we're not going to find anything." Simmons nodded back, confirming the comment, and Rich whispered, "Damn feds always think they know everything."

About a year ago, when Alan was a sergeant assigned to the patrol division, Michael Simmons had contacted him and requested that he join a special task force that dealt with helping families who have experienced the loss of a loved one. Simmons had told him that their specialized unit recruited people who could show great compassion and understanding for those who grieve. Alan agreed to join and assist the group, then later he discovered that the organization was not affiliated with the federal government. It was "a much larger organization," as Simmons had described it, and Alan soon learned that the group not only cared for those who grieved the loss of their loved ones but also actually escorted the souls of the dead down the path that led to their final resting place.

Simmons was not from this world; he was, in fact, from that place beyond life, the place where one goes after one dies: heaven, paradise, the afterlife, nirvana—whatever you prefer to call it. Alan was never completely clear on how Simmons came back to the living as Simmons had told him that he had once been alive. At first, Alan had speculated that perhaps Simmons was a ghost, but he soon changed his assumption as Simmons didn't seem to be a spirit that would materialize when needed. Alan would have thought him to be a living human being if it weren't for his ability to access the afterlife. He always seemed to show up when death was at hand, and, in fact, he always knew when death was about to occur. Simmons had the ability to speak with those who died and lead them through the dark hallways connecting the world of the living to the afterlife, an ability and a duty that was bestowed onto Alan. Before meeting Michael Simmons, Alan would have never believed that a person who was still alive could enter the afterlife and return until Simmons had finally showed him the fantastic place where people go after they die. Within heaven, as Alan called it, he had learned many things regarding the Light and the Darkness. He had learned that everyone is given a role in the next life that contributes to the epic struggle of good over evil. Alan had found himself caught up in a great battle within this realm and had discovered his role in the conflict.

Rich and Alan quickly surveyed the small farmhouse and found nothing of interest. They thanked the McCallisters and apologized for the inconvenience as they exited through the front door.

Turning to Rich, Alan said, "I'll catch up to you in a few. I'm going to see what the feds know."

Rich nodded and headed off in the direction of the barn. Alan walked down to the roadway, where he found Simmons sitting in his car. He made his way around to the passenger side and got in. Simmons had a concerned look on his face that Alan immediately recognized. "So how many did you have to lead into the Light?"

"None," replied Simmons. "Not even one."

Alan shook his head, looking somewhat confused. "None?" he asked, perplexed. "Not even one? What does that mean? If you didn't lead them, then . . . "

Simmons interrupted, confirming what Alan was about to say. "Yes, someone else did—and not to the Light, or I would have known about it. They were led into the Darkness—or so I presume."

Alan pondered the thought for a moment. "All nine of them were led into the Darkness?"

Simmons corrected him. "All *ten* of them were led into the Darkness. I was supposed to lead the eleventh, but he survived."

Alan was taken aback by the comment. "All of them were led to the Darkness, without even a chance of the alternative? How can that happen? What were they doing that placed them on their path?"

"Either what they were doing or what they had already done. I don't know, but their fate was carved very clear; their path was set with a definitive course," Simmons said in a low monotone.

Alan continued, "We only have nine bodies. The tenth isn't here. We believe it may be a boy named Johnny Bartel. Who is the eleventh, the one who survived?"

Simmons replied, "His name is Curtis Norman. He's a local boy who lives just outside of town with his mother."

"How did he survive?" asked Alan.

"I don't know."

"Do you know where he is now?"

"No," replied Simmons in a concerned tone.

"What about Johnny Bartel?"

"He's dead."

"I assumed that. I was inquiring whether you know where we could find his body."

"Find Curtis; he should know where Johnny's body is."

Alan nodded and sat silent for a moment, taking in the new information and trying to decipher the meaning of everything he had seen and heard this evening.

"The McCallisters said that a storm blew up and they ran for the cellar. They even witnessed one of the boys being sucked up by the wind, yet there are no trees, bushes, or structures damaged. What kind of tornado strikes with such precision to do that?" asked Alan, although he wasn't sure he really wanted to know the answer.

Simmons shook his head, but before he could comment, Rich Blane was standing outside the car. Simmons and Alan got out.

"Never seen anything like this before," said Rich, looking around. "This is bad, real bad, and worse yet, it seems unexplainable. We may never figure this one out. What do you think, Special Agent . . . "

"Michael Simmons," replied Simmons, noticing that Rich was waiting for an introduction. "I do think there's an explanation for this, but you're right—it's very bad."

"We're looking for a young man named Curtis Norman," said Alan to Rich. "He may have been here when this happened, and we need to track him down. Let's start with his mother's house—they live on one of the old farms just outside of town."

"Let's go," replied Rich, as he began walking toward Alan's car.

Simmons said to Alan, "I'll be in touch soon. Contact me if you find Mr. Norman."

"Will do," replied Alan, as he headed toward his car.

As Alan and Rich were about to pull away, a detective ran up to the driver's side window. He was wearing latex gloves and carrying a large thick rope that had a noose tied on the end. Alan rolled down the window, and the detective said breathlessly, "Glad I caught you guys before you left. I found this up near the fence bordering the bean field. I think it has some blood and skin on it. What do you two think?"

Alan shook his head and looked over at Rich, who he could see was just as puzzled. "No idea," said Rich. "Bag it and test it; we'll see what the lab can determine."

The detective nodded, "The medical examiner's here and is transporting the bodies in for emergency autopsies. Hopefully we'll know something tonight or tomorrow morning."

Alan rolled his eyes and commented, "Fifty feet up in a tree, dropped from a high altitude. I can assume the cause of death, but perhaps it will shed some light on other areas."

The detective nodded in agreement again, and Alan directed, "Tell Captain Lee we're heading into town to follow up on a lead of a potential survivor, and we'll call him if we find anything."

"Will do," replied the detective, as he turned and left.

Alan drove away and started back down the road that led to town. He was still contemplating his involvement with the whole ordeal as he said to Rich, "I'm still wondering why we're even here. Do you really think that somebody killed these victims and then threw their bodies up in the trees and on the rooftop of the house? It seems like a natural disaster to me. Why not call in the State Emergency Management Agency or FEMA?"

"Lee wants to make a name for himself," said Rich. "The local sheriff was dumbfounded when he discovered that he had nine dead victims to deal with. He called in for help, and Lee wasn't going to pass it up. Hey, that's the way it works, and besides, we do have a stabbing—although I doubt that a shoulder wound killed him. And what about the rope and noose? Something else was going on here besides that storm."

"Yeah, you're right," replied Alan. "Something else was going on here. I'm just not sure that I really want to know what that was."

Rich laughed at Alan's comment, and they continued to drive toward town.

CHAPTER 3

The Missing Victim

C URTIS NORMAN COLLAPSED on his bedroom floor. Every muscle in his body ached, not to mention his neck, which was cut and bruised from where the rope had nearly strangled him. He was exhausted but would not close his eyes. Lying on his back on the floor, he stared out the window and said out loud, "Pop, if you can hear me, I want you to know that I did like you said. I did what was right, even when they tried to kill me. I still did what was right." Tears ran down his face as he held up the watch on his wrist to examine the new crack on the crystal.

Rain trickled down outside his window, and he jumped every time there was a clap of thunder. As he lay there, he saw two distinct and steady beams of light that moved across his room and illuminated the far wall. He heard the sound of an engine out front and determined that someone had just pulled into the driveway. He knew it couldn't be his mother, because she was already sleeping, and the old beat-up truck she drove had been parked out back since he arrived home.

Curtis heard two car doors close and footsteps approaching the front porch. Reaching under his bed, he retrieved his shotgun, then got to his knees and grabbed two shells that were sitting on his nightstand. Loading the gun, he carefully crept toward the small window on the opposite side of his room. He slowly raised his eyes and the barrel of the gun just enough to peer over the edge of the sill. His gaze caught two figures approaching the front porch; both were wearing sports jackets and ties.

As they drew closer, the glint from something shiny hanging from the waist of the taller man made Curtis realize they were cops. With a sigh of relief, he pushed the shotgun back under the bed and went to answer the door. He opened it before either man could knock, because he didn't want them to wake his mother, but it was too late. He heard his mother walking down the hallway behind him. Curtis could now see that the two men were indeed police officers; each wore a gun and a badge on his hip.

It was around 5:30 AM when Alan and Rich approached the front door of the small farmhouse. Alan knocked, and a light came on from within. A woman in her late forties, with blond shoulder-length hair, answered the door. Her face was thin and leathery, and Alan could tell she had been sleeping. She looked at Alan and Rich and stared confusedly at the badges on their waists.

"Are you Mrs. Norman?" Alan asked politely.

"Yes," responded the woman, with a puzzled look.

"I'm Lieutenant Alan Crane, and this is Detective Sergeant Rich Blane. We are with the Major Case Squad, and we need to speak with your son, Curtis," said Alan.

"Well, yes . . . I know," replied the woman.

Now it was Alan and Rich who looked confused as Alan inquired, "Ma'am, you said you know. I'm not quite sure I understand."

"I know," she repeated. "The other two officers who were just here said they needed his help. He left with them."

Alan was surprised by the comment, and a sense of urgency came over him as he turned to Rich. "Did Lee send anyone else over here?"

"No," replied Rich. "He assigned it to us. I heard him say it myself."

"Get on the phone with him and confirm it," said Alan, as he turned back toward Mrs. Norman.

"What did the other officers look like?"

"Oh, I don't really know," she answered. "I wasn't paying much attention. Guess they looked kind of like you two. You guys all look the same to me." She paused for a moment, then said with a tinge of concern, "Is there a problem?"

Alan was choosing his words carefully because he didn't know the correct answer to this question. "Perhaps," he stated. "How long ago did they leave?"

"About thirty minutes ago or so. Why? What's wrong? Why do you ask?" Mrs. Norman asked anxiously.

Alan realized that his next question was the last thing he could ask, or Mrs. Norman would become really suspicious that the other officers' visit concerned him greatly, so he said in a calm voice, "No reason, just trying to coordinate our investigation. Could I see Curtis's room?"

Mrs. Norman shrugged, obviously accepting Alan's reason. "Sure, this way." She led him down a short hallway past a small bathroom and came to a doorway. "Curtis tried to be quiet and not wake me up, but I heard someone talking at the front door. The other two officers said that there was a bad accident and they needed Curtis to identify some boys who had been killed. They said they'd have him back within an hour or so." She turned and looked at Alan to confirm what she had just said.

Alan picked up on her subtle cue and replied, "Yes, we have numerous casualties, and we think they're local boys. We appreciate the help."

"That's terrible," she said as she opened Curtis's bedroom door. "I hope they weren't—" she stopped suddenly and screamed at the sight before her in the middle of the room. Alan pushed past her, and Rich, who had been making his phone call to Captain Lee near the front door, ran into the room. In the center of the tiny bedroom was a body lying facedown. It appeared to be a young man. Alan walked around the side of the corpse and noticed that his face was a pale white. Rich flipped on the lights as Mrs. Norman walked up behind Alan.

Alan kept his gaze fixed on the boy as he asked in a low whisper, "Is this Curtis?" Mrs. Norman began to sob, and Alan turned and placed a hand on her shoulder to comfort her.

"No," she said in a cold, frightful whisper. "It's Johnny—Johnny Bartel."

∼

Alan looked over at Rich and could see that he shared Alan's feeling of anxiety.

"Did you get in touch with Lee?" asked Alan.

"Yes."

Alan wanted to ask whether Lee had sent other detectives over earlier, but he didn't want to alert Mrs. Norman. Rich could tell by the look on Alan's face that he wanted to ask the question, so he shook his head. Alan immediately understood and nodded in confirmation. Sighing, Alan said, "Tell Lee we found another body and to get the crime scene crew over here."

Within fifteen minutes, multiple crime scene–processing vehicles pulled up in front of the Normans' small house. Crime scene technicians flooded the hallway and bedroom where Johnny Bartel was lying lifeless. An assistant medical examiner showed up next, and shortly after that, Captain Lee himself. The captain had a foul look on his face, and Alan knew that he was feeling the stress of not being able to explain what was going on. Alan was unable to feel any sympathy for him; he knew that the good captain continually promoted himself to the press as an unsung hero, and it appeared that this case was blowing up in his face.

"How's it going, Captain?" Alan asked, with a slight tinge of vindictiveness.

"Oh just wonderful, and thanks for asking," responded Lee, gritting his teeth in frustration. Alan could tell he was irritated by the snide question.

Lee pushed past Alan and proceeded toward the room where Johnny Bartel's body lay. Rich came up behind Alan. He had a smirk on his face because he had overheard the banter between Alan and Lee.

"Yeah, it just keeps getting worse for him," Rich commented.

"Oh, really? What happened now?"

"Well," Rich explained, "crime scene finished with some of the bodies already, and they were transported for emergency autopsy. As you know, Lee demanded that autopsies be conducted as soon as possible, and he just received the preliminary results."

Alan raised his eyebrows as he looked at Rich. "And?"

"And the cause of death seems to preliminarily be greater myocardial infarction."

"English, please," Alan requested.

"It seems they died from massive heart attacks, or heart failure," Rich translated. "No broken bones; no contusions, abrasions, lacerations, punctures, or blunt trauma." Rich lowered his voice and continued, "I heard they didn't even have any bruising. That's damn creepy, if you ask me."

"What!" Alan exclaimed, turning pale. He was still in a daze when his cell phone rang.

Slowly flipping it open, he answered the call. It was Simmons, who said, "I'm heading over to the house. Meet me out front."

"Okay," replied Alan. He hung up and walked toward the front door. He went outside and saw a car approaching.

The driver's side window lowered, and Simmons said with concern, "Get in, we need to talk." Alan complied and anxiously waited to see what was going on.

"Were you aware that we have multiple bodies that were supposedly caught in a tornado? And that those victims are preliminarily dead because of heart failure?" asked Alan, astonished.

"I'm aware of that," Simmons answered as he looked down.

"Any ideas?"

"Not yet. We have to go into town. There's someone we have to help."

Alan nodded because he understood what Simmons meant. He had been recruited a year ago to fill the role of guide for souls that needed to reach the world beyond life, for those who have died and are in need of help walking through the passageway that divides the realm of the living from the Realm of Light. He had led many of them to their destination, and some were not so easy to lead. The manner in which a person had lived determined the extent of the journey. Those who were good and chose to do what was right had a very short walk, but those who had spent their lives taking the wrong path had a much longer journey, involving numerous obstacles and hardships before they reached heaven. Those who had led lives that were vile, dark, and evil never met with Alan or Simmons at all, for their fate was sealed, and they descended into the Darkness.

"Who are we leading?" asked Alan.

"A man named Alexander Burnstein. He's the store owner in town," replied Simmons.

The car turned into the main portion of town, which didn't amount to much. There was a small post office that sat next to a little brick building with a sign that read CITY HALL on the topmost row of bricks. Past City Hall sat Burnstein's General Store. As they entered through a set of old weathered wooden doors, Alan noticed that the sign on the front indicated that the store was still closed. Scanning the area as they made their way farther inside, they saw an elderly man lying facedown on the floor near the cash register and figured that this must be Mr. Burnstein. The man had numerous puncture wounds on his back, and a large pool of blood surrounded his head, neck, and midsection.

"What happened?" asked Alan.

"Don't know yet," replied Simmons. "Let's ask."

"Mr. Burnstein," said Simmons. "Let me help you up." The man sat up and Simmons took him by the arm to help him to his feet. Alan knew that although Mr. Burnstein appeared to be alive and well, the entity that he was speaking to was Mr. Burnstein's spirit. His physical body would soon reappear on the floor once his spirit was escorted to the world beyond life.

Alan had always envisioned a spirit as something translucent, without any physical form, perhaps mostly invisible. Since his experiences with Michael Simmons began, he had come to realize that they appeared more like those of the living. In fact, the first time Alan had encountered the spirit of a dead person he was startled with disbelief. He initially thought that this person had returned to life from a nonsurvivable death.

"Oh . . . is he gone?" Mr. Burnstein inquired.

"Who would that be?" asked Alan, staring curiously.

"The young man who cut my throat, that's who! He was extremely mad," Mr. Burnstein answered.

"Yes," said Simmons. "He's gone. Do you by any chance know who the young man was?"

"Yes, I recognized him. I've seen him around town. His name is Johnny; not sure about his last name."

"Follow us, Mr. Burnstein," Alan instructed, as he began walking toward the back of the store. The three of them reached a small door in the back of the building used for unloading supplies. Simmons reached down, turned the handle, and pulled it open. All three stepped through into a dark, black marble hallway. As Mr. Burnstein looked around, he said, "Oh . . . I see now. I wasn't sure if he had killed me, but I guess this confirms it."

"Everything will be fine, Mr. Burnstein," Alan reassured him. "We'll get you where you need to go."

"Oh, thank you," said the old man gratefully. "How I will miss my store and the many nice people in Mossy Grove!"

"You will see them eventually." Simmons smiled. "There are many nice people where we are going."

The three continued down the long hallway until the door they had come through could no longer be seen.

"When did Johnny attack you?" Alan asked.

"Yesterday morning. He must have been hiding in the store."

"Did Johnny say anything when he attacked you?" Alan wondered whether Johnny Bartel had indicated any type of motive for the murder.

Mr. Burnstein stopped, pressed his index finger to his lips as he thought for a moment, then replied, "He had a look of fear on his face, and he said that he had to kill me. He said that God told him that I had to die. Then he went on with some other babbling and such."

"What kind of babbling?" asked Alan, in an attempt to get Mr. Burnstein to be as detailed as possible.

"Oh, some more nonsense about God," replied Mr. Burnstein. "He said something about how God came to him in the wind or something like that. He went on and on . . . nonsense . . . a very disturbed young man."

Alan looked at Simmons and could tell that he was very concerned with what Mr. Burnstein was saying.

"Did he say what God looked like?" Simmons wanted to know.

"Oh, he babbled on and on about the awesome power of God's wings and the mighty wind that picked him up and told him to kill me." Mr. Burnstein paused and then added, "He doesn't know God. My God is kind and compassionate and stands for what is right and good. That young man better repent, or he may wind up in hell, although I'm not sure he can atone for murder."

Simmons said in a low and somber voice, "I'm sure he's already there."

"Was Johnny alone?" Alan asked.

"He's the only one I could see," replied Mr. Burnstein.

As Alan recalled the condition of Mr. Burnstein's body, he inquired, "Did Johnny stab you in the back several times?"

Mr. Burnstein looked a bit confused and he shook his head. "No, he dragged the knife down both sides of my neck. He never stabbed me in the back."

Alan looked at Simmons with some concern. Simmons shook his head to indicate that he couldn't explain the multitude of stab wounds.

The three continued a bit farther, until they came to an old wooden door with a wrought-iron handle. The door frame glowed yellow, and as they came very close, they noticed that the yellow glow was actually radiant shards of light emitting from the edges.

"Here we are, Mr. Burnstein," said Alan. "We will see you soon."

"Thank you, boys. You have shown an old man the way, and I appreciate it," said Mr. Burnstein, with a huge smile on his face.

Alan smiled back. "Just doing our job." He grabbed the handle and pulled the door open, which allowed a brilliant warm light to spill out into the hallway. Mr. Burnstein stepped through, and Alan closed the heavy door behind him. As they made their way back, Alan glanced over at Simmons, who was staring at the floor. His face was long as the two walked out into the store once again.

Alan stood by Mr. Burnstein's body and studied the two huge gashes down both sides of the neck where the blood must have poured out and drained the old man of his life. He flipped open his cell phone and punched in Rich Blane's number.

"Blane," said a voice on the other end.

"Rich, it's Alan. You had better tell Lee to get some people down here to the general store. It looks like we have another body—an elderly male in his seventies."

Rich exclaimed, "What! Are you kidding—another body!"

"Yeah, tell Lee to get some people over here as soon as possible."

"Will do," said Rich. "Did this one actually have a legitimate heart attack?"

"No, his throat was cut, and he was stabbed a number of times."

"Oh." Rich sounded surprised. "This thing just keeps getting better and better. By the way, how did you find this one?"

The question caught Alan by surprise, but he covered it up well. "A lead called into the feds—you know, the agent we met earlier, Michael Simmons. Anyway, he received a tip that led us here."

"Oh." Rich seemed to be satisfied with the explanation. "I'll let Lee know and get the crime scene crew on its way."

Alan hung up the phone.

"What's this all mean, Michael?" asked Alan. "Mr. Burnstein said that Johnny was rambling about God and the wind. What does this mean?"

"I don't know yet, but I'll contact you when I find out more. I don't like it at all."

"His throat was cut and he was stabbed numerous times in the back. Why?" Alan queried, as his eyes continued to pass over the gruesome scene. "Could this be something from the world beyond the living, perhaps from the Darkness?"

"Not likely, but I'm not sure," Simmons answered. "There are very specific rules about interaction with the living. These rules are set in place by the Light, and they cannot be breached—or so I thought. I'm unsure right now, but I have a theory that may contradict those rules."

"Let's hear it, then," Alan urged.

"No, not yet. I have to research the matter." Simmons shook his head. "And I sincerely hope my theory is wrong."

Three crime scene technicians and two detectives arrived. Alan led them back to Mr. Burnstein's body, and as the lights of the store were flipped on, he could see the horrific scene in its entirety. He continued to look over everything until something on the floor surrounding the body caught his attention. Carefully walking close, he studied the multiple sets of footprints scattered about on the laminated hardwood floor, highlighted and outlined by the victim's blood. He had seen this before.

He said to one of the crime scene techs, "What do you make of the multiple sets of footprints?"

The tech shook his head. "I don't know, but I can tell you that this one is a woman's shoe, probably a designer high heel. See the pattern?"

Alan looked at the distinct markings in the blood that depicted the flat curved front pattern of a woman's shoe accompanied by the small round mark of a spiked heel.

"What kind of nut commits a murder in high heels?" Alan asked, bewildered.

"Don't know," replied the tech, "but after all the crazy crap I've seen today, nothing surprises me."

"E-mail these pictures over to me as soon as you can," directed Alan.

"No problem."

Alan followed Simmons outside. They left in Simmons's car and headed back to the Normans' house. As the car stopped in the street, Alan could see various television camera crews assembling on the front lawn. He got out as Simmons remarked to him, "I'll call you when I know more." Nodding, Alan walked away toward the front porch, where he could now see Captain Lee and Rich standing. Moving around the outside of the crowd to avoid the cameras and the reporters, he slipped inside the doorway of the tiny house. Rich followed him.

"What's going on?" Alan inquired.

"Lee is grandstanding, as usual," Rich informed him. "He's about to dazzle the press with his superior investigative intellect," he added sarcastically.

Alan shook his head in disgust, and the two wandered back out to hear what Lee had to say to the press. Five microphones were set in front of the captain as he began his rant.

"I'm Captain Paul Lee, commander of the Major Case Squad."

Alan rolled his eyes as Lee bellowed out his official title to emphasize that he was important and in charge.

"We have multiple casualties and are still investigating the exact cause of death. We do have one young man in this house who we preliminarily believe has been stabbed to death, and we just received word that another stabbing victim has been found in town," Lee said, then cleared his throat.

Alan turned to Rich and whispered, "Johnny was stabbed?"

"Yes," replied Rich, "multiple times."

Alan continued to listen as Lee kept speaking.

"We have a suspect we are currently looking for. His name is Curtis Norman. He's twenty years of age, a white male, approximately five feet eleven inches tall, approximately two hundred pounds, blond hair and blue eyes, and is considered armed, physically violent, and dangerous. Please contact law enforcement if you see this individual. We will be providing a picture within the next hour."

A scream came from the hallway as Lee finished his speech. Alan saw Mrs. Norman run by and out onto the porch. She was screaming at Lee. "My son did not do this, and you know it! And he's not on the run—your people took him!" Two detectives grabbed her by her arms and pulled her back into the house. Some of the members of the media began talking among themselves, and Lee could see that he needed to quell this quickly. He told the news crews standing in front of him, "That's the suspect's mother; she is obviously distraught. We are still seeking Mr. Norman as our prime suspect."

Alan turned to Rich and muttered, "This isn't right. Do you really think Curtis Norman's our suspect?" Alan was positive that Curtis didn't kill Mr. Burnstein, but it would be hard to explain how he knew. Rich shrugged his shoulders and responded, "Well, we did find a knife in his room that we believe will match the wounds on Johnny Bartel, and who knows? It may have also been used on the victim at the store."

"What about the two cops who showed up and picked up Curtis?" Alan reminded him. "How does that fit in?"

"Well . . . " replied Rich, pausing to come up with a reasonable answer, "That's what Curtis's mother said, but who knows, maybe she's lying to cover for him."

"And Johnny's body in Curtis's room?" asked Alan.

"Maybe Curtis killed him and dragged him into his room. His mom tells him to split before the cops get there. Then she drums up some story about two mysterious cops who show up and take him away," Rich offered, as though he were poking around in the dark trying to find a light switch.

Alan retorted, "And his mom invites us into the house and leads us to the body of Johnny Bartel? She leads us right to the body? If she was going to cover this up, why did she let us in at all? She didn't have to. Come on, Rich, you saw the look on her face when she saw the body lying in Curtis's room. You saw her reaction—she wasn't making that up."

Rich nodded and slowly agreed. "Yeah. Well, if she's not making it up, then I have no idea how this happened. I mean, can you come up with an alternate series of events?"

Alan shook his head in frustration. "We need to find Curtis—and fast."

Walking back down into the room where Johnny Bartel's body was still lying, Alan studied the multiple stab wounds that were located near the shoulder area, then walked back into the hallway and headed toward the front door. Captain Lee came back into the house with a smile on his face that made Alan cringe. "Good work on finding that other body, Crane," Lee said as he approached Alan.

"Yeah, thanks," replied Alan in the most insincere tone he could muster. As Lee walked by him, Alan asked, "So, Captain, did you get the autopsy results back on Johnny Bartel yet?" Alan knew that he hadn't, since he'd just left Johnny's body in the next room.

"Not yet," said Lee. "The body's still here. Didn't you just come out of the room?"

"No, I saw the body earlier but didn't know that it hadn't been sent off yet," Alan lied. He knew that Lee would not be able to restrain himself from inquiring further into Alan's curiosity if he knew the truth.

"Why do you ask?" Lee was now squinting his eyes at Alan, studying his response.

"Oh, no reason." Alan reveled in playing games with Lee. "I just thought some of the wounds appeared to be superficial shoulder wounds, and I wasn't sure that any would have been fatal."

Lee looked disgusted and sputtered in frustration, "Superficial . . . what . . . they looked fairly deep to me . . . and positioned in multiple places that would have struck major organs."

Alan looked at Lee coolly and calmly said, "Oh, you may be right. I just didn't want you to jump to any conclusions, just in case."

"Just in case what?" said Lee agitatedly.

"Well, you know, just in case something silly came back from the autopsy—like the cause of death being heart failure. Then what would all those stab wounds mean?"

Lee became enraged. "You go screw yourself, Crane! I'm going to throw you off this unit! I'm going to get rid of—"

Alan interrupted, "Ah, but would that be a good political move, Captain Lee? You know that my department wouldn't be happy, and what reason would you give? Perhaps because I wanted to be extra thorough in the scope of this investigation to save this unit from embarrassment later on? Tell me, would that be your reason?"

"Like I said," Lee hissed, "go screw yourself!"

"Actually, Captain," said Alan with a smirk, "I think that's your role, and one that you are succeeding at quite well, without my help."

Lee pushed his way past Alan and entered the room beyond. Alan could hear him telling the crime scene technicians to unzip the bag so he could look at the victim's back once more. Rich walked back down the hallway with a big smile on his face and told Alan, "Come on— before you give the captain a heart attack, we better leave and go look for Curtis."

CHAPTER 4

The Imprisoned Evil

CLYDE RICHARDS SAT ON ONE SIDE OF HIS CELL and wondered why his new cellmate was in prison. They had brought him in the middle of the night, and he hadn't had a chance to speak with him. Clyde had been arrested and convicted of armed robbery five years ago. As he looked over the newcomer this morning, he noticed that he was a small man, clean shaven and clean-cut. Clyde would have guessed him to be in for some type of white-collar crime: fraud or perhaps embezzlement. The only thing that kept him skeptical was the strange tattoo the man had on the back of his forearm. It was entirely black and in the shape of a diamond. The mark seemed to move, and Clyde wondered what type of ink was used to give it such an illusion. The man stirred and eventually sat up, rubbing his eyes.

"So you're awake," Clyde remarked.

The man ignored him.

"Hey, buddy, better start making friends in here—it may save your life," Clyde warned.

The man nodded slightly but seemed unimpressed as he replied, "Yeah, whatever. I'm not afraid to die."

Clyde contemplated the man's words; perhaps he had misjudged this one based on what he looked like. Perhaps this guy was a real psychopath. Clyde knew that it was an unspoken rule not to directly ask someone what he was in for. Some would kill you just for inquiring, so he chose his words carefully as he lowered his voice: "So what's your story?"

The man smirked slightly as he sensed that Clyde's curiosity was rising, "Homicide," replied the man. "Multiple homicides."

Clyde scoffed, "Oh, bullshit, what are you really in for?"

The man coolly repeated, "I told you, homicide. You remember a gas station clerk by the name of Nick Swanolski?"

"Uh, yeah, I do remember the name," Clyde recalled. "He was killed in a robbery, if I recall. I remember seeing it in the paper. So you killed him in a robbery?"

A sinister grin spread over the man's face as he confided, "No, I killed him after the robber had left."

A confused look came over Clyde's face. "What? Why in the hell would you kill him after the place got hit? You mean you didn't make off with any money?"

"No, not a cent."

"What kind of psycho are you? I robbed a liquor store to get myself here, but I needed the money. You said you killed a clerk—a teenage kid, if I remember—but you had no reason?"

"There was a reason, but it's not important."

"You're a real nut," said Clyde. "If what you say is true, then, well . . . I admit, I'm no angel . . . but you—"

The man cut him off. "That's right, you are no angel, and I may have use of you just yet."

Clyde became angry and growled, "Hey, nobody uses me! Unless you want me to kick your ass right here, you better change your attitude. I don't care how many people you killed, I'm twice your size, and—"

The man interrupted Clyde again and said calmly, "You're right,

I apologize. What I meant is that I need your help, and you will be rewarded. Care to hear what I have to say?"

Clyde thought about the man's offer for a moment. "Hmm, reward, you say. You mean like some money or cigarettes? Hell, why not? Let's hear it. First you can start by giving me your name."

His cellmate stood up and extended his hand. "Patrick Kent. Nice to meet you."

Clyde shook his hand. "Clyde Richards. Now let's talk business."

~

Patrick Kent smiled as he thought how easy it was to manipulate the weak-minded. The cell door slid open to one side with a thunderous clap as a guard outside yelled, "Let's go! Chow time—move it!"

Clyde walked onto the tiered walkway outside their cell, and Patrick followed. A long line of prisoners formed in front of them and behind. Neither man spoke. They continued walking until they entered a large open cafeteria with heavy picnic tables. As Patrick made his way through the line for breakfast, he turned up his nose when a man behind the food counter slopped some runny yellow mush onto his plate. The man noticed his look and grunted, "What's wrong, sweetheart, not what you usually get at the country club?"

Clyde looked back at Patrick, then over to the food server and said, "Pipe down—the man's got some friends."

The food server raised one eyebrow. "Better hope he's worth it."

Clyde walked over to an empty table, and Patrick followed. As Clyde sat down, he said, "You better have some connections that can hook us up with something good. You're already becoming a pain in the ass, and I'm not taking a hit for you. You need to keep your mouth shut and your eyes down. There ain't much to ya, so I'm thinking you wouldn't last but a few seconds in a fight."

In the same arrogant manner that he had displayed in the cell, Patrick replied, "Their idle barbaric rhetoric has no meaning to me, and I'll prove to you that I have heavy contacts who will help us."

Clyde looked unimpressed as he began eating the mush on the plate. Patrick pushed his plate forward and scanned the room. An elderly black man with a short gray beard carried his tray of food down the center aisle of the room. Patrick noticed that all the prisoners said something to him as he passed, but he could not hear the words.

As he neared the table, Clyde asked him, "Preacher, can you bless me?"

The man looked at Clyde and said, "May God bless you, my son, and keep you in His good graces."

Clyde added, "And what about my friend here?" as he motioned toward Patrick.

The man's eyes met Patrick's. "No, your friend hasn't asked for God's blessing. Tell me friend, do you wish to be blessed by God?"

Patrick retorted sharply, "No."

The preacher stared him down. "That's what I thought."

Patrick gazed at the man with sincere hatred in his eyes.

Clyde quickly interjected, "Thanks, Preacher, and have a good day."

"Same to you Clyde," the preacher responded, without taking his eyes off Patrick. He abruptly turned away, continued down the isle, and sat down at the end table.

Patrick continued to stare at him. "Who is that man?"

"His name is Elijah Johnson; we call him 'the preacher.' He's the only source of faith we have in this hellhole," Clyde added accusingly, "so you better show him some respect, you idiot."

"I don't think so," replied Patrick. "When we return to our dingy little cell, I will work on getting us better accommodations."

Clyde laughed, "Okay, Mr. Big-Shot Pansy. You better come through with something, or I'll sell you to the highest bidder."

The morning meal ended, and they made their way back to the holding block. As the two entered their cell, a guard appeared and said, "Kent, come with me. You have a visitor." Patrick smirked at Clyde as he exited the cell. About thirty minutes later, he returned and asked Clyde, "Now, what kinds of things are of value here?"

Clyde rolled his eyes and challenged, "How about drugs? You think you can score some pot, or better yet, an eight ball—or maybe a kilo? Let's see you pull that off. Then once you get that, how about some women?" Clyde laughed. "Yeah, let's see you get some women in here." He was now howling with laughter because he knew his request was impossible, but he wanted to taunt Patrick for his arrogant demeanor. Patrick nodded and replied, "Okay," then drew a cell phone from his pocket and made a call.

Clyde was dumbfounded. "Hey, how the hell did you get that in here? You can't have that! In fact, we'll be in very deep shit if they find that in here, you idiot!"

Patrick held up his left hand to silence Clyde and began speaking to someone. Clyde's attention was drawn from the conversation to the door of the cell. He turned pale with fear as he stared out and saw a tall gentleman in a gray suit with two guards.

"Warden," he whispered, as Patrick continued to talk on the phone, "I have nothing to do with this. I—"

"Mr. Kent, Mr. Kent," the warden ordered, "get off the phone." Patrick nodded and finished up his conversation and closed the phone. The warden continued, "Mr. Kent, I'm not sure what you've done to accomplish this, but I'm not happy with it at all."

Clyde sank down on his bed, and his hands began to tremble. The warden looked to his left and motioned to one of the guards, who yelled, "Open 232." The door slid open, and Clyde placed his head down in the palms of his hands. The warden and guards stepped inside.

"I have a court order here to move you and your cellmate to our protective custody wing. Like I said, I'm not sure what you've done, but

I'm not exactly happy about it." The warden paused for a moment, then added, "Nevertheless, I must obey an order from the court. You and your cellmate will follow me."

Clyde stood up, looking shocked. They were led out of the cell block and up a long flight of stairs to a hallway. As they reached the end of the hallway, the warden pointed to a door on the right. It was a wooden door, and Clyde could see no locks anywhere on it. Patrick opened the door, and Clyde followed him in. The warden looked disgusted as he turned and left with the two guards.

Clyde looked around the large room. It contained two double beds, a refrigerator, a stove, a television, a computer, and two more doors. Clyde was speechless as he made his way over to one of the doors and opened it. He peered in to see a large bathroom with a tub and a shower.

"Yes," said Patrick, "I can see you're impressed. My bathroom is over here. You can take that one."

Clyde was about to tell Patrick that he was sorry for ever doubting him, but just as he opened his mouth, there was a knock at the door. He made his way across the room and swung it open to see two women dressed in miniskirts, fishnet stockings, and low-cut sleeveless halter tops. They were carrying two large bags.

Clyde was now in total awe as one of the women said, "Heard you two want to party," and she drew forth two large bags of white powder. The other woman took out two bottles of whiskey and a twelve-pack of beer. Clyde turned back toward Patrick, who looked bored. "You can have them both," he said coolly. "I have some other work to do."

CHAPTER 5

An Optimistic Clue

I T WAS NOW AROUND MIDMORNING when Alan and Rich canvassed Mossy Grove, which took about twenty minutes since the town was so small. They visited a number of farmhouses, where they interviewed many of the owners. Rich had obtained a photograph of Curtis Norman from his mother, but it wasn't really necessary because everyone knew who he was and what he looked like.

As they approached one of the last houses, Alan noticed that it was quite large and well kept. He also made note of the name over the doorway, Bartel, and knew that this must be Johnny Bartel's home. Alan knocked and waited. After a few seconds and no response, he knocked again, this time a bit louder than before.

Still no answer.

Rich stepped up to the door and knocked as Alan said, "I'll be right back. I'm going to have a look around."

He made his way around the back of the house and looked through the windows to see if he could observe any movement from within. *No signs of anyone,* he thought. As he began walking back around to the front, he noticed a trash can sitting near the side of the house. Removing the plastic lid, he peered inside. He discovered a plastic trash bag within and undid the tie. The smell was overwhelming, and he thought for a moment that he would give up on anything that might be inside because it was making him somewhat nauseous.

After taking a deep breath and holding it, he dumped the can over, and the contents of the bag spilled across the ground. Moldy food, an old paintbrush, a broken glass, and a newspaper were among the junk now lying on the grass. As he kicked at the debris, which scattered even more, several pieces of paper folded in half caught his eye. He bent down and carefully unfolded them, using his pen. The first three pieces appeared to be an article on the advance of the white supremacist movement. The fourth appeared to be a printed website page for something called the Optimist's Corner, and the last piece was a confirmation of member-ship with Johnny Bartel's information displayed at the top. He pulled two latex gloves out of his pants pocket and put them on. Carefully, he picked up the papers and carried them around front, then opened the trunk of his car and took out an evidence bag.

As he placed the papers in the bag and sealed it, Rich came down toward the car and asked, "Find something?"

"Probably not," replied Alan. "But we'll check it out anyway. Did you see anyone inside?"

"Nope, and I just put a call into Lee, who said they've come up empty on locating Curtis on the outskirts of town."

Alan nodded. "Hey, what is today?"

Rich looked confused. "Today?" he repeated.

"Yeah, what day of the week is it?" Alan clarified.

Rich laughed, "Man, you've been working too many hours. It's Thurs-day now—Thursday morning."

"Oh." Alan yawned. "Thanks. I couldn't remember. Guess I'm tired." Alan could feel the stress of the recent events weighing heavily on him; it was now causing physical exhaustion as well as mental fatigue.

"Take me back to my car, and let's get out of here and get some rest," Rich concluded. "I'll clear it with Lee on the way, and we'll come back this afternoon. We're out of leads on our end, anyway."

They drove back to the McAllister farm and as Rich got out of Alan's car, he said, "Let's meet back at your department at around three this afternoon."

Alan opened his mouth to reply, but instead he let out a long yawn, then rubbed his eyes, which were now burning, "Okay, I'll see you then."

Rich closed the car door, and Alan pulled away, heading for home.

$\sim$

As Alan made his way back to Riverston and rounded the corner onto his street, he could barely keep his eyes open. He pulled into his driveway and lumbered out of the car. Walking into his house through the garage entrance, he saw Alison in the kitchen standing in front of the stove, making grilled cheese sandwiches for lunch. Their four-year-old daughter, Missy, was sitting at the table with a fork in one hand and a huge smile on her face. She watched and smiled as Alison placed a small plate with a sandwich and a couple of chips in front of her. Missy giggled with excitement as she started eating.

"Would you like some?" Alison asked Alan as he made his way over to the table.

"No thanks, dear," replied Alan. "I'm too tired to eat."

"I can see that," she said. "You need to go to bed and rest."

"I will. I need to look something up first, and then I'll lie down."

He pulled his laptop computer over to the table and waited for it to boot up. After all the desktop icons popped up, he went on the Internet and searched for the Optimist's Corner. It took only a few minutes to locate the website, which described a nonprofit organization that aids convicted felons and others with criminal records in obtaining jobs.

Alan pondered this for a moment, then crossed the room, picked up the phone, and called dispatch.

Dispatcher Jennifer Roberto answered the phone, and Alan said, "Jennifer, I need you to run a subject named Johnny Bartel. I need a full criminal history on him."

"Okay, do you have his date of birth?"

"Yes, May sixth, nineteen eighty-six," he replied.

After a minute or so, Jennifer said, "I can't find any criminal history on your subject."

Alan was perplexed. "Are you sure?"

"Yep. I have nothing—he's clean."

"Okay, thanks, I appreciate it. I'll be in later."

He hung up the phone and wondered why Johnny Bartel was trying to enroll in an organization that helped ex-cons obtain employment when he had no criminal past. As he sat back down at the table in front of his laptop, Missy said, "Daddy, my friend is coming over today."

"Oh, really? What's your friend's name?"

"His name is Peter and he goes to my school. We play puzzles and blocks together."

"Oh, wow, that will be a lot of fun. When is Peter coming over?" asked Alan as he looked at Alison.

"I don't know," replied Missy.

Alison smiled. "His mother is dropping him off in about thirty minutes. I have to take him home later this afternoon."

"Well, you and Peter have a good time."

Missy giggled as she got down from the table and ran off to her room. Alan made his way to his bedroom to lie down and rest for a while. He stared up at the ceiling for about twenty minutes before he sank into a deep sleep.

Alan began to dream, and he saw himself floating far above the ground. He continued to glide and noticed a large field below him with a small barn in the center. Before long, the wind around him began to swirl wildly, and he noticed the sky begin to darken. As he watched the dirt blow from the ground and spin violently, he had the sensation that he was moving faster and faster across the field, which never seemed to end. Soon his body began to spin and dip in an erratic manner, and he felt dizzy, as though he'd drunk a bottle of cheap wine. Fear gripped at his chest, and he felt the sensation of free fall while he plummeted fast toward the ground. As he neared the point of impact, his body was jerked upward, and he felt the writhing pain of a large tree limb under him crush his chest from the collision.

Alan jolted awake and sat straight up in bed, with sweat dripping from his forehead and soaking his back and his neck. He looked over at the clock, which read 2:00, then he climbed out of bed and staggered a bit as he tried to gather himself. He slowly made his way back to the kitchen, where his laptop was still sitting open. Moving the mouse to bring the computer out of sleep mode, he noticed that the Optimist's Corner website was still open. He clicked the button for the home page, and a news story popped up with the headline MULTIPLE MURDERS— LOCAL SUSPECT STILL AT LARGE. A picture of Curtis Norman was shown to the right. Alan continued to read:

> Members of the Major Case Squad are seeking a suspect who may have murdered as many as eleven people in the small town of Mossy Grove. The suspect's name is Curtis Norman, and he is a twenty-year-old white male who is considered to be armed and extremely dangerous. Captain Paul Lee, commander of the Major Case Squad, is urging the public to contact law enforcement as soon as possible if they happen to see anyone resembling Norman.
>
> Lee commented, "This person is extremely dangerous, and I have no doubt that we will bring him to justice as we always do, but I must urge people not to approach him if he's spotted. Please call the Major Case Squad or local law enforcement if you think you have seen Mr. Norman."

A recent photo was provided and will remain posted on this site until the suspect has been apprehended.

Alan shook his head in disgust as he said to himself, "Eleven people—I guess he caused most of them to have a heart attack. Lee's an idiot." Alan continued to look at the picture, whispering, "Where are you, Curtis? What really happened?"

Suddenly he was interrupted by a small hand tugging at his pants leg. He looked down to see Missy and a four-year-old boy standing next to her.

"Daddy, this is Peter. He's my friend."

"Oh, hi, Peter. Nice to meet you," said Alan.

The boy smiled and replied, "Hi" in a soft tone, then looked away.

"Daddy, what are you doing?"

"I'm working."

"How can you be working if you're not at work?" asked Missy.

Alan contemplated the question, then responded, "Well, I'm working at home. I'm trying to figure some things out."

As Alan spoke, he could see Peter moving closer, as though he wanted to hear what was being said. "What kind of things are you trying to figure out, Daddy?"

"I've lost something, and I'm trying to find it," replied Alan.

"Oh," said Missy. "What did you lose?"

Alan tried to think how he would answer. "I lost a person, and I'm trying to find him."

"And you don't remember where you left him?" Missy looked confused.

"No, I can't remember where I put him, and I'm very sad." Alan frowned so that both kids would understand.

Peter finally spoke up and said, "Oh, don't be sad. I can help you."

Alan was somewhat amused at the response. "Really? So how can you help me?"

Peter was excited about being able to help. "When I lose my shoes, my mommy always says to go back to the last place where I remember . . . um . . . where I remember . . . where I had them . . . where I had them last."

Peter continued to stumble through his explanation, and Alan smiled, thinking that the two of them looked so cute trying to help him with his investigation. As he picked up a glass of water to take a drink, Peter's words echoed in his head. A bolt of awareness struck him in the head like a brick.

"Peter!" Alan exclaimed. "You're a genius!"

He looked down at the boy, who was grinning from ear to ear, and then over at his daughter, who had her arms crossed and looked angry.

"Oh, and you," he said to Missy, "are the prettiest girl in the whole world, and the smartest."

She apparently bought the afterthought, and she smiled and hugged him.

Alison came into the room. "You're up already?"

"Yeah, hun, but I've got to go. I love you, and I'll be back after a while," he said as he kissed her cheek and headed out the door. He started his car and noticed that the clock read 2:58, and then remembered that he was supposed to meet Rich at his station at 3:00 PM.

He phoned Rich and said, "Hey, I'm on my way back out to the McCallister farm. I'll meet you there."

"Uh, okay," Rich answered. "You got something?"

"I'm not sure yet. Just meet me there, and we'll see," Alan told him.

Alan snapped his phone shut and quickly accelerated the car back toward Mossy Grove. Making his way down a narrow dirt road, he watched as the old barn appeared in the middle of the field. He parked his car, got out, took his gun out of its holster, and made sure he had a round chambered. Very cautiously, he walked toward the barn, and as he grew near, he saw something on the upper northeastern corner that immediately captured his attention.

Smoke.

Within seconds, he saw a flame erupt from the same side, and the top of the barn was also igniting. He sprinted toward the large rickety barn doors but found them locked. Just then he heard the sound of a car door open and looked back to see Rich running in his direction. Bracing his feet firmly on the ground, he yanked harder on the doors, but they still failed to open. Holstering his gun so he could grip the handle with both hands, he clenched his teeth, then yanked once more. A faint muffled shout came from inside the barn.

"Curtis!" Alan yelled through the door. "Are you in there?"

Another muffled shout came from beyond the door, and Alan knew that he had to get inside. Looking around, he spotted a rusted shovel nearby. He grabbed it and wedged the blade into the small gap between the frame and the door. Placing both of his hands on the handle, he began pushing, and as he did, he noticed Rich step up behind him to help. The door began to give way, the faded red wooden boards broke off one side, and the shovel slipped out, causing both men to topple to the ground.

Alan quickly stood up and kicked at the splintered wood to make an opening. Smoke poured out and burned his eyes, making it difficult to see. He entered and saw Curtis on the far side of the barn bound and gagged on a hay bale. Flames scurried up the sides and over the roof of the old structure, and the temperature was beginning to become unbearable. Plowing forward, Alan reached Curtis as Rich continued to widen the opening in the barn door. Alan grabbed the boy under the arms and dragged him forward. Flaming hay bales and support timbers fell around them as they staggered back to the narrow entrance.

With nearly all of his remaining energy, Alan flung Curtis through the opening, and Rich pulled him away from the barn. Exhausted and unable to focus, Alan attempted to push his way through the hole, but an enormous board crashed down on his right calf, cutting open the flesh and causing blood to spurt onto the ground. He fell through the makeshift entrance in the wall of the barn and grabbed his leg as blood rose up in between his fingers and dripped onto the dirt. Rich grabbed him and dragged him away to where Curtis was sitting nearby. The barn was now completely engulfed in flames, like prey being devoured by a huge furious beast.

"Man, you're cut bad," said Rich as he looked at Alan's leg. "I'll get some gauze. I have a first-aid kit in my trunk. Stay put."

Alan tore a portion of his pants leg off and tied the material around his calf tightly to stanch the bleeding. He reached over and removed the duct tape from Curtis's mouth.

"Thanks," said Curtis. "I thought I was dead."

Alan looked at the boy and noticed a large black abrasion around his neck. "What happened to your neck?"

Choking, and through labored breathing, Curtis replied, "They tried to hang me . . . Johnny Bartel and the others. They were part of this hate group. They wanted to kill the old man in town who owned the general store because he was Jewish. I told them I wouldn't do it, and they tried to hang me." Curtis paused to catch his breath. "But I stabbed one of them in the shoulder and got away . . . and ran. They were all distracted, so I ran." He heaved as he tried to continue talking.

"What were they distracted by?" asked Alan, wincing in pain from his injury.

Curtis continued to draw short breaths as he spoke. "There was a storm outside, and a twister blew up. Then everyone ran out of the barn. I made my way out and dragged the guy I had stabbed, too. Everyone was scattering and trying to make it to the cellar, but the twister was too fast, and it was on everyone."

Alan was confused. "*On* everyone? What do you mean?"

He noticed extreme fear come over Curtis's face: his eyes widened and his cheeks paled. "It was on everyone, like it was chasing them—like it was alive and trying to eat them. It got every last one of them, then came back for me, but it left me alone." Alan saw the young man staring upward as though he were in a trance. His voice quivered as he continued. "I watched it . . . circling . . . moving forward like a cat that stalks a bird. And then there was something . . . something inside . . . it was . . . "

Just then several cars pulled up in the road, and several men in suits entered the field. Two detectives picked Curtis up by the arms while two others pointed their guns at his head. They cut his hands free from the ropes that bound them and quickly applied handcuffs. Captain Lee swaggered up and said, "Good work, Crane. Don't move. I have an ambulance that should be here in a few minutes."

Rich arrived with the gauze and started wrapping Alan's leg. Then the four detectives pulled Curtis away toward the cars that were parked on the dirt road.

"Captain," yelled Alan, "I need to speak with you."

Captain Lee turned toward Alan. "Yes, what is it?"

"I don't think Curtis did this. There's more to it. I need to interview him," Alan said, as Rich applied the last bit of gauze.

"I have two other detectives who are handling the interrogation. Just supplement the report with the details of your findings," replied Lee.

Alan shook his head in disgust. He could see that it was no use to argue with Lee.

"Where will you be holding him?" asked Alan.

Lee turned around once more. "Guess we'll take him to the county jail for now."

As Lee walked past Alan, another man approached and said, "Good job, Alan. Lucky we got here. That phone call barely gave us enough time, and I was afraid that our suspect would die before we arrived."

Alan recognized the man as Detective Mason Bernard, who worked at the same department as Captain Lee and Rich.

"What phone call?" Alan inquired.

"The phone call we received at the department. An anonymous caller advised that we should get over to the McCallisters' barn. Didn't Lee tell you?"

"No." Alan tried to put this in perspective. "So Lee had a call telling him to get over to this barn?"

"Yeah. Well, actually, it came into dispatch. I was riding with Lee and overheard the conversation while he was on his cell phone."

"Did they say anything else?" asked Alan.

"Don't think so."

"Did Lee tell anyone else about this phone call?"

"Don't think so," Mason said, shaking his head.

Alan nodded as Captain Lee's intentions seemed to become more suspicious than ever.

He reached in his pocket for his phone and called Simmons. As he waited for Simmons to answer, two paramedics arrived with a gurney and began to move him onto it.

"Hello," said Simmons.

"Michael, it's Alan. We have Curtis. They're taking him to the county jail, and I'm going to a hospital, I believe. The closest one is in Riverston."

Simmons replied, "Okay, I'll meet you at the hospital."

"I'm okay, if you're wondering. I have a fairly deep gash on my leg, but I'll live."

"Indeed you will, and that's why I didn't inquire. I'll see you at the hospital."

Alan hung up the phone as the paramedics loaded him into the back of the ambulance.

Before the doors closed, he yelled out to Rich, "See what you can find out from Curtis. He told me that the others tried to kill him and that they were planning on murdering the store clerk, Mr. Burnstein. Find out what you can and let me know."

"Will do," replied Rich, adding, "and you get that leg taken care of."

Alan lay back and tried to forget about the pulsating pain in his calf as the ambulance doors slammed shut.

~

Alan was moved into a small curtained-off area of the hospital just off the waiting room, and a nurse entered and began to cut away the gauze on his leg. As she carefully peeled away the bandage, the burning sensation came back and Alan winced in pain. He could feel fresh blood begin to flow as some of the sores were reopened.

A doctor entered the room. "So we have a nasty cut, I hear."

"Yeah, that's what I hear," said Alan, as he grimaced and tried to fight off the pain.

"We'll get you something for the pain, and I'll be right back to stitch that up."

"Sounds good. Thanks, Doc."

The doctor and the nurse left the room, and a moment later Simmons came around the curtain and said, "So they have Curtis?"

"Yes, he's on his way to the Boone County Jail, according to Captain Lee."

"And where did you find him?" asked Simmons.

"He was tied up in the McCallisters' barn. Someone set fire to it."

Simmons contemplated this information, and Alan continued. "There's more; apparently, Lee had received an anonymous phone call telling him to go to the barn. I'm not sure what that means."

"Me, neither. What did Curtis say?"

"He said that some of the others tried to kill him but were distracted by the storm that blew in. Curtis claimed that the tornado chased the others as though it were trying to catch them, but it left him alone. Then he told me that he saw something inside it."

Simmons was quiet for a moment, then asked, "And what did he say he saw inside the vortex?"

"Don't know. That's when Lee's crew dragged him off. I think Lee's dirty. He was quick to get Curtis out of there, and he didn't want me to interview him any further. And I don't think he told anyone about the anonymous phone call."

"Let's not jump to conclusions just yet," Simmons cautioned. "But we do need to get over to the jail and speak to Curtis right away. Let's go."

"I don't think I'm going anywhere real soon," Alan reminded him, pointing to the bloody wound on his leg.

Simmons looked down and placed his hand on the wound. A warm sensation shot through Alan's leg, and he could feel tendons and flesh moving. Alan looked down in astonishment as the large puncture disappeared, and he bent his knee several times and reveled at the lack of pain.

"It's amazing," said Alan, as he continued to move his leg. "I can't believe it."

The doctor reappeared in the room holding a needle and thread. The nurse came in behind him with a syringe and said, "This should help the pain." She moved the sheet that was covering Alan's leg and dropped the syringe. "What . . . what happened . . . where is the wound?"

The doctor leaned over her shoulder as her words caught his attention. His eyebrows raised, and he looked over at Alan's face, then at his leg.

There was an awkward moment when no one spoke. Finally, Alan said with a slight laugh, "Well, I guess you guys are better than I thought. I appreciate it, and have a nice day."

He jumped up from the bed and walked beyond the curtain. Simmons smiled and nodded at the doctor and nurse, who were speechless.

"Well, I must be going also," he said as he walked out.

CHAPTER 6

The Escaped Prisoner

A LAN AND SIMMONS ARRIVED AT Boone County Jail in Simmons's car and parked in the secured lot assigned to law enforcement. They made their way through the main entrance and up to a large reinforced bulletproof window where an in-house deputy sat.

The deputy spoke through a microphone mounted on the desk. "Can I help you?"

"Lieutenant Alan Crane and Special Agent Michael Simmons. We're here to see a prisoner named Curtis Norman."

The deputy nodded and moved in front of a computer screen. He began typing on the keyboard on the counter and replied, "Okay, he just came in; let me see where he is."

He continued typing, then picked up a nearby phone. Alan could not hear the conversation, but as the deputy hung up he said, "Looks like they moved him into isolation, for some reason. Take the elevator around the corner to the second floor, and booking should be able to tell you where he is."

Alan and Simmons entered the elevator and headed for the second floor. When the doors opened, they stepped out into a small waiting area with another reinforced window on the right. They walked up to the intercom and waited for the deputy on the other end to speak. Alan told the deputy who they were and requested to see Curtis Norman. Once again the deputy picked up the phone and began talking. When he was finished, he said, "Gentlemen, come through this door and wait by the booking counter. A supervisor should be with you shortly."

Alan waited until he heard the sharp popping noise of the heavy steel door's unlocking mechanism activate. He shouldered the door and heaved it open, then walked back to an open area where a large metal bench was bolted to the floor. Two people were handcuffed to I-bolt rings on the seat of the bench, both clad in fluorescent orange jumpsuits. One of them was a skinny man who was slumped forward and looked unconscious. The other was a huge muscular man with a shaved head and a wide assortment of tattoos up and down each arm. Alan made his way over to the booking counter, where another deputy was seated.

"We're waiting to see a prisoner named Curtis Norman. Are we at the right place?" Alan asked.

"Yep," replied the deputy. "In fact, he—"

A voice behind him interrupted. "Deputy Johanson, I need to see you in here right away."

Alan looked beyond the counter to the figure who stood in the doorway. It was another deputy, and from the chevrons on his arm, Alan could tell that he must be the on-duty supervisor. Deputy Johanson walked into the office and shut the door. As the door closed, Alan overheard the supervisor say, "You didn't give them a copy of that paperwork, did you?"

Alan peered over the counter and noticed a document lying face up. After a quick look, he saw Curtis Norman's name near the top and immediately recognized it as a court order. Reaching over the counter and grabbing the paperwork, he placed it on a small copy machine behind him, then quickly pressed the start button, made a copy, and returned the original back in its place behind the counter.

"Hey," said a voice behind them.

The large tattooed man was looking up at Simmons.

"Yes?" Simmons looked at him curiously.

"You lookin' for a kid named Curtis?"

"Yes, we are," replied Simmons. "Have you seen him?"

"Yeah, he was just here. Young kid, maybe nineteen or twenty, said his name was Curtis. Some deputies took him out the door over there."

"Where does that door lead?" asked Simmons.

"It goes out to the sally port where they park the police transport vans. It looks like they were taking your friend somewhere else."

Just then the door to the back office swung open, and the supervisor came out, with the deputy following. Alan quickly stuffed his copy of the court order into his pants pocket and patted it flat.

The supervisor approached them. "I'm Sergeant Sam Billings. Can you join me in my office?"

"Sure," replied Alan as he and Simmons walked behind the counter and entered the office.

Billings shut the door and said guardedly, "I have some news about the prisoner who was here, but I need to keep this very confidential."

"Of course," replied Simmons.

"It appears that Curtis Norman has escaped."

"What!" exclaimed Alan.

Billings drew a deep breath, "We just recently discovered he was missing, and we're doing everything we can to locate him."

"May we see his cell?" asked Simmons.

Billings hesitated, as though he hadn't expected this type of request. "Well, I'm not sure . . . you see, we are trying . . . "

Simmons interrupted his bumbling speech. "We need to verify the escape and document this for our report. We need to be on the same page. If not, this could get very complicated, especially if or when the media finds out."

Billings looked at them with despair, and Alan noticed that he was becoming pale.

"Yes, of course," replied Billings reluctantly. "Right this way."

He led them through a series of doors to a cell block with double bunks. As they passed, Alan asked, "I thought your deputy said Curtis was in isolation."

"Hmm." Billings seemed to choose his words carefully. "He must have been misinformed. Mr. Norman was being held here."

He pointed to an empty cell. Alan could clearly see that two cinder blocks had been pushed out, and sunlight was streaming into the small room. As the door clanked open, Alan ran to the gaping hole and looked out.

"What?" he cried in disbelief. "This would have taken days or months to do! There's no way he did this, and look . . . look here!" He stuck his head through the opening and looked around. "It's nearly thirty feet down! He would have broken his leg when he hit the ground!"

Billings looked defeated and out of answers. "I don't know what to say. This is where he was."

Alan protested, "You expect us to believe that Curtis Norman arrived here a short while ago, dug through this reinforced wall, and plummeted thirty feet?"

Simmons interrupted, "We have what we need. We will document this, and we appreciate your time, Sergeant Billings. Can you show us the way out?"

"Uh, certainly," replied Billings, looking relieved. "Follow me—this way."

Alan said nothing, but his teeth were clenched as they made their way out of the jail back to the secured parking lot. As he got into Simmons's car, he blurted out angrily, "Why the hell did you stop me? You know he was lying!"

"Perhaps he was incapable of telling the truth at this time."

"What's the difference?" Alan demanded.

"Perhaps he doesn't fully know the truth, and besides, he wasn't going to give us any further information. Now let's have a look at that paperwork."

Alan retrieved the document from his pocket. He flattened it out and scanned the wording.

"This is a transfer order from a state appellate court ordering Curtis Norman to be detained at Midvale Minimum Security Prison in Jamestown," said Alan. "That's only twenty minutes away."

"Let me see this order."

Alan handed the paper over as he commented, "Why would an appellate court judge be ordering a prisoner transfer?"

Simmons shook his head. "Look at the bottom, and tell me if you see anything odd."

Alan took the order back and looked down near the bottom, where a signature block displayed CHIEF JUSTICE ANNETTE ANDERSON, EASTERN APPELLATE DISTRICT.

"Yes, as I said, it's signed by an appellate court judge, and it's the chief justice, to boot," said Alan. "I can't figure it out. Can't you do something to help us out? Can't you see into the future? After all, you did heal my leg, and—"

Simmons cut him off. "No, it doesn't work like that. There are limitations to intervention, and I have no more information than you do at times."

"That's too bad."

Alan took his cell phone out and punched in a number. Rich Blane picked up on the other end.

"Detective Blane speaking."

"Rich, it's Alan."

"Hey, did you hear about Curtis's escape?" asked Rich.

"Yeah, I did, but I think there's more to it. Do you know anything about Chief Justice Annette Anderson?"

"The appellate court judge?" asked Rich.

"Yeah, that's the one," confirmed Alan.

"No, not really. Why do you ask?"

"I have a court order signed by her to transfer Curtis to another facility."

"What?" said Rich, confused. "How'd you get that?"

"From Boone County Jail," replied Alan. "Found it behind the counter in the booking area."

There was a moment of silence, then Rich said, "I was told that Curtis escaped."

"Yeah, I saw the cell he allegedly escaped from," said Alan skeptically.

"You did? So what did you see?"

"Two cinder blocks removed from a reinforced cell wall and about a thirty-foot drop to the street below. There's no way it happened like that. It would have taken months to get through the wall, and the drop would have caused some serious injuries."

"Hmm," said Rich, trying to digest what Alan had just told him. "Well, this complicates things."

"I'll bet Lee has something to do with this," Alan accused.

"You may be right, but we'll need to talk about this in confidence. I'll do some checking around and let you know what I come up with."

"Sounds good; I'll catch you soon."

As Alan snapped the phone closed, Simmons said once again, "Do you see anything else odd about the document?"

Alan looked down and affixed his eyes to the signature once again. He began to shake his head, but as he did, he gazed at the right corner and stopped.

"The date," he said in a low voice. "It's dated a week ago."

~

Alan and Simmons arrived at Midvale Minimum Security Prison, parked Simmons's car, and went in the large doors to the foyer. They approached the main area, where another in-house officer sat behind a reinforced window, and Alan pushed the button for the intercom.

"Yes, sir," said the guard behind the glass.

"I'm Lieutenant Crane, and this is Special Agent Simmons from the Major Case Squad. We need to speak to a prisoner named Curtis Norman."

"One moment, sir," said the guard, as he reached for the phone. He spoke with someone for a short time, then said, "We don't have anyone by that name registered here. Are you sure that's the name?"

"Yes, that's the name," replied Alan.

"What time would he have come in?"

"Within the last hour or so," replied Alan. "He's a white male approximately twenty years of age."

The guard began typing and focused on the computer screen in front of him.

"We had a twenty-year-old white male brought in about an hour and a half ago. He's listed as a John Doe, for some reason, no identification, and he was either unconscious or wouldn't talk. It shows he was transferred again. They left here about twenty minutes ago."

"Does it say where he was transferred to?" asked Simmons.

"No," replied the guard, puzzled. "This doesn't make sense. It's very atypical, unless perhaps the transfer information hasn't been entered yet. I can try to get a hard copy of the order, if you need it. It will take some time, but I can call you when I track it down. Do you have a number I can contact you at?"

Alan rattled off a cell phone number, and the guard scribbled it down.

As the two left the prison, Alan said, "I don't like this, not in the least bit. Something is definitely wrong here."

Simmons nodded in agreement, "The guard won't call you."

"What?" asked Alan, startled. "Why would you say that?"

Simmons sighed. "Because he won't find that order."

"How do you know?" queried Alan, still very puzzled.

"I just know."

CHAPTER 7

The Silent Suspect

ALAN RETRIEVED HIS CAR FROM THE FARMHOUSE with Simmons's assistance and then followed him back to Alan's office located within the Riverston Police Station. Glancing over his e-mails, Alan noticed that he had one from one of the crime scene technicians who had worked the Burnstein murder. He opened it and found numerous pictures of the scene with a variety of blood-splattered footprints. Gazing at the picture that depicted the print resembling a woman's high-heeled shoe, he quickly picked up the phone and made an internal call.

"Clint here," said a voice on the other end. Clint Rogers was a veteran detective with the Riverston Police Department and one of Alan's close friends. He always had a way of bringing a case together, even if he was a bit unorthodox at times.

"Clint, I need to look at the photos from the Franconi murder."

"The nun?" asked Clint.

"Yes," replied Alan. "Can you bring them in when you get a chance?"

"Sure thing, boss."

A few minutes later, Clint entered the office with a large manila envelope. "Here are the pictures," he said, laying them on the desk.

"Thanks." Alan opened the envelope and began thumbing through the photos. He stopped when he came to one that depicted several sets of footprints on the ground. After scanning the picture for a few minutes, he noticed the very thing that he had thought he remembered. Among the multitude of marks on the floor throughout the victim's spattered blood was the familiar print of a spiked-heel shoe.

Clint leaned over the desk to see what Alan was looking at and said, "Hey, I got a detailed analysis from the crime scene unit and lab on the possible shoe types and sizes."

"Excellent." said Alan. "Can you grab those?"

"Back in a minute." Clint left the office, returned a short time later, and handed Alan a two-page document.

"Well, it appears that at least one of our suspects is a woman. There's a positive match for a 'Jessie Allen' spiked high-heel shoe on this list."

"Eh, could be a cross-dresser," remarked Clint with a smile.

Alan half smiled and rolled his eyes as he said, "I guess that's a possibility, so I won't rule it out."

As Alan, Clint, and Simmons stared at the list, the phone rang.

"Lieutenant Crane."

"Alan, it's Rich. They found Curtis."

"Where?" asked Alan. He couldn't believe what he was hearing.

"Down near the river. He apparently stole a car after he escaped from jail, and the car turned up on North Westmeyer Road."

"Did he say how he broke out of jail in that short amount of time?" asked Alan incredulously.

"No," replied Rich. "He's not saying anything. He's dead."

～

Alan drove his car down a remote gravel road that led very close to the riverbank. He and Simmons got out and made their way down toward the water, where Rich Blane and two crime scene technicians stood over a dark mass of black hardened remains. The sandy ground slowed them as they walked, and Alan nearly fell when his ankle turned on an uneven portion of the beach.

"Here he is," said Rich.

Alan looked down at the body, which hardly resembled a corpse. "How do we know this is Curtis?"

"Found this about ten feet away," replied Rich, holding up a torn blue backpack.

Alan took the backpack and opened it. He looked through the contents: a pair of jeans, some old sunglasses, some worn tennis shoes, and a beat-up watch with a broken crystal. Searching the pockets of the jeans, he discovered a tattered brown leather wallet. He looked inside and found a driver's license belonging to Curtis Norman. Alan shook his head in disbelief.

"Where did you find this?"

"Over here. I'll show you."

Rich stopped a short distance from where everyone was standing and pointed at the ground. Alan gazed at the spot. "Any ideas on how he was burned?"

"Nope," said Rich.

"Does Lee know about this?"

"Yeah," Rich answered. "He was here but left about five minutes before you arrived."

As Simmons looked at the body, he observed, "The fire was very hot."

Alan refocused on the charred corpse and noticed that it had partly melted, fusing the arms to the torso and the legs to each other as though someone had poured the body out like pancake batter onto a hot griddle.

Simmons looked over at Alan. "I assume Mr. Norman had only one arm?"

"What?" replied Alan in shock.

"The left arm is missing," Simmons clarified.

Rich quickly turned to look at the body again. The crime scene techs were approaching with a long black body bag.

"Did anyone tamper with this prior to our arrival?" asked Alan.

"Don't think so," said Rich. "There was nobody around when we first got here."

"Was Lee here before you?"

"Well, yeah," said Rich, slightly skeptical, "but come on now, you don't think he did anything . . ."

"I'm not saying that—just trying to cover all bases."

As Alan continued to look around, he noticed that the sand around the body appeared to be unblemished.

"If this fire was so hot, how is it that the ground is undisturbed? It looks like he was burned somewhere else and moved here."

"Let's have a look around," suggested Simmons.

Alan and Simmons began walking down the beach as the crime scene techs zipped up the body bag and loaded it into a van. Rich got on his cell phone and began talking, and Alan noticed that he appeared to be upset.

Rich yelled down to Alan, "Hey, I got to go. I'll catch you later."

Alan nodded and waved as Rich departed.

As Alan and Simmons continued to walk down the beach, Alan noticed among the pile of branches and other debris that had washed ashore, a dark object that appeared to be a small black log. They drew closer, and Alan noticed that the texture and color were the same as the blackened body they had just left behind.

"Michael, it's an arm! Doesn't it seem kind of funny that this guy, burnt to a crisp, is missing an arm, and all of a sudden here it is?"

"There are no coincidences, Alan. Everything happens for a reason— you know that."

"I guess we should bag it up and get it over to the medical examiner." Alan hesitated, looking to Simmons for his approval.

"Do you think that is the best course of action?" Simmons countered.

"Maybe not," Alan admitted. "Something feels wrong here. I'm not sending this to the lab. We're taking this with us. I need to do some checking around first so I can make sense of all this before I turn anything over to someone else. I have a friend, Nigel Stewart, who works in a private lab, and I'm sure he'd do me a favor. I'm going to have him look at this. He might be able to tell us when and how this body was burned. I've seen more than my fair share of gruesome remains in my time, but I can't imagine what would cause a body to burn to this extent. Nigel's really good. He'll be able to tell us what happened, if anyone can, and I can trust him to keep it to himself.

"I know that you see more than I do, Michael," Alan continued. "Why can't you just wave that magic wand of yours again and save us the trouble of having to find all of this out piece by piece?"

"Alan, you haven't listened. As I've said before, it doesn't work like that. We learn things in life one piece at a time. To do otherwise is not in the order of nature, and there are limits to what I can and will do. The more you develop, the more you will recognize the importance of learning in the right way. Knowledge obtained in any other way will surely lead to a falling from the path that makes knowledge good and right."

Alan pondered all the things he had learned from Simmons, but he still felt some resentment as he thought of all the good that could be done with Simmons's abilities.

Looking around, he made sure that everyone had departed the area. Seeing no one, he opened the backpack that contained the only link to the identity of the burned body, alleged to be Curtis Norman. He carefully picked up the charred arm and deposited it in a large evidence bag, which he sealed up and placed in the backpack. He and Simmons walked to his car as he contemplated what he would do next.

Alan started the car, then looked over at Simmons. "Let's get this to Nigel before someone thinks to come looking for the missing arm."

As they drove to United Technologies Laboratory Services, Alan hoped that his propensity for acting on instinct would not cause him to make a mistake for which he'd be sorry. But he knew that to understand what had really happened to this person—and more important, why—he would have to investigate without the fear of discovery by those whom he had come to mistrust.

Luckily, Nigel was working late at the lab preparing for a long three-day weekend. They arrived just as he was preparing to depart.

"Nigel, how about a few minutes for an old friend?"

"Hey, Alan. Let me guess. You have another one of those 'suspicious blood samples' that winds up being no more than marinara sauce from someone's last meal."

"No. This one's a little more challenging."

He reached into the backpack to retrieve the evidence bag that contained the arm. As he opened the evidence bag and carefully pulled out the limb, he noticed Nigel raise his eyebrows as he affixed his gaze on the black remains. Alan carefully placed it on the table in front of them, and he now noticed that the ring finger was missing. Nigel was taken aback at the sight. "Am I going to get in trouble for this?" he asked.

"You might not want to publicize it."

"So I *am* going to get in trouble." Nigel smirked.

"*Trouble* is a relative term, Nigel, and I really need this one."

Nigel continued staring at the charred arm for a moment before he said, "Okay, I'll do it. Give me a couple days."

Alan smiled, "Thanks. Call me when you know something."

∼

Alan and Simmons got back in the car, and Alan sat there for a moment staring at the cheap watch with the broken crystal that had been among Curtis Norman's belongings. As he flipped the watch over, he noticed an inscription: HONOR THE LIGHT. Alan found this strange and said to Simmons, "This inscription that's on Curtis's watch says 'Honor the Light.' Does that mean anything to you?"

Simmons shook his head. "Not sure. Perhaps there's more to it."

"Yes, maybe we should speak with Mrs. Norman."

Simmons nodded and they headed back toward Mossy Grove.

As the car pulled up to the tiny Norman house in Mossy Grove, Alan noticed that it seemed much more peaceful without the reporters and numerous police officers who had been there previously. They approached the door and knocked. After a moment or so, Mrs. Norman answered.

"Mrs. Norman," said Alan, "we need to ask you a few more questions about your son. "

"Have you found him?" Mrs. Norman cried, fighting back her tears.

Alan looked over at Simmons to get some indication of how he should respond. Simmons shot him a look to caution him against telling her that Curtis was gone.

Alan continued, "Well, not exactly, ma'am. We found this." He held up the watch, and Mrs. Norman took it to examine it closely.

"That's the watch that my husband gave Curtis just before he died."

Alan nodded, then proceeded, "I noticed an inscription on the back that says 'Honor the Light.' What does that mean?"

Mrs. Norman paused, then sighed. "It's something that my husband used to say. It's from a poem. It doesn't really mean anything."

"Do you remember the poem?" asked Simmons.

"Not really, but I may have it written down. Do you need it?"

"We would like to see it. Perhaps it will help us find your son," Alan stated.

"Let me see if I can find it. I'll be right back. Make yourselves comfortable."

Alan and Simmons sat down on the tattered brown couch in the living room. A few minutes went by, and Mrs. Norman returned with a folded piece of paper that she handed to Alan.

Alan unfolded the page. It was worn around the edges and faded, as though it had been subjected to dampness—probably from being in the wallet of her late husband. He flattened out the page and read the handwritten text:

Honor the Light of the day
When the fires loom in the distance
When the waters rise
When the winds blow strong
And the earth shakes underfoot
A kind word from a friend
A helping hand from a stranger
Gives us the strength to weather the storm
And guard that which is right
From those who do wrong
To walk the path of victory

As Alan finished reading, Mrs. Norman said, "You can have it if you think it will help you find my son."

He carefully folded the paper and placed it in his shirt pocket. "We'll keep looking for your son and let you know as soon as we discover anything."

"Thank you both," said Mrs. Norman.

They returned to the car, and Alan read the poem aloud so that Simmons could hear the words.

"What does this mean?" asked Alan.

"The 'Light of the day' may refer to the Realm of Light, pertaining to what is right and just. Strength is derived from the Light, which is based on kindness and compassion, as the references to helping another and speaking a 'kind word' imply. 'Weathering the storm' and the 'path of victory' both refer to the battle between the Light and the Darkness. I'm not completely sure about the rest. I'll need to do some checking."

Alan nodded as he took in all that Simmons was saying. He continued to stare at the paper, and suddenly he paused on the word *fires* as he recalled the horrible sight of the charred body they had discovered earlier.

"Fire," he muttered.

"What?" asked Simmons.

"Fire!" Alan said louder. "Curtis's body was burned, but it wasn't the first time someone had tried to set him on fire, and . . . " Alan stopped in midsentence, opened his cell phone, and quickly called Rich.

∾

"Blane. Who's this?"

"Rich, it's Alan. Did you get any preliminaries on the McCallister barn fire investigation?"

"Well," Rich hesitated, "a complete fire investigation wasn't actually done."

"A complete fire investigation wasn't done?" Alan repeated incredulously. "What exactly does a 'complete fire investigation' mean?"

"Other than the fire department putting the fire out, nothing else was done."

"What! You mean to tell me that no one did *anything*?"

"I think the fire marshal was going to send somebody out to do an investigation, but Lee told him not to waste his time."

Alan couldn't restrain himself from blurting out in sheer disgust, "You mean to tell me that someone burned down a barn, nearly killing our prime suspect, and no one bothers to do anything to investigate that?"

There was a pause on the other end of the phone, so Alan continued, "So *now* are you willing to believe Lee is dirty?"

"What do you want me to do, Alan? I work for the guy. Do you think I'm just going to walk up and accuse him of covering up an investigation? You gotta be crazy."

"No, I don't expect you to do that. *I*'ll do that."

"Look. Give me some time to come up with something solid, and if you're right, I'll help you nail him."

"All right, Rich. You do some checking, but this thing isn't going to lie around forever. You get back to me as soon as you learn something. By the way, what kind of shoes does Lee wear?"

"Why the hell would you ask me something like that?"

"I need to know—it's important," said Alan sincerely. "And I want to know his shoe size, too."

"All right, all right," Rich said reluctantly. "I'll find out and get back to you as soon as I can. I'll catch you later."

"See ya," Alan signed off, and he proceeded to make another call. A woman answered. "Boone County Central Dispatch."

"This is Lieutenant Alan Crane with the Major Case Squad. I need to find out if there was a fire investigator called out to work the McCallister barn fire last week."

"Hold on for a moment. Let me check the log and see if we had anyone assigned to the call."

Alan waited as the dispatcher checked to see who was on the scene.

"Lieutenant, the report says that Ross Woler from the Boone County Fire Protection District was on the scene. Do you need his number?"

"Yes, please, that would be great."

Alan copied the name and number down, then thanked the dispatcher for her help and hung up.

He turned to Simmons. "Something's just not making sense here. Rich Blane just told me that the fire was never investigated because the fire marshal's office was told not to come out, but I just checked with the dispatcher at Boone County, and she gave me the name of the fire investigator who was on the scene. It doesn't add up. The fire investigator was on the scene, but he decided not to investigate it? And beyond that, how can an investigator with any experience fail to conduct an investigation of an incident of that magnitude?"

Simmons stared blankly at Alan. "That's probably worth looking into."

Alan nodded and made one more call. He punched in the number for Ross Woler and waited for him to pick up.

"Boone County Fire, this is Ross."

"Ross, this is Lieutenant Alan Crane with the Major Case Squad. I need some information on the fire out at the McCallister farm. I understand you were there on the scene."

"Yeah, I was there. What do you want to know?"

"Can you tell me if an investigation was done by your agency?"

"Well, I started to look into it, but I was told by someone from your group that there was no need, that the Major Case Squad would take care of anything that needed to be done."

"Do you remember who that was or what he looked like?"

"Honestly, Lieutenant, there were so many people running around out there that day, I don't remember. All I recall is that the guy told me that he was from the Major Case Squad, and he was wearing credentials that said so."

"Do me a favor. Check with your people and see if anyone remembers who that was, then give me a call. I need to do some follow-up on the fire."

Alan gave Woler his cell phone number and thanked him for his time before hanging up. He turned to Simmons, who had been listening to Alan's half of the conversation, and said, "Someone has to remember something about this. It just happened a week ago."

"I'm confident that someone knows," Simmons said with a furrowed brow, "but we may never find them."

"Let's head back to the McCallister barn and take a look around."

CHAPTER 8

The Missing Barn

WHILE THE DAY SEEMED TO DRAG ON, THE extended daylight hours that summer provides encouraged Alan and Simmons to continue on. They arrived at the McCallister farm just before dusk. They made their way down to the site where the barn once stood, and Alan stared in shock. The dirt had been freshly plowed to erase all signs of where the half-burned structure had stood only a week ago.

Alan ran to the patch of newly turned earth. As he scraped the ground looking for any sign of remnants, Simmons walked up behind him.

"You won't find anything," Simmons said confidently.

"What?" asked Alan. "How do you know?"

"I know," Simmons declared somberly.

Alan looked at him and could tell that this conclusion was definite. As he surveyed the field, he noticed a large tractor with a flat blade on the front. "I bet that's what they used."

"Perhaps, but it depends on who did this."

Alan looked confused. "You're talking in circles, as usual. What do you mean?"

Simmons paused and pointed at the ground. Alan walked closer and bent down to see a small two-inch crack in the ground that led to the place where the barn once stood. "What is it?"

"The earth cracked here," replied Simmons. "It fractured as though from the impact of a tremendous force."

"What could have done this?"

"I don't know, but it wasn't that tractor," Simmons asserted. "The forces of nature far exceed that of humanity, regardless of science, technology, and human understanding. The only thing that can come close is the passion of man related to the commitment to do what's right or what's wrong, influenced by either the Light or the Darkness."

Alan stared blankly. "What do we do now?"

"The answer will come to us, but we may have to be patient."

Just as Simmons finished speaking, Alan's phone rang. "Lieutenant Crane."

"Lieutenant Crane, it's Ross Woler. I checked around but couldn't locate anyone who could recall the detective who stopped the investigation. I did, however, collect some wood fragments from the barn before I was called off. I wanted to call you and see if you needed them."

"Absolutely," replied Alan. "I'll be over tomorrow to collect what you have."

"I'll secure them for you."

Alan snapped the phone shut. "Perhaps this will shed some light on what's going on."

Simmons smiled. "Yes, perhaps it will. I'll meet you tomorrow after I do some checking."

"Sounds good," replied Alan. "I'll get you back to your car so we can go home."

~

The next morning, Alan awoke early, relieved that it was Friday. Alison and Missy were already up, and he met them in the kitchen.

Alison smiled. "All ready for another day of detective stuff?"

Alan paused, then replied, "I guess so."

"Well, at least it's exciting."

Alan frowned, "Yeah, I guess you could say that, but I'd settle for one unexciting day this week. It wears on you after a while, you know. All those people who die, all the grief and despair, and then there's the issue of the criminal justice system. Too many times I've seen those who are guilty go free."

"Well, it's not forever," said Alison.

"Yeah, I know." Alan looked over at Missy, who was eating some cereal and grinning.

"Daddy, can I come to work with you today?"

"Not today. Daddy is too busy today."

"But you said I could come with you to work. Remember? You said that you'd take me to work with you, and then we'd go to lunch together, just you and me. "

"I know, honey, but today is just not a good day for that."

"Ple-e-ease, Daddy."

"I'll tell you what. I'll take you for ice cream on Sunday."

"Ice cream . . . ya-a-ay!" exclaimed Missy, and she began singing a song about how she loved ice cream.

Alan looked at Alison and laughed as Missy continued with her elated tune. He left the house upbeat, reflecting how his daughter could make him smile no matter how much the world seemed to drag him down.

Flipping open his phone, he scrolled down the recent call list to Ross Woler's phone number and called it. Woler answered right away.

"Ross, it's Lieutenant Crane. I want to meet you to pick up that evidence."

"Sounds good, I have a meeting I have to make at nine, but I can meet you around eleven, if that's good."

"No problem," said Alan. "I need to go by the office, and I'll swing over to the fire department after that. What station will you be at?"

There was a pause, and Woler finally responded, "I'd rather not meet at the station. I'll give you my address. Can you meet me at home?"

Alan copied down the address and hung up.

Having a couple of hours to kill before he met with Woler, Alan went to the station to check his e-mail and phone messages. After sitting down at his desk, he noticed the red light on the corner of the phone blinking, indicating that he had voice mail messages. He punched in his password and listened to the first message through speakerphone. All he could hear was the sound of garbled voices and static.

Alan hit a key to replay the message and listened once more. Moving his ear closer to the speaker, he turned up the volume to hear if he could discern any words. The display screen on the phone indicated three options for the voice mail: Save, Next, and Delete. Alan's finger moved toward Delete. His hand hovered over the phone as he contemplated listening to the message again. Finally, he selected Save and went on to the two remaining messages.

The next message was from Rich Blane. "Alan, it's Rich. I may have some more information regarding that topic we discussed yesterday. Call me, and I'll fill you in." Alan hit Delete, and the final message came over the speaker.

"Alan, it's Nigel. Call me, I have some . . . ," there was a pause, then "just call me." After Alan finished listening to Nigel's message, he hit Delete and quickly called Nigel's cell phone.

"Nigel Stewart."

"Hey, it's Alan. What did you find out?"

Nigel replied, "Hold on one minute." Alan heard footsteps and a door close. Nigel lowered his voice and said, "I got some information for you on that arm you brought in."

"I'm listening."

"I think I've discovered the chemical makeup of the accelerant used to burn this person. It was benzene, polystyrene, and gasoline." Nigel paused for a moment, then continued in an even lower voice, "Alan do you realize what this is?"

"No, enlighten me."

"Historically speaking, it was called Greek or Roman fire by some and Byzantine fire by others. The Byzantines actually wrote the recipe into their military manuals."

"So some ancient chemical compound was used?"

"Well, not exactly. The substance that was used was a new and improved form of the older versions of the chemical."

"Nigel, I need you to speak in plain terms. Act like I know nothing about chemical compositions or historical references, because actually I don't."

"It's a new form of napalm. It's called napalm-B. This is why the body was in the condition you described. It burns extremely hot, crystallizing the outside and causing the inside to petrify."

"Who the hell would have access to something like this?"

"Someone with some heavy connections, perhaps a military contact."

As Alan was pondering the possibilities, Nigel continued excitedly, "There's something else."

"Let's hear it."

"After I identified the chemical composition, I did an X-ray to see if by chance anything would show up."

"And?" Alan waited for him to continue.

"There was an anomaly on the X-ray that appeared to be a pin."

"What kind of pin?" asked Alan.

"Probably from wrist surgery," Nigel surmised. "Whoever this was must have torn some tendons or ligaments and had a pin placed in his wrist to reattach them. I carefully extracted it and found that it was composed of mainly titanium, which is why it survived."

"Okay, anything else?"

"Yeah, I knew that some of these types of pins usually contain serial numbers. So after a quick look under an electron microscope, I discovered a number sequence inscribed on two of the four sides that may give us an indication of where it came from. I'll write up a brief synopsis and get it to you, but . . . " Nigel paused.

"But what?" Alan prompted.

Nigel's tone became very serious, "But I don't want my name attached to this, Alan—understand?"

"I hear you," replied Alan. "I'll keep it low-key."

Chapter 9

Unexplainable Clarity

A S ALAN TOOK A MOMENT TO GATHER HIS THOUGHTS, he once
again was interrupted by the sound of his phone's incessant ring.

"Hello."

"It's Michael. I have to talk to you."

"Yeah, I need to talk to you, too. I just talked to Nigel over at the lab
and—"

Simmons interrupted, "That will have to wait. I'll be by in ten minutes to pick you up. We have another matter to attend to that can't be
delayed."

"But Michael—"

"It'll have to wait. We have to help someone. Someone you know."

"All right, but come right over. We have to talk."

"I'll be right there."

Ten minutes later, Simmons stopped his car in front of the police station, then yelled to Alan, who was standing out front, "Get in, we have
to get going."

As they drove off, Simmons said with great concern, "I did some
checking. Curtis Norman never walked into the Light."

"But the body we found, wasn't it—" Alan began.

Simmons interrupted, "I don't know, but I know he never crossed into the Light."

"Could he have been led into the Darkness?" Alan wondered.

"I don't think so."

"Perhaps he's still alive." Alan looked confused.

"Perhaps," said Simmons.

For what seemed an eternity, neither one spoke as they both tried to think of what might have happened.

Alan finally broke the silence. "I got a call from Nigel Stewart, who said that the arm we gave him had been burned by a substance composed of benzene, polystyrene, and gasoline, which forms—"

"Yes, napalm. I'm familiar with it. I've seen it do many horrible things." Simmons finished Alan's explanation. "It's been used for centuries in one form or another. I remember it from the Byzantine era and World War II, when it was used to foster terror. It destroys completely."

"Exactly. I had hoped to get some DNA from the arm to help us identify the victim, but Nigel said there was nothing but charred and petrified flesh. But there is one thing," Alan continued. "Nigel found a surgical pin in the arm. He was able to get a serial number off of it, and I'm supposed to pick up that information from him later today, but right now we need to meet with a fire investigator who has more evidence from the barn fire in which Curtis nearly died. We need to get over there as soon as possible."

"There's no rush, Alan."

"What do you mean there's no rush?" asked Alan. "I have to meet him at eleven, and it's almost eleven now."

Simmons sighed heavily and replied, "He'll wait."

Alan's furrowed brow hinted at his exasperation as he asked Simmons, "How do you know if he'll wait? You don't even know him."

"I know who Ross is."

"So you've spoken to Ross. He's told you about the evidence."

"No, not yet, but I suspect that we'll both be talking to him very soon. I told you that we had someone who needed our help, someone you already knew. Where do think we are going now?"

Alan slammed his fist on the dashboard. "Every time I start getting close to the truth, someone dies. I'm starting to think that maybe it's my fault."

"You know better than that, Alan. You know that there is a reason for everything that happens, and everything relates to the Illissia Finistonus —the way of the Light, or as you would call it, God's plan."

Alan said nothing but recalled his talks with those much wiser than he from the "other side." He remembered hearing about the larger plan that guides everything that occurs in life, then reminisced how he had struggled with accepting the occurrences of human suffering relating to the concepts of free will and this "guiding plan."

Simmons interrupted Alan's thoughts. "Perhaps Ross Woler will be able to tell us who killed him."

Alan said with unusual confidence, "No, he won't."

Simmons waited a few seconds, then replied, "You seem sure of that. How do you know?"

A wave of satisfaction came over Alan as he sensed a change and listened to the words fall from his lips. "I just know."

Alan saw a tiny smile on Simmons's face and knew that his moment of clarity had briefly reversed their roles as student and teacher.

～

As they pulled into Ross Woler's driveway, Alan noticed that there were no cars at the house. They approached the door, and Alan took his gun from his holster. Simmons shook his head. "No need for that." Alan put the gun back in the holster, and the two went through the front door, which was standing slightly ajar.

As they made their way through the foyer, Alan saw numerous broken items, papers, and other things scattered everywhere. He carefully walked through an archway to the right that led into a dining room. A china cabinet had been overturned in one corner, and shards of broken glass were strewn about the floor.

"Looks like someone was in here looking for something," said Alan.

"Yes, it appears that way."

They made their way through the room and pushed open a swinging door into the kitchen. As Alan surveyed the room, which had been completely ransacked, his eyes finally fixed on the gruesome scene near the table. Lying on the floor in a pool of blood was Ross Woler. The all-too-familiar scene, including a variety of stab marks and wounds on the body and twelve sets of footprints in the blood around the body—made Alan shake his head in disgust. He peered hard at the footprints. He noticed that they were left in all directions, but they all seemed to be the same size and shape as one another. He was startled as a voice said, "Glad you made it." Alan looked up to see Woler's spirit standing to the right.

Simmons asked, "I don't suppose you know who did this?"

Woler replied, "I was hit from behind, and I didn't get a good look at him."

Alan nodded. Woler's answer confirmed what he had already known. He looked over at Woler and said, "You said you didn't get a good look at *him*. Was there only one of them, and was that person male?"

"I had just poured a cup of coffee, picked up the phone, and dialed you, Alan. Just as the phone connected, a man's forearm grabbed me from behind. I then felt an intense burning in my back, and I fell to the ground and lost consciousness as the life flowed through the wound."

Alan looked down at the corpse and observed, "Your neck was slashed."

"I died from the wound in my back. I'm unaware of any wounds to my neck."

Alan stood for a moment attempting to figure out this puzzling aspect of Woler's death. "You didn't hear anyone rummaging through the house?"

"No."

"It looks as though someone had gone through your home looking for something. They have overturned and destroyed every room with great intensity."

"This must have been done after I was gone," Woler concluded. "I wonder if they were looking for the evidence you were coming over to retrieve."

In all of the confusion, Alan had almost forgotten about the wood samples that Woler had collected from the barn fire. He said excitedly, "Yes, perhaps they were trying to locate the evidence. Where is it?"

"It's in the trunk of my car."

Alan recalled that there were no vehicles in Woler's driveway. "Is your car here?"

"Not my department-issued vehicle. Our support staff had come over to pick it up for service yesterday. I had forgotten that you were coming over to pick up the evidence. I tried to call you, to let you know before you got here, but I didn't make it in time. The car is due back tomorrow."

Alan recalled the garbled voice mail he had received and now realized that it must have been Woler trying to contact him as his life was ending.

"Where do your cars go for service?" asked Alan.

"Anco Tire and Auto over on Fifth Street."

"Does anyone else know that the evidence is in that car?"

Woler shook his head. "I don't believe so."

Alan nodded and Simmons said, "Well, let's get going."

The three stepped through the door that usually led to the garage and entered the hallway of polished black marble beyond. After a short walk, the familiar door to the other side came into view.

Woler opened the door, and the brilliant illumination poured through. Alan felt the warm light on his face, and Woler stopped to say some final words before he disappeared.

"I go now to join the great battle. As police officers and firefighters, we are seen as brothers and sisters united for a common good. But in the end, all of humanity is divided between those who serve the Light and those who serve the Darkness. Unfortunately, not all of our brothers and sisters may fall on the same side, but most of us will."

Alan nodded. "Yes, perhaps you're right, and I have my suspicions about those who serve the Darkness. I will do my part to see that justice becomes reality for those who degrade our good name."

Woler smiled. "I know you will."

As the door closed, Alan sat for a moment pondering what lies on the other side, beyond life. He had been in that world and seen its wonders. It gave him a great sense of peace knowing that Woler would be very happy among the Light, for he would be assigned a very important duty. *A sense of purpose always nurtures one's soul,* he thought. Some who pass on become those who actually fight the seemingly never-ending battle between the Light and the Darkness. Others who pass go on to mentor and teach the ones who fight. All who are in the world beyond life are filled with honor and pride for their contributions to the realm in which they exist.

Pondering the thought of this predetermined assignment, Alan remarked, "You know, Michael, some may argue that the lack of choice in the responsibilities that you are given after you die may be a bad thing."

Simmons replied, "There is no lack of choice."

Alan mildly disagreed. "Sure there is; after all, when you die you're given a specific assignment, specific abilities, and power along with a specific rank or classification. At least, that's been true in the examples I have seen. How is there any choice in that?"

Simmons explained calmly, "Alan, you know the answer to that question. Everyone has absolute control over the things you speak of. All among the living can choose their course in death. They make this decision in life. They forge this path from the time they spend here, and it's absolutely their choice to be good and do what's right . . . or not. That is the power they all have before they die. You know this to be true, and many here speak the words to ask for the direction of the afterlife and the ways of the Light."

Alan nodded when Simmons reaffirmed that the answer was in front of him, but as Simmons finished his last sentence, Alan became confused and asked, "How do those here ask for guidance?"

Simmons turned and faced Alan. "Haven't millions of people in your own faith uttered the words 'Thy will be done on earth as it is in heaven?' Haven't those words been spoken and sung time after time? People of other beliefs have made similar proclamations referring to 'guidance through the light' as they search for clarity. Doesn't that mean that those here cry out for the will of the Light or God, as you say? Those here ask for their duties and orders, for their sense of direction, guidance, and comfort. And the question is answered, but perhaps many choose not to listen."

Alan took a deep breath as Simmons's comments permeated his consciousness and brought clarity about the entire concept. His mind wandered back to the time when he journeyed to the other world and met with those who fought the Darkness. Alan recalled the warriors whose power and rank were based on how much kindness, compassion, and love for others they had shown during their lives. "You're right," Alan admitted, and the two stepped back into the study where Woler's lifeless body lay in a pool of blood on the floor.

Alan phoned Clint Rogers.

"Detective Rogers."

"Clint, it's Alan. Get officers over to three eighty-four Chestnut Street. We have a dead firefighter, and I'll need you over here as soon as possible."

"What!" exclaimed Rogers.

"Firefighter named Ross Woler. He's been stabbed. Get over here fast."

"Will do, boss. See you in a few minutes."

Alan continued to survey the body. His eyes fixed on the two large slashes that ran down both sides of the neck. As he looked over the stab wounds, he noticed that there seemed to be only four or five, unlike in the other murders. He again surveyed the footprints that surrounded the body. Alan bent down to get a closer look, then made another phone call.

"Detective Sergeant Blane," a voice answered.

"Rich, it's Alan. Did you ever find out the shoe size and brand worn by Lee?"

"Yeah, but it wasn't easy. I knew that he kept an extra pair of shoes in his office and that they were identical to the ones he wore in case the first pair got dirty or something. I then had to sneak into his office and—"

Alan cut him off. "Rich, Rich, what did you find out?"

"Sorry," said Rich discontinuing his rambling. "He wears a size eleven wingtip made by Olsen and Marks. The brand emblem is on the center of the sole along with the name."

Alan nodded. "You better meet me over at three eighty-four Chestnut Street in Riverton. There's been another murder."

There was a pause on the other end, then Rich finally asked, "What happened?"

"I'll tell you the rest when you get here."

Alan stared down at one of the bloody footprints before him. The same print was tracked throughout the entire scene, which led Alan to conclude that Woler had been killed by one person. Alan continued to look at the clear outline of the shoe. It appeared to be approximately a size eleven, and he could see the words *Olsen and Marks* on the center of the sole.

CHAPTER 10

On the Trail of a Murderer

AFTER SIMMONS HAD DRIVEN HIM BACK TO HIS OFFICE, Alan bid him good-bye and told him that he needed some time to think about the things that had transpired. He knew that he had to find the reason for Woler's death. The evidence that Woler had spoken about held a clue to his murder as well as to the others.

Alan's fists tightened at the thought of Captain Lee, convinced of the role that he had played in killing the firefighter and perhaps the others. His anger and frustration rose as he realized that he lacked the proof to bring him to justice. Lee had been very careful in hiding his involvement and had gone to great lengths to conceal his guilt.

Alan jumped into his car and departed for Anco Tire and Auto. He entered the front of the large automotive shop and made his way up to the counter. A clerk standing near a cash register asked, "Can I help you?"

Alan quickly flashed his badge. "I hope so. I'm Lieutenant Alan Crane from the Riverston Police Department, and I'm looking for a car that was brought in for service. It should belong to the Riverston Fire Department, specifically to a firefighter named Ross Woler."

The clerk grabbed a clipboard from the counter and began thumbing through the sheets. He shook his head. "Hmm, I don't have any fire department cars that were brought in today. Hold on one second, let me ask someone in the shop." He walked over to the door that led to the garage area and opened it, then yelled, "Hey, Roy."

Alan could see a man in a greasy jumpsuit look up from under the hood of a large black truck; he assumed that he was one of the mechanics. The man yelled back, "Yeah?"

"Hey, did we have any of the fire department cars come in today?"

The mechanic walked toward the office door, scratching his head with a dirty socket wrench. He seemed to be deep in thought. "Um . . . you know, I think I saw one come in early this morning, but someone picked it up before we could get to it."

Alan overheard the comment and asked, "Did you get a look at the person who picked it up?"

The mechanic pressed his lips tightly together and shook his head slightly. "Not really. I saw him from a distance. He was a tall guy in a jacket and tie. I assumed he was one of the people in charge over at the fire department."

"Damn," said Alan. "You didn't happen to see which way he went when he pulled out of here, did you?"

"Sure didn't," replied the mechanic.

Alan was disappointed but thanked the two men and returned to his car. As he was putting his seat belt on, his cell phone rang. "Lieutenant Crane."

"Alan, it's Rich. I put the word out about Ross's car being missing, and I got a phone call from Schmitty's Scrap Yard. Apparently someone dropped it off there earlier today."

"How did you know Ross's car was missing? I never said anything about his car, and I've just discovered that it's not here at the service station like it should be."

There was an awkward pause on the other end of the phone, and Rich finally came up with an answer. "What do you mean? Lee told me that Ross's car was gone. He said he had spoken to you. It was very shortly after you called me to tell me about Ross's murder."

"Lee never talked to me. You know what that means, Rich: he's in on this. I've been telling you this all along. And another thing, he wears the same type of shoe as the one that was tracked all over the crime scene in Ross Woler's blood."

Rich took a deep breath. "Wow, I guess you were right. What now?"

"You sit tight and keep an eye on him. I'm going over to see if I can find that car, but when I'm done, I'm going to nail that bastard to the wall."

"I'll keep a line on him and let you know if he does anything else suspicious," Rich promised

"Good," said Alan. "I'll catch you in a little while." He headed toward the junkyard.

As Alan drove down a long gravel road that led to Schmitty's, the white dust became so overwhelming that he had to roll up his window. He slowed down as he passed through the open gate of a large chain-link fence, and he nearly passed by the small office on the right because of the thick white dust clouds that followed him in. Parking the car, he stepped out and tried to catch his breath as he gagged on the dry chalky taste of lime. He waved his hand in front of his face in a meager attempt to clear the air immediately in front of him.

As the dust finally began to settle, he realized that he was parked on a large concrete slab that was actually a scale used for weighing deliveries that came into the yard. Alan could see a woman sitting at a desk behind a plate-glass window just beyond the scale. She had short greasy brown hair and puffed on a cigarette that hung from her lips. He made his way up to a small door to the left of the window. As he entered the small dirty office, he looked around. The woman turned to him and said in a gravelly voice, "How can I help you?"

Alan quickly showed her his credentials, "I'm Lieutenant Alan Crane of the Riverston Police Department, and I'm looking for a car that may have been brought here recently. It should be a newer model Ford Crown Victoria, and it belonged to the Riverston Fire Department."

The woman immediately knew what Alan was talking about. "Oh yes, I remember the car from this morning." She rummaged through some paperwork on the desk until she retrieved a small piece of paper, which she held up. "Hey, we did everything by the book. See, I have the title."

Alan held up his right hand to assure her that his intentions were not to accuse her of any wrongdoing. "I'm not concerned with that, but I would like to know who brought the vehicle here. Did you get a good look at him?"

The woman shook her head. "No, not really. I can't remember him. He handed me the title through the drop-off window, then parked the car at the far end of the yard like I told him to."

"I need to get to that car quickly. Where is it, exactly?"

"Straight ahead. Stop when you get to the crane. Ask the operator to point it out to you."

"Very good, I'll be right back. I may have some additional questions for you."

He ran out of the tiny office, got back into his car, and followed a narrow dirt pathway. The car bounced wildly as he traversed the horribly uneven terrain of the junkyard and attempted to avoid the mounds of sharp ground steel that would surely shred his tires. After a moment, a large crane with a giant flat electrical magnet hanging from its boom came into view. Alan parked off to the side of the makeshift road and approached the huge piece of machinery. As the operator saw Alan, he turned off the enormous engine that sputtered and clanged.

Alan identified himself, then said, "Hey, I'm looking for a car that came in recently. The lady in the office said it may be down here. It's a newer model fire department–issue Ford Crown Victoria. Can you show me where it is?"

The crane operator nodded. "Yeah, I can show you what's left of it. I put it through the shredder a little while ago." The crane operator led Alan over to an engine block that was placed off to the side of a large mound of steel.

"That's it?" Alan asked. "This is all that's left?"

"Yep," replied the operator. "The rest of it was ground up into tiny pieces about the size of baseballs."

"Why would you shred a brand-new car? Wouldn't it be worth more if you just resold it?"

"Hey, that's not up to me. You'll need to speak to Rosey about that."

"Rosey?" Alan echoed.

"Yeah, Rosey. I assume you met her at the front desk when you came in."

"Yes, I did. The lady at the front. I did meet her, but I didn't get her name. Thank you for your time, and I'll check with Rosey about the other information."

"No problem," replied the operator, as he made his way back to the crane.

Alan drove back to the office and spoke to Rosey again.

"So why did you shred a perfectly good car that was nearly brand-new?"

Rosey looked up from her paperwork. "Because the guy who dropped it off paid us to shred it. He insisted that we shred it as soon as possible, and he gave us a substantial amount of money to make sure it happened."

Alan became slightly angry. "And you didn't find that the least bit suspicious?"

Rosey continued to puff away on her cigarette and said defensively, "Hey, I told you he had a title. That's all we need."

Alan sighed with disgust. "Okay, so how much is the *substantial* amount that this guy paid?"

Rosey became agitated. "Hey, I don't have to tell you."

Alan's anger increased. "Look, that car was involved in a murder. I wouldn't think that you would want a great deal of publicity on this matter, so why don't you cooperate and tell me what I need to know before I have this place swarming with cops, the press, and who knows, maybe even the EPA? I'm sure they would want to take a good hard look at how 'environmentally friendly' your junkyard is."

Rosey blurted out, "It was around ten thousand in cash. It was much easier to take the cash than for us to try to resell—"

Alan interrupted. "Ten thousand!"

Rosey nodded. "Around ten thousand, give or take a few hundred."

"Okay, but you didn't get a look at the guy who dropped it off?"

"No," Rosey reiterated. "But," she continued as she held up her index finger to indicate she had come up with a new idea, "I can pull up the video surveillance for that period, and perhaps we can see who it is."

"Excellent," said Alan. "Let me see it when you get it up on the screen."

Rosey began clicking the computer mouse and typing various things on the keyboard. Finally she said, "Here it is."

Alan strained to see the tiny upper-right corner video clip on the quad screen. The front of a new red Ford Crown Victoria entered the picture. As the midsection of the car stopped on the scale, the familiar white chalky dust cloud rolled in along with it, completely masking the camera's view. Alan thought he could see the car door open but could not make out even the slightest detail about the driver.

"I can't believe this," he said despairingly.

Rosey shook her head. "I'm sorry. I guess this doesn't help you."

"No, it doesn't," replied Alan. "Well, thanks anyway."

He started to leave, but as his hand was on the doorknob, a piece of paper on the corner of the desk nearby caught his eye.

"Rosey," Alan inquired, "do you happen to give receipts for vehicles that you purchase?"

Rosey nodded. "Oh, yes, I forgot about that. We also have them sign the receipt." She thumbed through a stack of papers, pulled one out near the bottom, and handed it to Alan. "Here's the one for the car you were looking for."

Alan took the receipt. "Thank you, Rosey."

"Will that help you?"

"I'm not sure." Alan drew his breath in sharply, stunned to see the signature block. It read R. BLAIN.

CHAPTER 11

The Attempted Setup

ALAN GOT INTO HIS CAR AND immediately called Rich Blane. As soon as the detective answered, Alan demanded, "Rich, how do you sign your name?"

"What?" asked Rich, taken aback.

"How do you sign your name?"

"Uh . . . I sign it Richard Blane. Why in the hell are you asking me something like—"

Alan cut him off. "Rich listen to me carefully. I think someone is trying to set you up. How do you spell your last name?"

"What!" yelled Rich. "Set me up for what? Are you kidding me? I—"

"Rich! How is your last name spelled?"

"It's *B-L-A-N-E*. Now tell me what's going on!"

"I've just come from the scrap yard, and the car was shredded along with the evidence from the fire. The video surveillance didn't pan out, but I did manage to pull a receipt where the person who dropped the car off had to sign. The signature block shows 'R. Blain,' spelled *B-L-A-I-N*."

"No good son of a—"

"Rich!" Alan yelled again. "You need to keep yourself together and watch your back. I know Lee is behind this, and I'm thinking he's trying to pin it on you. I need to get into his car and possibly his office."

"It's got to be him. He always spells my name wrong, and just as you described. I can make some calls and see what I can do for a search warrant. You think you have enough?"

"Don't know," replied Alan, "I've got the shoe prints, but that's circumstantial at best without a detailed lab analysis."

"I'll start drafting an affidavit, and we'll see if we can get someone in the courts to play ball."

"Okay," replied Alan, "but keep your head down and meet me at my office as soon as you can. I'll—" Alan's cell phone beeped as another call came in. "Hold on one second, Rich."

Alan clicked over and heard Simmons's voice. "Alan, there's been another murder, and we need to go."

"Oh, no!" Alan exclaimed. "Not now! I'm in the middle of something that I need to act on right away. Can you give me a few hours?"

"No," Simmons declared firmly. "There's another person who has been murdered in the same manner as the others. I am growing increasingly concerned with what all this means, and we need to help her as soon as possible. We need to get going, and I'll have you back in a timely fashion."

Alan knew what Simmons was referring to when he said "timely fashion." Those from the world beyond had some limited abilities to alter or preserve time so they could walk people to the Realm of Light and not lose a moment of time in the realm of the living.

"All right," Alan conceded reluctantly. "Meet me at the office, but we need to make this quick." Alan switched back to Rich, who was still waiting.

"Rich, get that paperwork together and hang out in my office until I get back. I have an emergency situation that I need to attend to right now."

"Will do," replied Rich.

~

Alan pulled up in the police department parking lot to find Simmons waiting in his car. He got in and asked, "So who needs help this time?"

"Her name is Eva Stevenson. She's a pediatric surgeon."

"I've heard of her. She's developed some new technique that's saved hundreds of babies. Why would someone want to kill her?"

"Don't know," replied Simmons. "We'll see what she has to say."

They arrived at a large medical building and entered through the two glass doors in front, which were unlocked. Alan looked up at the enormous entryway and saw two large half-circle staircases that led up to the second level. He walked closer to the center of the room to study a large decorative fountain that was fed by water flowing from somewhere on the second floor. Simmons flipped on some lights, which illuminated the entire entryway, and Alan could now see a red tinge in the water that streamed from above.

Blood, he thought, as he gazed upward to where another fountain formed the upper basin for the waterfall. The two men made their way up the stairs, and Alan stared at the body of a middle-aged woman lying facedown at the far end of the fountain near the edge of the overflow. Her neck was slashed like the other victims' necks, and the water slowly undulated, dispersing the blood that oozed up from the stab wounds in her back. As he continued to survey the scene, something more shocking caught his attention and made his pulse quicken. Written on the ceiling above where they stood was something strange. Alan wondered if it was a different language:

ɘnɒɿƆ nɒlA

"Is that written in blood?" Alan asked anxiously.

Simmons peered up. "It appears so."

"What does it mean? Is this from your language—the divine language?" Alan thought back to his time in the other world, when he had discovered that everyone can speak the universal language of the afterlife. There were also certain words that he had learned, along with their translations, from a man who had been assigned as his teacher and mentor in the world beyond.

Simmons shook his head. "No, I don't recognize it."

"Alan Crane," said a voice behind them, which made Alan instinctively turn and place his hand on the butt of the gun under his jacket.

He looked up to see Eva Stevenson's spirit standing in front of them and sighed in relief. "You scared the crap out of me! We were just trying to figure out what these words mean."

Eva nodded and said, "Sorry . . . Alan Crane."

Alan nodded. "Yes, yes . . . I'm Alan Crane. Pleased to meet you."

Eva shook her head and clarified, "No, I'm speaking of the words—*Alan Crane.*"

Alan looked puzzled as he said, "I don't quite understand."

Eva pointed to the water near the edge of the fountain on the opposite side, where her body was lying. She said, "Look into the water."

Alan and Simmons peered into the water as a sense of realization and fear came over him. The reflection clearly showed that the words on the ceiling were reversed:

Alan Crane

His breathing quickened, and he asked Eva, "Is that written in your blood?"

"Yes, I believe it is."

"And I don't suppose that you were the one who wrote it?"

"No, and I didn't see who wrote it."

Alan continued to stare at the water as though he were in a trance. "Someone is playing with me," he murmured. Waving his hand over the surface of the water caused the haunting image to distort for a moment, then re-form.

Simmons grabbed him by the shoulder to catch his attention. "It appears so, but let's tend to the matter at hand."

Alan composed himself, turned to look at Eva, and asked, "Did you see who killed you?"

"I saw one of them," she replied.

"What did they look like?"

"He was short with a dark complexion and a short greasy-looking beard. He spoke with a thick accent, and it seemed that the others were angry at him for showing his face."

"What did he say?" Alan retrieved a notepad and pen from his pocket.

"He said something about a door, but he was very hard to understand. As soon as he said it, I heard someone else say, 'She's still alive, you idiot!' The second voice was that of a woman. I felt someone grab me from behind, and that was all I remember."

Alan scribbled down the information. "Did you recognize either voice or the man?"

"No, I have never seen him before, and the other voice did not seem familiar, either."

"Can you tell me what type of accent he had?"

"It sounded Hispanic or maybe Portuguese."

"Okay, I guess we'll be going, then," Alan concluded as he looked over at Simmons.

The three stepped through an office door on the western wall. As they walked through the short, dark, black marble hallway, Alan asked Eva, "Why would anyone want to kill you?"

She shook her head and replied, "I can't think of any reason. Most of my work involved saving children. I didn't have anyone who had shown any hatred toward me."

Alan nodded and opened the doorway that led to the other side.

Once Eva was gone, the two men returned to the scene and began to look around for more evidence of what had occurred. As Alan was bending down to try to see whether there were any bloody footprints present, as at the other crime scenes, he heard something very faint that got his attention. "Did you hear that?" he asked Simmons.

"Yes, I did."

They both stood up and listened more intently, and Alan could hear a faint sound like someone's voice. Alan ran to the opposite side of the floor, where more office doors ran along the wall.

"I think it's coming from in here," he told Simmons. He tried to turn the knob, but the door was locked. He sized up the heavy reinforced office door and determined that forcing it open would most likely not be an option. Simmons reached down and grasped the handle. He turned the knob and pushed the door open with ease. Alan frowned. "Nice— I'll expect an explanation on that later."

The two walked through the door into the large waiting area of a doctor's office. As Alan approached the reception window, he noticed business cards on the counter with Eva Stevenson's name printed on them. Simmons went through one of the side doorways and into the back of the office, and Alan followed. At the back of the office, in a small room with a table and four chairs, the body of a younger woman lay face up on the floor. Numerous gunshot wounds peppered the front of her torso. In the corner of the room, a cabinet containing numerous bottles and medical products stood open.

"Oh, thank you for finding me," said a voice from the area near the cabinet.

Alan could now see the woman's spirit standing in front of them. She walked closer to where her body was sprawled upon the floor.

"Who are you?" asked Alan.

"I'm Emily," she replied. "Emily Austin. I'm Dr. Stevenson's receptionist."

Alan turned toward Simmons and asked, "Did you know about this one?"

Simmons shook his head.

"What happened, Emily?" asked Alan.

"A man came in the office and shot me."

"Did you get a good look at him?"

Emily paused for a moment, then replied, "Well, not a good look. I didn't quite see his face, because it was dark in the room, but I think he was a cop."

Alan felt his heart leap. "Why would you think that?"

"He was dressed in a suit, and I saw a badge clipped onto his belt."

"Can you describe the badge?"

"Gold," she replied, "I believe it was gold. As I said, I couldn't see his face in the dark, but I got a glimpse of the badge, and when he first pointed the gun at me, I noticed a large ring on his finger—like a class ring or something."

Alan was somewhat confused. Emily's account was not adding up. "Emily, it seems that you were fairly calm when he was pointing the gun at you. In fact, most people who have a gun pointed at them and who believe they are about to die only focus on the gun itself. And you were able to see a ring and the badge on the man's waist, but it was too dark to see his face?"

Emily looked down, somewhat ashamed, and replied, "Well, I wasn't afraid once I saw the badge. I assumed that he was going to arrest me or something. I put my arms up to surrender, and then he began shooting. I fell and died before I had a chance to realize what was happening."

"I'm confused. Why did you expect him to arrest you? And by the way, why were you sitting in the dark?"

Emily sighed heavily. "Look, I've made some mistakes. I have been addicted to pain medication for a very long time. Dr. Stevenson always keeps some in the cabinet back here. I was in here to get some, hoping that nobody would see me."

Alan turned to Simmons. "Could this be why you didn't see this one?"

Simmons nodded his head. "Perhaps."

Alan turned back to Emily, "Can you describe anything else about the ring he wore?"

"No, not really. It was on his left hand, the same one he was holding the gun with."

"So he was left-handed?"

"Yes, I think so," replied Emily.

"Okay, Emily," said Alan. "Let's get going. We have a long walk ahead of us." As he opened the door that led into one of the examination rooms and stepped through into the marble hallway, he said to Simmons, "This may take some time."

Simmons nodded in agreement.

Alan remembered the people he had escorted through the hallway who hadn't led the most upstanding lives. They weren't necessarily bad people, but they had made mistakes while still among the living. Their hallway always offered a variety of interesting and difficult obstacles.

As the three continued for a distance to where they could no longer see the door they had initially come through, what Alan had predicted actually happened. The hallway split off to the left and to the right. He could not see the end in either direction, so he held up the badge that hung around his neck. Simmons had given him the badge when they had met, and although it had no markings or identifying organization on it, the illumination that it projected always made it easier to see through a dark and musty corridor.

After a short pause, Alan instinctively turned to the left, and the others followed. At times, Alan wondered whether Simmons actually knew the correct way to go but would allow him to lead them down the wrong path to make it a learning experience. As they neared the end of the hallway, he noticed the look of caution on Simmons's face and decided that Simmons did not know the correct path.

They came to a doorway, and Simmons began backing up slowly.

Alan knew why. The door in front of them had no illumination emitting from the edges, and as they approached, the light that shined from his badge was actually drawn into the frame, like smoke being sucked up by a fan. Alan grabbed Emily by the arm and said, "Okay, we've come the wrong way. We need to go back."

Emily looked a bit confused. "There's the door. Shouldn't I go through?"

"No," replied Alan as calmly as he could muster. "This isn't the right door."

A look of enlightenment came over Emily. Her eyes got wide, and she whispered, "Okay, let's go back, then."

The three backed away slowly and began walking in the direction from which they had come. Alan knew that the Realm of Darkness was beyond the door they had just encountered. He had previously encountered a fork in the hallway leading to two different doors. In that situation, it always seemed that the door that led to the Darkness was always easier to locate than the door that led to the Light.

The three soon passed the point where the hallway forked and continued down the fork on the right. After a substantial distance, the hallway ended in an opening that led to a narrow room beyond. Alan seemed to recall that the obstacles in such places always related to the mistakes that the person had made while alive. "Emily, tell me more about your addiction and stealing the pain medication."

Emily looked down at the ground. "Oh, I'm so ashamed. I was addicted for a long time. It ruined my life. I stole money and drugs to keep myself medicated. I pushed my family away when they reached out to help me. I was so bad at one point that I pawned a solid gold locket that was my grandmother's."

"Did you ever try to get help?"

"Not by my own accord." Emily hung her head. "My mother and father signed me up in a program, and I was supposed to stay at this center for twenty weeks. It was a step program that started off slowly, then increased in intensity to make a critical life change. I had been in trouble for stealing and agreed to go into the program rather than going to jail. My father worked it out with the court. I never completed the entire program and ended up spending about four months locked up. Once I got out, I started stealing and popping pills again."

Alan nodded as he led them into the room. He stopped at the back wall, where a ledge about knee-high rose and continued back about two feet. All three of them stepped up on the ledge and walked to the back, where they found a similar ledge that was approximately waist-high and extended back another four feet. Once again they climbed up, and Alan concluded that they were climbing a giant set of stairs that increased in size as they ascended. Alan struggled as he threw himself up onto the next step, then helped Emily up. Simmons leapt upward with ease and landed in a kneeling position.

As they continued upward, the stairs became so tall that they actually had to boost one another up. On the seventeenth step, Alan stood on Simmons's shoulders while Emily climbed up onto Alan's shoulders very cautiously and with extreme difficulty until she reached the next level, which was very wide and deep. Once she was on the ledge, she rolled onto her stomach and reached over to grab Alan's hand and pull him up. She strained as she continued to grip him, and Simmons pushed Alan's feet up over his head to move him forward. Alan rolled onto his back, and then quickly got to his knees.

He looked down at Simmons and said, "How are we going to get you up here? I don't think I can reach over far enough, even if Emily is holding on to my legs." To Alan's surprise, Simmons scaled the slick wall like a bug climbing the side of a house. Alan looked at him with some contempt as he noticed that he wasn't even winded. "Why the hell didn't you go first if you can do that?"

Simmons explained calmly, "I can't go first."

"Well, why not?" Alan demanded.

"It doesn't work like that."

Alan began to breathe deeply, trying to catch his breath, and said in frustration, "Yeah, yeah, I know, it doesn't work like that. That's what you always say. Do you have a book with the rules in it so I can read how all of *this* works? Then perhaps I can stop asking you to do things you 'can't do.'" Alan made quotation marks in the air as he said "can't do."

Simmons smiled. "Sorry, no rule book."

"Figures."

The three walked to the back of the ledge, and Alan's heart sank as he saw that the next step was not connected to the previous one. Instead, there was a ten-foot gap in front of them. He stared down at the seemingly endless hole below the staircase. As he dropped a penny over the side, he knew that he would not hear it hit the bottom—if there even was a bottom. Turning toward Emily and shaking his head, he asked, "I take it that you quit your rehabilitation around week eighteen?"

As Emily looked over at the huge void between them and the next ledge, she replied, "Yep, and now I wish I hadn't."

Alan agreed. "I wished you hadn't, either."

Emily began to cry, and Alan thought that perhaps he hadn't been as sympathetic as he should have. "Emily, I'm sorry. Don't worry, we'll make it. We've been in similar situations. We need to figure out a way to get over there."

He continued to survey the distance to the other ledge, then realized that there was still another obstacle even if they figured out a way to traverse the hole. The other ledge was very narrow, perhaps only two feet wide, with another missing step on the far side. If they were to try to jump, they would have to get a running start, then stop precisely on the next ledge without falling off the back end.

Everyone sat in silence for a moment, looking at the obstacle in front of them. Emily finally said, "Throw me over there."

"Excuse me?" asked Alan.

"Throw me over to the next ledge. When I was very young, my mother signed me up in gymnastics. I attended for about five years, and I was excellent at the balance beam. Throw me over, and I'll try to catch my balance."

"Are you crazy?" said Alan. "First of all, you could very easily fall off the other side. Second, I don't think I'm strong enough to throw you that distance."

"He is." Emily pointed at Simmons.

Simmons stepped forward and nodded to confirm what she had said. He placed his hands around Emily's waist, and she stretched out her hands to balance herself.

"I don't like this," said Alan.

"Do you have any other suggestion?" asked Simmons.

"Nope, go ahead and toss her," Alan conceded reluctantly.

Simmons flung Emily into the air, and she landed squarely on the next ledge, using her outstretched arms and bent knees to break her fall. She stood up and smiled.

Alan said, "That's good, but it doesn't get us over there. What are we going—"

Before he could finish, Simmons had picked him up and leapt with him onto the next ledge. Alan let out a yell and looked extremely angry once Simmons set him down on the slim ledge. "What the hell? I thought you couldn't go first!"

Simmons replied, "I didn't go first. I didn't say that I couldn't go second."

Alan pointed a finger at his face. "Okay, just stop talking. You really drive me up a wall sometimes!"

Simmons grinned and prepared to throw Emily to the next step. The three continued the same routine until they finally made it to the top, where the ledges ended and a short hallway continued. As they entered the corridor, Alan could see a doorway at the end where light was flowing from the edges of the frame. They drew closer, and Alan noticed an object hanging from the ceiling just in front of the door. The shards of light streaming from the doorway made the object glisten and sparkle, which projected an array of colors on the dark walls. When they came very close, Emily ran to the object and took it in her hand.

"I can't believe it. It's my grandmother's locket." She opened the tiny clasp and peered inside at her mother and father's picture. She smiled and began to cry. She quickly affixed the locket to her neck and said to both of them, "Thank you so much. You've helped me find my way. I will always remember you."

Alan smiled. "You're welcome, and I expect we might see you again sometime." With that he opened the door, and Emily stepped through. He turned to Simmons. "Now let's get back to our crime scene. Since it didn't occur in Riverston, I'll have to call the appropriate jurisdiction, which is Evansville."

Evansville bordered Riverston. It was a much larger city, with a population of about 60,000 people. Its police department had around 100 police officers, including his friend, Detective Rich Blane, and the very person whom he would soon accuse of being a corrupt cop, Captain Paul Lee.

CHAPTER 12

The Ring

ALAN AND SIMMONS WALKED BACK TO where Eva Stevenson's body lay in the fountain. Alan phoned Rich Blane.

"Blane."

"It's Alan. Did you make any progress on the search warrants?"

"Yeah, I think we'll get them. Are you still meeting me over at the station?"

"No, change of plans. I got a . . . " Alan paused as he tried to think of how he could explain his knowledge of Eva Stevenson's murder. "I got another tip from the FBI agent I've been working with about an incident at the Gateway Medical Building in your city. We just arrived and found the building unsecured. There's been another murder. You may want to notify your department and meet me over here. I have more things to discuss regarding the situation with your captain."

"Another murder!" exclaimed Rich. "This just keeps getting better by the minute." His tone was sarcastic. "I'll notify our dispatch center, and I'll meet you over there in a few minutes."

"Sounds good, see you in a few."

Alan and Simmons made their way down toward the entranceway to the building. Within minutes, Alan could hear car doors slamming and people approaching. A man in a suit hastily pushed open the heavy electronic door and walked briskly toward Alan and Simmons.

"How the hell did you know about this!" the man blurted out accusingly.

Alan looked at him, feeling a surge of contempt.

Lee!

Before Alan could think about what he should say, he sharply retaliated, "Perhaps I should ask you the same thing."

Captain Lee paused for a moment and turned his head to the side, looking bewildered. Alan realized that this was not the time for the confrontation that he so much desired. Before Lee could respond, Alan said, "Agent Simmons here received information from an informant that there was suspicious activity occurring in this medical facility. He contacted me and asked if I could show him where the building was. I escorted him over here, and we found the front door unsecure. I called as soon as I discovered the bodies."

"What kind of suspicious activity?"

Simmons looked at Lee and replied, "That's classified—a matter of national security. I can't discuss the details."

Alan almost laughed as he watched Lee's face intensify with anger. He knew that Lee's ego would not be able to handle someone telling him that he wasn't important enough to be privy to something confidential.

"I'm the commander of the Major Case Squad, and there's been a murder here!" Lee yelled at Simmons.

Simmons nodded and smiled. "Okay."

Lee clenched his fists, and Alan couldn't help but smile. A simple okay was worse than any obscenities or derogatory comments that Simmons could have made. It was a false acceptance that really said, "That's nice, but I don't care"—or that's the way Lee would have interpreted it, anyway.

Just as Lee was about to start in again on Simmons, Alan interrupted. "Mur*ders*. There's more than one body here."

Lee looked at Alan briefly and turned back toward Simmons, about to begin yelling again. There were now several people pouring into the building, and Alan pointed up the stairs toward the fountain where Dr. Stevenson's body was still lying.

Once again, before Lee could speak, Alan said, "Perhaps you didn't hear me, I said there's more than one body here."

"I heard you, Crane!" yelled Lee agitatedly.

Alan noticed that this was the third time he had tried to relay that there was more than one murder and Lee had not been surprised. Because Alan had told Rich there had been another murder but hadn't told him about the second victim, this confirmed his suspicion that Lee had previous knowledge about this incident. Lee's response should have been focused on the multiple deaths, but instead he seemed to be more concerned with what Alan and Simmons knew. This added to Alan's belief about Lee's involvement and guilt. Lee began to lecture Simmons again that he should have been informed about the suspicious activity. Alan noticed the gold badge that hung on the right side of Lee's waist, which meant that he must wear his gun on his left side.

"I wasn't aware you were left-handed," Alan observed.

Lee stopped his rant briefly and looked at Alan with disgust. "What?"

"You're left-handed. I never noticed that."

Lee shook his head and glared at Alan as though he wanted to spit on him. "What the hell does me being left-handed have to do with anything, Crane?" Lee pulled his jacket back and rested his left hand on his gun.

"Nothing," replied Alan. "Nice ring you have there."

Lee brought his left hand up to display the large gold ring. His demeanor changed somewhat as he said in a calmer voice, "Oh, it's the ring I got when I graduated from the FBI National Academy." Alan knew that Lee could be distracted by talking about himself. "Yes, I was selected to attend a few years ago—great program."

Alan's contempt grew even more as he thought about Lee attending the FBI National Academy. It was probably the highest professional certification that one could attain in law enforcement, like a lawyer passing the bar exam or an accountant becoming a CPA. The FBI National Academy was an advanced course for senior-level law enforcement officers. The course entailed ten weeks of intensive training and testing with the various units of the FBI. Getting in was extremely hard; only one-half of 1 percent of law enforcement worldwide was accepted. This was something that Alan aspired to do in his career, and the thought that Lee had been given the opportunity and privilege to attend made his stomach turn.

"Captain," yelled a voice from overhead.

"I'll be right up," said Lee, and he began to ascend the stairs.

"The other body is in an office in the back," yelled Alan to Lee, "just in case you didn't know or don't remember."

Lee turned and glared at Alan for a moment, then his hand shot down and quickly pulled his pistol from his belt. Alan was caught off guard but quickly drew his gun and pointed it down at the floor, unsure of what the captain was going to do. He anticipated a gunfight, but Lee never raised his weapon. Instead he said, "Have you cleared the rest of the building?"

"No," replied Alan, somewhat relieved but still keeping his gun ready.

Lee seemed not to pay much attention to Alan's actions. He nodded and continued up the stairs. When he reached the top, Alan could hear him gathering a couple of officers to help him with a building search.

Alan put his gun back in his holster and took a deep breath.

A hand on his shoulder caught his attention, and he looked behind him to see Rich.

"You okay?" asked Rich.

Alan nodded. "Yeah, I'll be fine."

"I hope to have those search warrants by Monday. I'll be in touch, but until then, watch your back."

"Oh, I am, believe me," Alan declared. He watched as Rich began to climb the stairs.

"Let's leave," said Simmons. "There's no more we can do here."

Alan nodded as the two disappeared out the front doors and headed back to Alan's office.

CHAPTER 13

Duty Calls

SATURDAY MORNING CAME, and Alan was eating breakfast with his family. He had left his cell phone in the bedroom, not wanting to deal with anything work-related for the time being. After all the recent events, he knew that the weekend would not offer him a reprieve, and he anticipated a call. As he continued to eat, he could hear the distinct ring from the other room. Alison heard it as well and said, "Your phone is ringing."

Alan nodded. "Let's finish breakfast."

"What if it's an emergency?"

"It's always an emergency," he said wearily. He looked over at his daughter, who was eating a bowl of cereal and smiling after each bite. "Is that good?" he asked. She said nothing, just nodded and smiled even bigger so that Alan could see the food in her teeth. Grinning back at her, he forgot about his phone, which had stopped ringing. Picking up the steaming hot mug of coffee he had just poured, he sipped it slowly and began to relax, only to be interrupted by the ringing of his phone again about thirty seconds later. Grudgingly, he stood up and walked toward the bedroom, saying, "Sometimes I wish I didn't own a cell phone."

"You don't," Alison retorted humorously. "It's the department's phone, remember?"

"Yeah, that makes it better. I guess it's the job that drives me crazy at times."

"So you wish you didn't have a job?" she probed, trying to spark a certain response or thought process.

Alan sighed. "No, I'm grateful for my job. I just sometimes wish I didn't have this particular job."

"Ah, so you want a different job. Perhaps one that doesn't bother you as much—especially on the weekends. Well, maybe your experience in law enforcement could open up some new opportunities."

Alan replied cynically, "Yeah, right—my experiences."

"Well, you have encountered many interesting things through your work, haven't you?"

Alan thought about this last question for a moment. "You have *no* idea."

"Perhaps you could write a book."

"Yeah, sure," he said with a laugh. "Take it from me, nobody would believe the experiences I've had—they'd lock me up in the nuthouse."

Alison smiled. "Well, then you'll just have to write a novel—since you'll have all that time sitting in the padded room at the nuthouse."

"I'll keep that in mind," Alan laughed.

"Hey, at least I got you to smile," Alison pointed out, and Alan realized that this had been her goal from the beginning of the conversation.

He nodded and continued smiling. "I'll be right back."

As he reached the nightstand where the phone was still connected to the charger, it stopped ringing. He reached down and opened it up to see the display indicating two missed calls. As he walked back to the kitchen, he heard his home phone ring and his wife answer. She held out the phone. "It's Clint."

Alan frowned as he took the phone. He tried not to sound rude, realizing that it wasn't Clint's fault. "Hey Clint, what's up?"

Clint started as he usually did. "I'm sorry to bother you on the week-end, but I got something you need to know about."

"Sure, what's going on?"

"I'm down at the old Gallo meatpacking plant. Patrol got a call about an open door and went in to see if someone had broken in."

"Isn't it abandoned?" asked Alan.

"Yeah, it has been for years. Anyway, when they started searching the place, we found multiple bodies—and when I say multiple, I mean we're still counting."

A call such as this would normally have made Alan jump to his feet in an adrenaline rush, but in light of recent events, he merely shook his head and sighed. "What number are we up to now?"

"Twenty-one, last time I checked."

"Twenty-one!" The adrenaline was now kicking in. "You have twenty-one bodies?"

"As I said, we're not done counting."

"Any idea how they died?"

"Not yet. I've glanced over a few of them, and they all appear intact, but it seems that they are all bloated."

"Bloated," Alan echoed in confusion.

"Yeah, you know, like a floater."

Alan knew that the term *floater* referred to a dead body that had expanded as a result of either gases leaving the corpse or some other environmental factor. "So have they been there for a while?"

"Can't tell yet, but the stench is unbearable."

"Wonderful," replied Alan sarcastically. "I can't wait to get there. I'll be down in a few."

"Okay, I'll continue to get a head count and try to find some ID on them after crime scene gets some initial processing done."

"Sounds good. I'll catch you on scene in a bit."

Alan hung up and told Alison what had happened and that he needed to go.

She kissed him on the cheek. "Go ahead, we'll be here when you get back."

"I know, but it's Saturday, and I've been at this all week . . . and . . . I miss you guys."

"We have tomorrow," said Alison. "We can do something after church."

"How do you know I won't get called out tomorrow?" asked Alan, frustrated.

"I'll ask God to give you the day off," she laughed.

Alan chuckled. "Okay, you do that, and let me know what He says."

He kissed his wife and daughter good-bye, then left the house.

CHAPTER 14

A Watery Grave

AS ALAN PULLED UP TO THE old brick meatpacking plant, he noticed a number of dark colored minivans parked outside. These were used by the medical examiner's office to transport bodies for autopsies. As he walked up to the main entrance, he noticed a large amount of broken glass strewn all over the sidewalk. Looking up, he could see that all of the windows in the upper portion of the building had been broken. The lower windows had been boarded up, and as he approached to get a closer look, a voice behind him said, "Glad you're here."

Alan turned around to see Clint Rogers standing next to a woman he recognized. "Dr. Catanick?" Alan asked.

"Yes," replied the woman. "I thought I should personally take a look around with this many victims and these . . ."—she paused for a moment, searching for the right words—" . . . well, unusual circumstances."

Alan nodded and remembered her from past cases. Andrea Catanick was the main medical examiner for the region. A year ago, Alan had recalled a case in which two bodies had been discovered with strange-looking wounds on their backs. The wounds had been dark black, and Dr. Catanick had described them as being burned by something very cold. She had been intrigued by the mysterious punctures, and Simmons had told her that they were searching for a serial killer who might be using a chemical to burn his victims. This turned out not to be the case; both victims had been killed by a weapon that was from the world beyond the living. Perhaps this was why Dr. Catanick had shown up at this particular scene. This suspicious event had probably piqued her interest once again.

"I noticed all the upper windows have been shattered," said Alan.

"Yeah, there's glass everywhere, and from the looks of it, the windows were pushed outward—not much glass on the inside," commented Clint.

"Let's see what we have inside."

As the three approached the front door, the putrid smell of death overwhelmed Alan. Dr. Catanick pulled a small jar of menthol gel from her pocket and unscrewed the lid. She held it out for Alan, who scooped a small amount out with his fingertips.

"You'll need more than that," she said.

Alan nodded, scooped out more, and rubbed it just below his nose. Clint did the same. As the three entered, Alan could see bodies strewn about the floor and crime scene technicians busy at work. He surveyed the building and noticed that the place was virtually empty, except for a few large steel tables and the long overhead cable system with numerous meat hooks hanging down from the ceiling. It looked like a scene from a horror movie.

Alan turned to Clint. "How many did we end up with?"

"Twenty-three here on the floor and seven more we're still trying to recover. The fire department should be here soon to help."

"What do you mean?" asked Alan.

Clint took a small flashlight out of his pocket and clicked it on. "There's no electricity. Everything was blown—circuits, fuses, everything." He pointed the light upward toward the rafters, and now Alan could see the outlines of seven more bodies dangling.

"What the hell . . . " he said, shocked.

"My feelings exactly," said a voice behind them.

All three of them turned to see Simmons standing in the entryway.

"Ah," said Dr. Catanick. "It's your friend from the FBI who always seems to show up when strange events happen."

Alan nodded and appreciated her keen sense of understanding, "Hello, Agent Simmons," he said, in an attempt to reinforce that Simmons was indeed from the FBI.

"Good day," replied Simmons.

A uniformed police officer and a crime scene technician approached the four quickly. The officer told Clint, "Detective, you may want to take a look at this."

Clint nodded, and they followed the officer to the far end of the plant. He led them down a short hallway and into what appeared to be the men's restroom. The room had been completely destroyed; the tile had been removed from the walls and the floor. As Alan looked around, he noticed that all of the toilets and sinks were missing; only twisted and mangled pipes remained. "What happened to all the plumbing?" asked Alan.

"Up there, sir," said the officer, pointing to the ceiling.

Alan had to strain to see past the rafters to the thick foamlike insulation, where he could see a portion of what appeared to be a toilet. He continued to look on in disbelief as he realized that the floor was littered with shattered pieces of porcelain. Everyone's mouth hung open except for Simmons's; the agent merely had a look of sincere concern on his face. Alan stumbled for the words. "It's like they exploded . . . like they blew up, or were launched from a cannon . . . what the . . . "

"You think the pipes blew?" asked Clint.

"I've seen pipes break before," Alan declared, shaking his head, "but I've never seen anything like this. The water pressure that would have been needed to do this is beyond anything that I can explain."

"I noticed that there were numerous puddles of water around the scene, almost like there was a recent flood," said Clint, pointing to some standing water on the floor.

Alan turned his attention to this; he hadn't noticed all of the random spots of water when they had first walked in because of the distraction of so many corpses. Scanning the scene, he began to see other things that supported the theory of the pipes exploding. There was water slowly dripping overhead, and the wood used to board up the lower windows seemed damp to the touch.

Dr. Catanick drew out the small jar and held it toward Simmons. "I'm sorry, I forgot to offer you some. The stench is overwhelming."

"Thank you, but I'm fine," replied Simmons.

Dr. Catanick nodded and commented curiously, "So the smell of the dead doesn't bother you. You're a man after my own heart."

Alan didn't know if she said this to Simmons to find out more about who he really was or if she was coming on to him. Either way, Alan found it quite amusing and added, "Oh, yes, Michael has a deep appreciation for death. I'm sure he would share it with you sometime if you asked."

Simmons seemed to quickly pick up on Alan's attempt to encourage the doctor to delve into his background. He smiled politely. "Perhaps some of the stench isn't coming from the bodies."

Alan was confused by this comment. Simmons was notorious for saying something and then waiting for someone to ask for an explanation. He wondered whether Simmons was playing devil's advocate to distract Dr. Catanick from asking him more questions.

"Perhaps it's from the raw sewage that's scattered all around us," Simmons offered.

Alan rebutted, "There are several bodies scattered about, and they've been here for some time, obviously—look how bloated they are."

The conversation was interrupted by another uniformed officer who addressed Alan. "Lieutenant, we've found some identification on one of the subjects." The officer led them over to where one of the bodies lay on the floor. "This is Mr. Martin Carnus. I called his name in and had dispatch run it through the computer. He has an extensive criminal history involving the distribution of narcotics."

"Martin Carnus," Alan pondered aloud. "Why does that name sound familiar, Clint?"

"The drug unit's been working cases on him for a while—he was a major distribution point, or so they thought. He's been involved in numerous methamphetamine operations and various violent crimes."

Alan remembered now. "That's right, he's a major local player, hooked on meth."

The officer added, "His driver's license lists him as six feet tall, weighing two hundred and fifteen pounds."

Alan looked down at the enormously bloated body and replied, "Looks more like three hundred and fifteen pounds now. Like I said before, these bodies have been here for a while—hence the foul smell about this place."

Dr. Catanick bent down to get a closer look. "Perhaps Agent Simmons is correct. Perhaps we are standing in a huge sewer and the stench is not from these bodies. As I look at Mr. Carnus, I am leaning more toward the theory that he has not been dead for any significant length of time." She pushed slightly on the chest area, and as she did, liquid bubbled up from the mouth and poured down both sides of the cheeks, like a plastic bottle full of water that has just been squeezed.

"Then why are these bodies so bloated?" asked Alan.

"Water," replied Dr. Catanick.

"Water?" Alan repeated. "Then what killed them?"

Dr. Catanick stood up, looking concerned. "Preliminarily, it appears as though they've drowned."

CHAPTER 15

The Dark Blade

SUNDAY WENT WELL BECAUSE Alison's prediction that Alan would not be called in to work came true. The time with his family was invaluable. He even got to take Missy for ice cream, as he had promised.

Monday morning came too quickly. He woke early, dressed, and went into work. The first thing he did in his office was to check his voice mail. Alan listened again to the saved garbled message that he now believed was from Ross Woler, the fire investigator who had attempted to call him on the day he was killed. He restarted the message and turned up the volume to hear if he could make out any sounds in the background.

Just before the message ended, there was a very short portion that sounded like someone's voice. Alan replayed the message and transferred it onto a digital recorder, which he then downloaded onto his computer. The computer's speakers were of better quality than the phone speaker, and as he played with the sound controls, he was finally able to make out the voice and what it said: "Evansville units prepare to copy— "

Then the phone went dead, but there was enough there for Alan to realize what it was—a police radio for the Evansville Police Department.

Whoever killed Ross Woler must have had a police handheld radio on, since the words were that of an Evansville Police dispatcher—the very police department where Captain Lee worked. Alan jotted down a note to remind himself to tell Rich about his discovery and to add this to the murder cases in which he believed Lee was involved.

He saved the garbled message once again and went on to the next voice mail. Rich Blane's voice came over the speaker and said, "Alan, I've got those warrants we spoke about. I will meet you at your office around eight o'clock."

Alan glanced at the clock in the lower right-hand corner of his computer screen; it read 7:39. He dialed dispatch, and a woman's voice responded, "Yes, Lieutenant."

"I'm expecting a Detective Blane from the Evansville Police Department to arrive shortly."

"He's here now," replied the dispatcher. "Do you want me to bring him back?"

"Yes, that would be great."

Within a few seconds, Rich appeared in Alan's office.

"I have the warrants right here, and I've notified my chief, who's initiated an internal investigation. The chief has directed me to turn the criminal investigation over to the FBI now that Lee is a suspect. I contacted the field office and let them know. I thought perhaps your friend who was on the scene of several of these incidents might be assigned, but the field office didn't seem to know who he was. Wasn't his name Michael Simmons?"

The question caught Alan off guard, and he had to think quickly, "Oh, well, that's because he's not out of the local office. He's dispatched from D.C. I should give him a call and see if he's going to help."

Rich nodded. "The Major Case Squad will still be handling the other murders they were assigned to, but our department will not participate because of the possibility of a conflict of interest. I did, however, seize the shoes Lee keeps in his office—you know, the ones that possibly matched our crime scene."

Alan nodded his approval, then added, "You'll want to seize the other shoes he wears into work just in case you have the wrong pair. You'll also want to seize his gun and see if it matches the ballistics in any of the shootings."

"Shootings?" said Rich, confused. "The only person who was shot was the assistant in Dr. Stevenson's office, Emily Austin."

"Well, you never know. I'd check it out just in case. Lee was acting suspicious when I saw him at the scene." He could not tell Rich that he had spoken to Emily after she had died and that she had described the gold badge and the ring that matched the one on Lee's left hand.

"Really?" said Rich, surprised. "What did he do at the scene?"

Alan had hoped that Rich wouldn't ask this. "He seemed extremely agitated and defensive about Special Agent Simmons and me discovering the murders prior to his arrival. I'm telling you, it was suspicious. I'd take the gun just to cover all of your bases."

Rich nodded. "Well, it's not our investigation, anyway. I'll pass it on to the feds, and they can take it, if they want. I'll tell them that we have reason to believe it may have been used in the shooting."

"I also have reason to believe that this voice mail I received was from Ross Woler the day he died. I think he tried to call me while the killer entered his home and attacked him."

"Why would you think that?"

Alan scrambled to think of an explanation besides telling him that Woler had spoke to him after he was dead. He quickly came up with a solution. "I saw my number on the caller ID feature on his phone for outgoing calls, and the time frame matched the time on the voice mail. Anyway, listen to this." He played the call back on the computer so Rich could hear the radio traffic that was recorded at the end.

"Wow! That's definitely one of our dispatchers. Lee must have had his radio in his pocket or something when he entered the house. That's very incriminating, and I'll let our Internal Affairs division know about it also."

"Is the captain married?" Alan wanted to know.

"Uh, no," Rich answered. "He's divorced. Why do you ask?"

"No real reason." Alan was purposely vague. "I noticed he wore a class ring on his left hand. He said it was from the FBI Academy. I was just wondering if anyone else would be home when the search warrant was served."

Alan flipped open his cell phone and called Simmons.

"Yes, Alan," said Simmons.

"Hey, I'm here with Rich Blane, and he has some search warrants that he's turning over to . . . "—he paused for a moment—". . . to your agency. I was wondering if I may be able to go along when those are served."

"I'm sure I can arrange something," replied Simmons. "I'll pick you up within the hour, and we'll go see what we can find."

"Sounds good, Rich isn't supposed to participate in the investigation, but perhaps we could bring him along to observe."

"Fine with me," said Simmons. "I'll see you in a few minutes."

Alan turned back to Rich and said, "I assume you would want to come along, since you've put all this work into the case."

"Certainly," replied Rich. "I appreciate the invitation."

～

Alan and Rich entered Simmons's car, which had stopped in front of the station. "I've received authorization to proceed with serving the warrants," said Simmons.

"Good," replied Alan. "Where to first?"

"I guess we need to go to Lee's house," replied Rich. "But I'm not going in if he's home. It would be . . . "—he paused for a moment—". . . well, you know, uncomfortable, since we work together and all."

"What's the address?" asked Alan.

"He lives over in Winding Lake Estates in Evansville. His address is one ninety-three Winding Creek Drive."

Within moments the three were parked in the street in front of Captain Paul Lee's home. Alan noticed that there were no cars in the driveway, and nobody appeared to be home.

Simmons and Alan approached the front door and rang the bell.

No answer.

Alan knocked harder and rang the doorbell once again.

Still no answer.

"Do we force our way in?" asked Alan.

Simmons smiled. "No need." He turned the knob and pushed the door open.

"Was that locked, or did you . . . " Alan began to ask as Simmons entered the house. Alan motioned to Rich, who quickly got out of the car and ran up to meet them.

"Where is the captain supposed to be today?" asked Alan.

"Supposed to be in training," replied Rich. "But I wasn't sure what time he had to leave his house."

Rich handed the copies of the warrants to Simmons, who folded them in half and placed them in his jacket pocket. Alan took out a small digital camera that he had brought along. The three made their way back to the bedroom, and Alan looked through the closet, where several pairs of shoes were arranged in an orderly fashion on the floor.

"It looks like he may be wearing the other pair of shoes that we need. None of these match the description," said Alan, as he shuffled through the closet.

"No sign of his gun," stated Rich, who was looking through the dresser drawers. "Most likely he has it with him."

Alan heard footsteps coming down the hall, and his hand went immediately to his weapon holstered on his waist. He thought for a moment that Rich was going to try to hide in the closet. Two men in dark-colored suits appeared, and the taller of the two said, "Hey, Simmons, sorry we're late."

"No problem," Simmons told them. "Let me introduce everyone, Alan, Rich, these are Special Agents Dockins and Stallworth from the FBI. Gentlemen, this is Detective Sergeant Rich Blane and Lieutenant Alan Crane."

The four nodded in acknowledgment, and Dockins said, "We'll take the other half of the house and the garage. You find anything yet?"

"Not yet," said Simmons.

The two agents left the room.

Alan continued to search through the bedroom but found nothing of interest. He, Rich, and Simmons then went back down the hallway to the kitchen. As Alan was opening a drawer near the stove, he heard Dockins call from the garage, "Hey, we got something over here."

Alan, Rich, and Simmons made their way into the garage, where Dockins was holding a ladder and Stallworth was standing on the top rung. Most of his body was hidden in the crawl space above the garage ceiling.

"What have you got?" asked Alan.

"Some type of knife," replied Stallworth. "It looks like it might have some blood on it, but it's hard to tell. Pass me the camera, Dockins."

Stallworth stepped a few rungs down the ladder so Dockins could hand him the camera.

"So you can't tell if there's blood on it? You need a light?" offered Alan.

Stallworth shook his head. "I got a light. It's hard to tell because the knife is a dark metal."

He grabbed the camera and ascended the ladder once more. Alan saw three bright flashes of light, and Stallworth descended the ladder carrying the camera in one hand and a clear plastic bag in the other. As he reached the ground, he held up the bag so Alan, Simmons, and Rich could see it. Inside the bag Alan saw a black curved blade that he immediately recognized from his travels to the world beyond life.

"It's not metal," Alan whispered as his eyes widened. "It's a type of obsidian stone. I've seen it before." Thoughts were racing through his mind as he recalled what this was: a weapon of the Darkness used by those who were evil and vile.

Stallworth seemed somewhat confused by Alan's comments but ignored them. Dockins hit the garage door opener button, and the door rose slowly. Stallworth walked to the edge of the garage and held up the knife, trying to get a better look at the blade. "I think I see some blood on it," he said as he strained to look at it closer.

Dockins pondered out loud, "Wonder if this is our murder weapon."

"It is," replied Simmons.

"You seem confident, Simmons. How do you know?" asked Stallworth.

"I just know."

The five of them continued to stare at the black blade with the ornately carved handle as the sunlight seemed to be drawn into it, consumed.

Alan, Simmons, and Rich sat in the parking lot of the Central County Police Academy. The training course that Lee was in was due to end at 3:00 PM, and it was 2:50 now. Dockins and Stallworth waited at the entrance while Simmons, Alan, and Rich sat in Simmons's car, which was parked next to Lee's car. They had decided that it would be better to wait until Lee exited the academy in order to reduce the drama that was going to occur when the FBI arrested him.

At 3:10 PM, Alan saw Lee walking out the front doors. Stallworth and Dockins approached him. Alan could not hear what they were saying, but he could tell that Lee looked confused yet seemed to be cooperating. He saw Stallworth reach into Lee's waistband and retrieve a pistol, which he handed to Dockins, who placed it in a plastic evidence bag. Lee began to argue and protest but allowed Stallworth to cuff him. They escorted him over to their car and placed him in the backseat, and the car sped off.

CHAPTER 16

The Boy and the Saint

JIMMY HOWARD'S SPIRIT SAT IN HIS WHEELCHAIR and looked down at his body sprawled on the floor. The twelve-year-old was no longer in pain but wondered why he was dead. He caught a brief glimpse of the twelve people who had run into his room. Each was armed with a peculiar looking black-bladed knife, and all were dressed in long, hooded robes that prevented him from seeing their faces. The robes had huge sleeves that hung down nearly to their knees. They had thrown him from his chair, slashed him across his neck, and repeatedly stabbed him.

He wondered why they hated him so much. Two of them spoke to each other with foreign accents while the others made motions for everyone to cease talking. They had left in a hurry while he was dying, so he had reached down from his chair and placed the bloody hands of his corpse against the hard rubber wheels of his chair in an attempt to pull himself back up—to no avail.

His mind flashed back to the time he truly realized that he was not like other kids. It was when he was seven years old. He remembered how elated he was to learn that he was invited to a birthday party of a friend in the neighborhood. Arriving at the party, he soon realized that he could not play with the other kids in the inflatable bounce house that had been set up in the front yard. He asked his mother why he couldn't go in as he pulled on her shirt and pleaded. She told him that he might get hurt, and it would be better if he just watched from his chair.

His uncle, Joe, who was also present, picked him up and said, "Don't be silly, he can play—watch and see." His uncle carried him into the huge bouncy room and began jumping. After a moment, Uncle Joe set him down in the middle of the undulating floor. Jimmy then realized that he could not play like the others. When his uncle saw him beginning to struggle, he picked him up and started bouncing. Jimmy laughed until his sides hurt, and that moment stuck in his mind permanently.

As he relived that day, he relished the bittersweet memory for a while, then realized how much he missed his uncle. As the life was fleeting from his body, he remembered the day two years ago when his mother had told him that his uncle had been in a car accident and died. Grief overtook him; he cried for a week after the funeral and gave up one of his most treasured possessions, a small necklace and medal that he laid across his uncle's chest as he wiped his eyes on his sleeves while his mother held him over the casket. The medal had been given to him shortly after he was born by his uncle and was inscribed SAINT CAMIL-LUS, PRAY FOR US around a portrait of the saint. On the reverse side of the medal was a symbol that looked like a six-pointed star with a triangle in the center.

≈

Alan gasped as he looked down at the bloody body of a twelve-year-old boy. He said in a surreal and angry voice, "They've killed a kid." A moment passed, and Alan spoke once again. "Why? Why a kid?"

Simmons shook his head.

Alan dropped his gaze and studied his surroundings. "This makes no sense. I know these murders are connected. I can count the twelve stab wounds in the back and see the twelve sets of footprints like at the other scenes. But a kid, why a kid?"

"Let's ask," said Simmons, as he spoke to Jimmy's spirit in the chair "What do you remember, Jimmy?"

"Twelve people came into my room and stabbed me."

"Do you remember what they looked like?"

"They had long robes and hoods. I couldn't see their faces. Two of them spoke with a funny accent; I think maybe it was Spanish."

Alan came close and knelt down to look at the boy at eye level. "Why do you think it was Spanish?"

"My tutor from school is from Mexico and speaks Spanish. That's what they sounded like."

Alan nodded. "Do you remember anything else about them?"

"They stabbed me with these black knives, then ran out of the room."

Simmons shot Alan a look of concern at the mention of the black blades. Jimmy said nervously, "My mother, where is my mother? She was downstairs, and she didn't come up to get me even after those people ran in here. Is she okay?"

A look of empathy came over Alan's face as he said, "Jimmy, your mother is—" "Your mother is fine," interrupted Simmons. "And she'll be coming up to see you soon. We all have a short walk to take."

"You'll have to push me," replied Jimmy. "As you can see, I can't walk. I've had cerebral palsy since I was born. I've never walked."

Simmons smiled as he said, "Yes, but today, Jimmy Howard, you will walk." With that, Simmons extended a hand and helped Jimmy to his feet. The boy stood speechless as an overwhelming look of joy enveloped his face. At that moment, a middle-aged woman entered the room and ran over to Jimmy.

"Mom!" yelled Jimmy, running to her for the first time ever.

She embraced him. "I'm so proud of you."

Simmons looked at Jimmy as he drew an object from his pocket, "I have something for you." Simmons handed the small necklace and medal over to him, and Jimmy looked at it in astonishment. Alan looked down at the medal that depicted the saint on one side and the strange symbol on the other.

"It's the medal that I left with Uncle Joe!" exclaimed Jimmy.

"Yes," said Simmons. "And when we arrive, I believe you will see your uncle once again."

Jimmy was grinning from ear to ear. "Well, let's go!"

The four of them walked through the closet door and down the short hallway to the door where Jimmy and his mother slipped into the Light. As Simmons and Alan began to walk back, Alan commented, "I didn't know that two people could go through the same door."

"Sometimes it's possible, if their lives were closely linked and their task in the afterlife will be, also."

Alan nodded. "I'm somewhat confused by the medal that you gave to Jimmy."

"Yes." Simmons had anticipated the question. "The medal depicted Saint Camillus, the patron saint of the ill, on one side and the Star of David with a triangle in it on the other."

"I'm confused. The saint would refer to one religion, and the Star of David would refer to another."

Simmons explained, "The medal of Saint Camillus was made among the living; the symbol on the back was placed there at a later time, and it is not the Star of David. Although it is very similar, it has a distinct difference: the triangle in the center. This symbol was created by those who have passed, and it represents those who walk among the Light. It represents a special order that aids those who fall in battle while fighting the Darkness. Perhaps the Star of David was derived from these concepts of protection and good."

Alan nodded as he thought about this, and the two stepped back through the closet door from which they had come.

$$\sim$$

"You mentioned an order that helps those who have fallen?" asked Alan.

"Yes," replied Simmons. "There's an order that attempts to retrieve fallen warriors from the Darkness."

Alan looked surprised. "So you send people from your world, the Realm of Light, to rescue those soldiers who have fallen in battle with the Darkness?" An image of the great battle that Alan had been involved in some years ago sprang into his mind. He could vividly see the hordes of the soldiers of Darkness flooding the field of battle, and he remembered how the small unit he was attached to survived through the help of elite warriors, as Simmons would call them. The memory of the giant winged soldiers with their glistening Roman armor and weapons made Alan realize the truth about the beings he thought of as angels.

"No, those in this group are among the living. They call themselves the Disciples of Light. Think of them as a type of special reconnaissance unit in your own military," Simmons elaborated. Alan was about to quiz Simmons on the Disciples of Light, but his phone rang.

"This is Alan."

"It's Rich. I'm down at the lab, and the ballistics from Lee's gun match the bullets found in Emily Austin's body. A DNA match also links the blood on the knife found in Lee's house to the murder of Ross Woler. I thought you would want to know."

Alan nodded. "Yeah, I figured it would."

"I'll catch you later," said Rich.

Alan snapped the phone shut and shook his head. "A dirty cop who kills people," he said in utter disgust. "I wonder if he's linked to these other killings."

"Perhaps," commented Simmons. "But I think there are other forces at work beyond Captain Lee."

"I agree, but he must have been motivated to kill Ross Woler to cover up the evidence found in that barn fire. There must be a link."

"I'm sure there's a link somewhere," said Simmons, "but I think this link is going to be much bigger than you are expecting. There are things in motion that I cannot explain—troubling things."

Alan sighed. "Sometimes there are no explanations."

"Untrue—there's always an explanation, it's just beyond my ability."

"You mean like how a tornado just kills people without knocking down any structures, or how twenty-three people drowned in a building, or how a barn disappears with no trace?"

Simmons nodded. "Yes, it's disturbing, and Captain Lee didn't cause any of that."

Simmons looked grim, so Alan decided to change the topic. "So what is this Disciples of Light organization?"

"It's a small group of people who are in key positions in your society and culture. They are privy to the existence of the world beyond the living and to the battles. They were once like you: they led those who died to the Light."

"So they got promoted, in a sense, then?"

Simmons looked upward for a moment, thinking about Alan's question, then he replied, "Not really; their role is just as important as what you do. They've just switched duties."

Alan was about to continue exploring the issue but was interrupted by his cell phone. "This is Alan."

"Hey, boss," said Detective Clint Rogers.

"Clint, what's up?"

"There was a flyer you submitted to the lab for prints last week."

"I did?" asked Alan, trying to remember.

"Yeah, it was a flyer from an organization called The Optimist's Corner addressed to Johnny Bartel."

"Oh, yes, I took it from the trash can by his home. It sounded like some type of motivational organization, and I couldn't understand why Johnny would have been involved—seemed suspicious, so I figured I'd grab it."

"Yeah, well it came back with two sets of prints on it—one set is his, and the other set belongs to a subject who's in jail for murder."

"What!" Alan exclaimed. "Who is it?"

"Our old friend Patrick Kent."

Alan's mind was racing as he got off the phone and relayed the information to Simmons. Patrick Kent was in jail for murder, and Alan had been the one who had solved the case, but that was only part of the story. Patrick was an evil person who had been leading those he recruited into the Darkness. He had been a leader among the army of Darkness that Alan had faced some years ago in battle. Alan had defeated Patrick's soldiers, then taken Patrick back to the Realm of the Living, where he had been imprisoned for his crimes.

"We need to head back to the station," he said to Simmons. "I need to research this Optimist's Corner organization."

Simmons nodded and remained silent. Alan wasn't sure what this meant, but he was confident that if Patrick Kent was involved, there were links to the Darkness.

CHAPTER 17

The Fire of Death

B ACK AT THE STATION THE NEXT DAY, Alan searched the Internet until he found the website for The Optimist's Corner. The main page was a cheerful display of young people smiling, with a short introduction of the organization below. Alan read it out loud to Simmons, who had stopped by:

> The Optimist's Corner is a motivational organization that challenges young people to fulfill their maximum potential. We offer one-to-one counseling and guidance to those in their youth who find themselves lacking self-confidence or a sense of belonging. Our service is free, and many of our students find themselves flourishing once they've completed our program. We do not take everyone; we are particularly interested only in those who do not have the life skills or faith to succeed.
>
> Some of our graduates go on to fill exemplary positions in society—just ask OC grad and billionaire record producer Jack Stone of Stone Records: "Hi, I'm Jack Stone of Stone Records, and I just wanted to tell everyone how The Optimist's Corner saved my life and made me what I am today—check it out."
>
> If you are feeling rejected, down-and-out, and want to join a real team with people who care, call us at the toll-free number listed below.

Alan's eyes continued to scan the page until it reached the bottom. "This doesn't seem like an organization that Johnny Bartel would have been affiliated with—or Patrick Kent, for that matter."

"Oh, I don't know about that," Simmons disagreed. "Who knows what haunted Johnny Bartel? Perhaps he was down-and-out, underconfident, and feeling like he needed to be part of a group. As for Patrick Kent, this organization sounds like the type of people he would prey upon: no self-confidence and a lack of faith."

Alan nodded as he continued to study the page. "Guess I didn't see it that way—maybe you're right. The flyer I had seized made comments about them trying to help people with criminal backgrounds."

"When you look at that description, you most likely see a good, positive outlook in an organization that claims it's there to help people."

"Yeah, pretty much," replied Alan, still scanning.

"But, in fact, the underlying message may be much different," Simmons analyzed. "They mention the positive factors of helping youth and the subsequent success, but I wonder why they concentrate on those who lack a sense of belonging."

Alan disagreed. "You're reading too much into it—perhaps they focus on that group of people because they think that those are the ones who are in need of the most help."

"Or they think that those are the people who are the least strong-willed —who are the most vulnerable to influence," Simmons pointed out.

"Ah," said Alan as he squinted to make out something at the very bottom of the page. "It says here that this is a division of a company called Aviance Inc." He quickly went to the website of Aviance Inc. Alan looked over the page and read some of the tabs aloud: "Aviance Motivational Division, Aviance Utilities Division, Aviance Medical Supply Division, Aviance Textiles, Aviance Sporting Goods Division— what *don't* these guys do?" He clicked on the sporting goods section to discover a display of multiple large sporting goods chain stores. He then called Clint Rogers.

"Hey, boss," said Clint, in his usual upbeat tone.

"Hey, Clint, you know anything about Aviance Inc?"

"Nah, never heard of it."

"Okay," replied Alan. "It's affiliated with The Optimist's Corner organization and a lot of other companies as well."

"Are we familiar with any of those other companies?"

"Yeah, some," said Alan as he glanced back at the computer screen. "Apparently they own all of the Sam's Sporting Goods stores across the country."

"I do some secondary security at Sam's. I'll do some poking around and see if I can find out anything about our parent company."

"Okay, keep me posted. Thanks, Clint."

Alan sat in silence for a moment, slowly tapping a pen on his desk. He brought his index finger to his lips as he contemplated his next move. Suddenly he remembered something, and he reached for the phone. Simmons raised an eyebrow, wondering what Alan's latest theory might be.

"This is Nigel," said the voice on the other end of the phone.

"Nigel, it's Alan."

"Where the hell have you been?" demanded Nigel, agitated. Then he lowered his voice. "I've had that report on the pin I found in that limb you submitted ready for days now—I thought you were going to pick it up."

"I know, I know. I'm sorry, Nigel—it's been really busy around here, but that's exactly why I'm calling you. I'll come over and grab the report in a few minutes, but I wanted to know if you found any company name on the pin."

Nigel let out a long disgusted sigh, and Alan could visualize him rolling his eyes as he talked. "Hold on—I'll grab it." A few seconds later he returned and said, "Nope—no name, but there are initials inscribed on one side: SMS. That may be the company—not sure."

"Thanks, Nigel—I'll be over in a few."

Alan hung up the phone and clicked on the Aviance Medical Division tab, which revealed a list of companies. His eyes rolled down the page until one caught his attention: Sinclair Medical Supplies. "This may be it, Michael—this may be the company that supplied the surgical pin in the body that was burned."

"Very good, perhaps that will give us some answers," replied Simmons.

"Yeah, I hope so," said Alan. He stood up. "Come on, we need to get the full report from Nigel and then get over to Sinclair's to see if they can trace the serial number." As Alan reached for the doorknob, the phone on his desk rang. He hit the speaker button and answered, "Yes?"

Jennifer Roberto the dispatcher, said, "The shift commander wanted me to inform you that they're responding to a fire down at the Mendello docks."

"Okay, and is the fire department on its way?"

"The fire department is on the scene and the fire is out, but there's more. We have eight fatalities, and the witness was . . ."—Jennifer paused, then continued—" . . . going crazy."

Alan glanced up and could see that Simmons shared his curiosity. "Describe what you mean when you say the witness was 'going crazy.'"

Jennifer seemed to struggle for the words. "The witness said some off-the-wall things. Swing up to dispatch and I'll let you hear the 911 call."

"Be right there."

The two hurried into the communications center, where three dispatchers were busy dealing with all the calls. Jennifer motioned to the two men to sit down at a vacant terminal, where she quickly accessed the 911 recording. Alan and Simmons listened intently.

"Nine one one, what is your emergency?" Jennifer's voice said calmly.

"They're burned . . . it burned them all . . . they're all dead!" a frantic woman's voice exclaimed.

"Okay, calm down, ma'am. I need to verify that you are calling from two oh three Front Street?"

"Yes," said the frantic voice.

"Okay, and you said someone was burned. Is there a fire?"

"Yes! It burned them all—we're in the office down on the docks!"

"Okay," replied Jennifer, still keeping her voice calm. "I have officers and emergency personnel en route. You said that someone burned them. Who burned what?"

"It killed them!" she screamed. "My boss, Lucio, and his brothers and sons—it killed them all—burned them up!"

Alan was familiar with the name Lucio. Lucio Mendello was a crime boss who ran the docks. He and his family were rumored to be responsible for dozens of killings and said to control most of the drug trafficking across the state. The recording continued:

"Okay," said Jennifer, "I want you to get out of the building and wait outside for our officers and the fire department."

"I'm already outside," sobbed the woman.

"Ma'am, you said that someone killed Mr. Mendello. Do you know who did this?"

"It wasn't a person," hissed the woman, thinking that the dispatcher wasn't listening to what she was saying. "I saw it coming. I saw it out the window. It came across the water . . . it was glowing like the sun . . . it was on fire. It came through the window!"

"Okay, ma'am, calm down, and watch for the officers."

"They're here now," said the woman through quick short breaths.

"Okay, I'm going to hang up, then."

The recording ended. Alan looked at Simmons as the two quickly made their way toward the door.

"See," said Jennifer, "I told you she was crazy. She saw some glowing fiery thing that came across the water; like that really happened—unless it was a missile or something," she added with a chuckle.

Alan hit the door hard, and he and Simmons ran toward his car.

"So you think it was a missile?" he said to Simmons facetiously. He was pretty sure he already knew the answer.

"Nope."

"That's what I was afraid of." Alan shook his head as the two quickly got in the car and headed off toward the docks.

CHAPTER 18

Lucio's Doom

A S ALAN PULLED THE CAR INTO THE PARKING AREA of the dock office, he noticed that there were no signs of the building being burned from the outside. He and Simmons got out of the car and were met by Fred Greenway, one of the local fire investigators. The perplexed look on Fred's face said it all.

"What have you got, Fred?" asked Alan.

Fred shook his head and stared at the floor. "Never seen anything like this."

Alan had expected a response like this. The three of them made their way over to a stairway that led up to the second floor, where Lucio Mendello's office overlooked the river and the docks below. As they ascended to the top of the stairs, the horrible aroma of burning flesh filled Alan's nostrils. They entered the room, and Alan could see eight corpses strewn about.

At first the room didn't appear to have been burned, but as Alan examined his surroundings further, he noticed several holes about four feet off the ground in all of the walls. The holes were large—about the size of a bowling ball—and had burn marks around the edges, as though a hot projectile had passed completely through them. Looking through one of the holes, Alan could see that whatever had made it had passed through not only the office walls but also the surrounding buildings. He walked over to where the corpse of an older man with a large dark mustache lay faceup. He recognized him at once: Lucio Mendello.

"Well, I guess we can rule out heart failure," Alan said to Simmons, who was surveying the other end of the room.

"Why's that?" asked Simmons as he came closer.

Alan pointed to the bowling ball–size burn hole in the center of the man's chest as he replied, "Because based on the positioning of that hole, I seriously doubt that his heart is still in his body."

Fred was now standing by them and said, "I have no idea how to label this one."

"We'll call it a homicide, and I'll get a detective assigned," replied Alan.

Fred nodded and left the room.

Alan turned to Simmons. "What the hell does this, Michael? A flame thrower? A torch? A bomb?"

"I don't know, but it was very hot and lethal. Let's go ask the witness what she saw."

Alan nodded, and the two made their way out to where an ambulance was parked in front. The rear doors stood open, and as the two men approached, Alan heard a woman yelling, "I'm not crazy! I saw it, you idiots! I saw it!" As he peered inside, he saw a woman in her mid-forties with bleached-blond, shoulder-length hair and tanned leathery skin. She was sweating profusely, and black streaks from her mascara ran down her cheeks. A police officer and a paramedic were also in the back, trying to calm her down.

"Officer, let me have a word with her," said Alan as he extended his hand for the distraught woman. After she stepped out, he led her to a nearby bench where he sat next to her. Simmons stood facing both of them.

"Ma'am, I'm Lieutenant Crane from the Riverston Police Department, and this is Special Agent Simmons from the FBI."

"Good, get those other idiots out of here—they want to take me to the nuthouse!" she sobbed. "Nobody believes me, and I'm telling the truth!"

Alan pulled a tissue from his pocket and handed it to her. "What's your name?"

She dabbed at her eyes, then said, "Nancy Correl."

"Tell me what happened, Nancy."

"Why?" she sneered. "So you can make fun of me? You won't believe me, either."

"Try me," said Alan calmly.

She drew a deep breath, and Alan noticed her hands trembling. "I was on the phone with Mr. Mendello's dry cleaner when I saw something out the window. At first I thought it was the reflection of the sun moving across the water, but then it kept getting brighter as it got closer. It seemed to glide just above the water like a huge bird."

Simmons interrupted. "A bird? Did it appear to have wings?"

She paused for a moment, trying to recall. "I . . . I couldn't tell . . . it was too bright to make out."

"Okay, so what happened next?" Alan said encouragingly.

"It moved very quickly and came through the window."

"I didn't notice the window broken," Simmons commented.

"It didn't break the window," she explained. "It came through it like light coming through a pane of glass. Then it stood upright. It was taller than the room . . . oh, you guys think I'm nuts, don't ya?"

"No," replied Simmons very confidently. He had a troubled look on his face as he said in a low voice, "You said it was taller than the room, and it stood up. Could you make out what it looked like once it was in the room?"

"Somewhat," she replied. "It looked almost like a giant man. It was taller than the ceiling because it went through the ceiling. Didn't you see the huge hole it burned in the top of the room?"

Alan and Simmons looked sheepish as they both shook their heads, embarrassed that they had forgotten to look up at the ceiling. Nancy continued, "Then it said something." She stopped talking for a moment, and, as her eyes widened, Alan could see a deep fear crossing her face.

She said nothing for a moment, then Simmons placed a hand on her shoulder and said, "It's okay, tell us what it said."

Her voice was but a whisper as she stared off into the distance. "It said, 'Welcome, Lucio, I've been waiting for this day to come.' Then it became very bright and hot . . . like I was standing too close to a fire . . . then it . . ." she trailed off, as though in a fearful trance.

Alan lowered his gaze to hers and said soothingly, "What did it do then, Nancy?"

With a blank stare, she replied, "It exploded, and I couldn't see. When I woke up, all the others in the room were dead." She began crying hysterically. "It was terrible! There were burn holes through them and all the walls. I don't know why it missed me."

Alan put his arm around her shoulder in an attempt to comfort her as he said, "It's fine now. We'll figure out what happened. I'm going to have an officer drive you home."

She nodded as Alan helped her up, and the three of them departed.

Alan and Simmons made their way back up to the office just as the crime scene technicians began arriving with all of their equipment. Looking up, Alan noticed a hole burned in the top of the ceiling, which was about ten feet overhead. The diameter of the hole was wide enough to drive a car through.

"What could have done that, Michael—Greek fire, or napalm, perhaps?" asked Alan, as he recalled the charred body found by the river that had been burned by napalm-B.

"No, I don't think so," replied Simmons. "This was something different —something that isn't from here . . . it's like," he paused, struggling to recall something. "It's like I've seen this before."

CHAPTER 19

The Wise Prophet

CLYDE RICHARDS STARED DOWN AT THE fistful of money that his cellmate had just handed him. He couldn't believe how connected this guy was: money, drugs, women, whatever else he wanted—and all from prison. It was like a dream come true. Clyde hadn't thought much of him at first; after all, Patrick Kent was a slimy, white-collar, yuppie type who claimed to be a murderer.

But after they had switched to a lavish room with a bird's-eye view of the entire prison yard and had access to whatever they wanted, Clyde decided that he might pay Mr. Kent a bit more respect. The $500 in cash that Clyde now held in his hand was a down payment for a job Patrick wanted him to do.

For some unknown reason, Patrick had great contempt for Elijah Johnson, the man who was known as "the preacher" because he always gave blessings to all the other prisoners. Everyone loved him because he inspired hope and faith, even in the darkest times. Ever since Patrick had rejected the preacher's blessing in the cafeteria that day, however, his hostility toward the man had only grown.

Clyde was now tasked with killing the preacher for Patrick, who promised him another $1,000 in cash upon completion. It was very late, and Clyde walked down the vacant cellblock to where the preacher's cell door stood open—just as Patrick had said it would be. Clyde looked in and saw Elijah lying on the bottom bunk with his head propped up on a prison-issued pillow. The top bunk was vacant—once again, just as Patrick had told him it would be.

Stepping into the cell, Clyde came closer to where Elijah was sleeping. He reached into his pocket and drew out a small .38 caliber revolver that Patrick had somehow obtained. The ability to sneak a gun into a prison was not a small feat, so Clyde knew that if he pulled this off, Patrick would be able to give him whatever he wanted. Raising the pistol, he extended his arm straight out and stepped forward until the gun was only two inches from Elijah's head. Clyde pulled the hammer back, and, as the cylinder rotated, he noticed that Elijah was smiling.

"I want to ask you a question." Elijah's voice was steady as he opened his eyes.

Startled by the voice, Clyde nearly dropped the gun, but he quickly tightened his grip and steadied the barrel once more, level with Elijah's forehead. As he looked into Elijah's eyes, he saw no fear, no hesitation, and no regret, only a look of pity as the man stared up at his executioner.

Elijah spoke once more. "Are you going to kill me, Clyde?"

A bead of sweat trickled down Clyde's face and dripped off his chin as he said, "Shut up! Don't say anything else."

In a steady and calm voice, Elijah repeated slowly, "Are you going to kill me?"

Clyde tried to get his senses about him as his finger slid onto the trigger guard and he began to squeeze. *Do it! Do it, you coward*, he told himself. Lowering his head as his conscience got the better of him, he pointed the barrel of the gun upward. He lowered the hammer slowly with his thumb, allowing it to rest on the unexpended round, and he slipped the pistol back into his pocket.

"No, Preacher, I'm not going to kill you."

Elijah beamed at him. "I'm very proud of you, Clyde. God bless you, my friend."

Clyde nodded as a tear rolled down his cheek. "Bless you, Preacher, bless you."

Clyde exited the cell quickly and walked back to his room, intent on returning the money to Patrick and telling him that he would not kill the preacher. When he arrived, he found Patrick sitting at a small desk in the corner of the room. Without turning around or making eye contact, Patrick sneered, "You coward. I knew you couldn't do it."

Clyde became angry and threw the money in Patrick's direction as he blurted out, "You go screw yourself, you slimy, little, yuppie bastard! I'm not killing the preacher."

Patrick continued to scribble on a piece of paper in front of him as he let out a long sigh and said, "Yeah, I guess I'll have to do it myself, but not right away. I'm busy with other arrangements right now."

Clyde became enraged and closed the distance between him and Patrick, who was still writing at the desk. "No, you won't," remarked Clyde, as he pulled out the pistol and pressed it to the back of Patrick's head.

In an instant, Patrick sprang to his feet, whirled around, and grabbed the gun in one hand while he plunged a large black dagger into the center of Clyde's chest. "Yes, yes, I will," he hissed. "I will also be able to walk you to where you are destined to go as soon as your life is drained from your body."

Clyde was fading fast as he looked into his killer's cold, dark, evil stare. He gritted his teeth as a sense of clarity overtook him, and he said, through the blood that gurgled up in his throat and spewed from his lips, "I'll walk with the preacher. You can go to hell."

Patrick looked thoroughly disgusted and spat in Clyde's face. "So be it," he said in a low demonic whisper as he let Clyde's lifeless body fall to the floor. "So be it."

CHAPTER 20

The Mysterious Pin

Aㅤ LAN AND SIMMONS MADE THEIR WAY TO the private lab where
Nigel worked and picked up the report along with the pin that was
found in the wrist of the charred corpse. Then they headed over to Sinclair Medical Supply to see if the company could track the serial number
on the pin. Alan and Simmons pulled up into the large driveway of the
corporate headquarters, where a huge sign out front displayed the company abbreviation, sms. Alan's phone rang as he was about to get out of
the car, and Clint Rogers excitedly said, "Hey, boss, I got something for
you regarding Sinclair."

"Funny you should call now, Clint. I just pulled into the parking lot."

"Yeah, well hold on before you go rushing in there. I need to fill you
in on something. As I told you, I've been working security on and off for
them for a few years now. I went back and checked my last pay stub, and
it does indicate that they are a division of Aviance Inc. I went online and
looked up the actual check through my bank account, and it shows the
Aviance Inc. logo, and it's signed by the CFO, Matthew Russ."

Alan prodded him impatiently. "Okay, Clint, where you going with
this?"

"Well, I guess they switched CFOs awhile back, because I went to my bank and accessed one of the checks I deposited when I first started work. That check was signed by their old CFO: Patrick Kent."

Alan sat stunned for a few seconds, then blurted out, "Thanks Clint." He turned to Simmons. "Patrick Kent was the old CFO of Aviance Inc. I need to find out who this pin is registered to, but now I'm worried about who we're really dealing with."

"Let's head over to my office," Simmons suggested. "I have someone who may be able to access the company's database without setting off any alarms."

A short time later, they pulled into the lot of the FBI field office, and Alan asked, "So everyone here thinks you are really with the FBI?"

"Almost everyone."

"Then there is at least one person here who knows who you really are? Do they walk people to the other side, too?"

"Not any more. They are part of the group I told you about, the Disciples of Light. I'll introduce you."

They made their way through the main entrance to an office in the rear of the building. The solid wooden office door had a placard displayed in the center that read SPECIAL AGENT IN CHARGE AMANDA GREGORY. As they entered, Alan saw a tall slender woman, who appeared to be in her early fifties, rise to greet them. She had short black hair and was dressed in a finely pressed skirt and suit jacket. Extending her hand, she firmly gripped Alan's as she said, "Pleased to meet you, Alan Crane. I've heard good things."

Alan smiled and nodded. "Thank you. I assume that you are Special Agent Gregory by the placard on the door."

"Indeed, and what can I do for you two today?"

"I need to access a database at Sinclair Medical Supplies in order to track down who this pin was registered to." Alan held up the small clear evidence bag, then thumbed through Nigel's report to retrieve the serial number that Nigel had recorded. He then grabbed a notepad and pen from the desk and scribbled down the number. Amanda sat down in front of a computer monitor and began typing and clicking the mouse. After about five minutes, she glanced over at the notepad and typed in the number.

She hit the enter button, then sat back in her chair, "This may take a few minutes." Looking up with a smile, she commented, "So you are the famous Alan Crane."

Alan looked puzzled. "Famous?"

"Oh, yes, I've heard of your accomplishments."

"And what would those be?" he asked curiously.

"You are one of the few among the living to ever become a Light Bringer and lead a seristrum—twelve units of the army of the Light—to victory over the Darkness."

Alan now knew what she was speaking of and could recall the events vividly. In his many travels to the world beyond the living, which Western religions call heaven, he became involved in one of the ongoing battles that occur between the Light and the Darkness. He found himself leading soldiers representing the Light to battle with those from the Darkness—those from hell. The Light Bringer was the title given to the leader of the group; it meant that he was the one who carried the Light and the power that gave each of his warriors the strength to defeat the enemy. His wit and resilience led the seristrum to victory over a particularly powerful enemy of the Light: an enemy who also turned out to be from the Realm of the Living, an evil and vile man named Patrick Kent.

Amanda looked mildly concerned. "Lieutenant Crane?"

"Oh, sorry, I was thinking about that day. It was like nothing I've ever experienced before. My apologies for daydreaming. It was a significant event, but I wouldn't label myself as *famous*."

"Well, you may not, but many others do," she rebutted. "Your story is one of faith and courage and serves as an inspiration."

"Thank you," replied Alan. "It's nice to know that it made a difference."

She glanced back at the computer screen. "Ah, here we are. Looks like your number is registered to a person named Travis Collins."

"I knew that wasn't Curtis's body," Alan declared. "That's why you couldn't tell he was dead and why we couldn't walk him to the Light," he said to Simmons. Turning back to Amanda, he asked, "Any way you can access more information about Mr. Collins?"

Amanda nodded and continued typing, "Wow, he has an extensive criminal history. Felony assault, armed robbery, and . . . second-degree murder."

"Hmm, well, no more of that, since he's dead. I guess society will be better off," replied Alan.

"What do you mean?" Amanda said as she continued scanning the screen. "He's not dead, he's incarcerated, currently serving two consecutive life sentences."

"What!" exclaimed Alan, and he began talking very quickly. "That can't be—he's dead. His body was burnt to a crisp. That pin was taken out of what was left of his wrist after it was crystallized by some type of intense heat."

"Sorry, but it says here he's in prison—Jackson Penitentiary. It's a maximum security state prison about forty minutes north of here."

Alan's gaze met Simmons's, and the two quickly walked to the door.

"Thank you, Special Agent Gregory."

She smiled at Alan. "Thank you, Light Bringer. Stay safe."

Chapter 21

The Trembling Earth

I T WAS DUSK, AND PATRICK KENT LOOKED out the window of his bedroom on the upper floor of the prison. He was particularly interested in the two figures approaching the front entrance. As they grew nearer, he noticed that one man was tall, with a badge hanging around his neck, and the other was a shorter man in a suit. The two walked at a quick pace, and, as more of their features came into view, he realized who they were.

"Damn it!" he yelled as he grabbed a cell phone from his pocket and made a call.

"It's me," he said agitatedly. "I don't know how in the hell they found us so quickly, but they're here."

The voice on the other end muttered something back, and Patrick yelled angrily, "Alan and Michael are here! We need to move fast and let the others know."

He snapped the phone shut and threw it across the room as he said aloud, "Damn you, Alan Crane—damn you!"

∾

Alan and Simmons hurried up to the main entrance of Jackson Penitentiary, where they quickly cleared security and were met by an in-house guard.

"I'm Lieutenant Crane, and this is Special Agent Simmons. We need to see a prisoner named Travis Collins."

The guard nodded and checked his computer monitor. "He's in cell block F. I'll have him brought into an interview room so you can speak to him. Come through the doors on your right, and you'll take the first hallway on the left. Wait there, and we'll be right in."

Alan nodded and thanked the guard. He and Simmons entered the doorway and made their way down the hall. They waited at the entrance to the interview room until they heard the locking mechanism on the door click. Alan pulled the door open, and each took a seat on one side of a small table in the center of the room. After five minutes, a guard appeared with a prisoner clad in a yellow jumpsuit. The prisoner's face was not in view because he had his head hanging low. The guard escorted him to a chair on the other side of the table and secured him to an eyebolt attached to the end of the tabletop with the handcuffs that were fastened to one of his hands. The guard left the room, and the prisoner put his face down on the table.

"Travis?" Alan asked.

"I'm not Travis," replied the young man with a southern drawl.

Alan noticed that his hair was blond and greasy, probably from not being cleaned for quite some time.

"You aren't Travis Collins?"

The prisoner raised his head and brushed the hair back from his bruised face. "No, I'm not Travis Collins," he repeated.

As Alan continued to gaze at his face, he searched his memory to recall where he had seen him before. In an instant it came to him. "Curtis . . . Curtis Norman?"

The young man became more alert. "Yeah. Hey, you're that cop that pulled me out of the barn."

"Yeah, it's me—Alan Crane. I've been looking for you everywhere. They transferred you to different prisons. They told me you had escaped and then eventually told me you were dead."

"What?" said Curtis, obviously shocked by what Alan had just told him. "They ran me all over the place. How did this happen?"

Alan sighed. "There was a dirty cop involved, but we got him—he's in jail now."

"I didn't kill anyone!" protested Curtis.

"I know. I believe you, Curtis, but right now we need to get you out of here."

Curtis nodded, and as Alan stood up to summon the guard, he heard a deep, low, rumbling sound that caused him to become very uneasy.

"Did you hear that, Michael?"

"Yes."

Alan hurried over to the door and found it unsecured. As he reached for the handle, he heard another rumbling sound that was louder and shook the walls. Looking out into the hallway, he heard someone yelling for help from around the corner just as another rumble shook the floor and walls once again. He and Simmons darted around the corner but were nearly knocked off their feet as the walls shook violently. The scream was very close. They continued forward toward the cry for help, and to their horror they saw that a large, deep crack had formed in the hallway and a man was holding on to the edge to keep from plummeting. Alan quickly grabbed his arm and heaved him up, then stared down into the deep crevice that had formed in front of them. He could not see the bottom, but a cold and vile black mist rose from below.

"What the hell is this, Michael?"

"It's the Darkness," replied Simmons. "It rises from below. We need to leave now."

The man they had helped up ran down the hallway and out of sight as Alan blurted out, "You don't have to tell me twice! Let's grab Curtis and get the hell out of here while we can."

They ran back to the interview room but found it empty, and just then another tremendous shock wave struck and threw them to the ground.

"Damn!" yelled Alan. "He's gone. We need to find him!"

"No time for that now," protested Simmons. "We need to leave."

Running back into the hallway, they made their way to the door that led to the main entrance. Alan yanked hard in an attempt to open it, but it was locked. He kicked at it and tugged, but it wouldn't budge. Another round of tremors struck, and once again they were both thrown to the floor. Simmons pushed Alan to one side and reached into his suit pocket, pulling out a white marble rod about a foot long and two inches in diameter. He ran his hand across the rod, and it lengthened to about five feet. It appeared to be pulsating with some type of energy, and Alan noticed that it was becoming brighter and brighter. Simmons raised it above his head and struck the door with tremendous force.

Sparks and brilliant light shot in all directions as the door exploded into pieces. They stumbled into the main lobby and found that the front doors were standing open. Running frantically and attempting to keep their balance through the shock waves that were now causing portions of the structure to come tumbling down, they made their way out. Alan was breathing hard, but fear kept him moving as he felt the horrible sensation of the ground falling away under his feet. A cold chill ran up his back, and the sensation of free fall was gripping him.

The dark mist was creeping up around his face just as something grabbed his hand and gripped it tightly. He looked up to see Simmons pulling him upward and climbing at the same time. They were about ten feet from the top of what was now a huge crater where the prison once stood. Simmons was continuing his vertical momentum, digging with his feet and still pulling Alan along by the hand.

As they came within two feet of the top, Alan noticed another hand reach down and grab Simmons's wrist. The hand pulled both of them up past the edge, and Alan lay on his belly gasping for air. Once he had caught his breath somewhat, he rolled over and sat up to see an elderly black man with curly silver hair standing near them. Simmons, as usual, didn't look a bit exhausted or strained from the rigorous climb.

"You," said Simmons, looking at the old man in surprise.

"Good to see you, Michael," replied Elijah.

"Good to see you, too. It's been a long time."

Elijah smiled. "Not too long. Five hundred years or so."

Alan sat stunned and speechless. He turned his gaze from the two men and stared down at the tremendous sinkhole that was now filling up with earth and debris.

"Come on, you two, we're not safe here. We need to get farther away," Elijah said as he helped Alan to his feet. The three made their way back to the parking lot where Alan had parked. Alan was glad to see that this area had not been affected, and as they reached the car, he breathed deeply, then asked, "Okay, what happened here? What *was* that? It looked like the ground swallowed up the prison."

Simmons said nothing but turned his gaze toward Elijah as though seeking his opinion. Elijah quickly picked up on his concern and said, "Yes, Michael, you are wise to be concerned."

Alan interrupted. "What did this?"

Elijah turned to him and said, as he lowered his eyes, "The Fallen."

CHAPTER 22

A Fallen Evil

A S ALAN CONTINUED TO STARE AT the huge hole that was once the prison, he stood stunned as the ground continued to fill in like the bottom of an hourglass being filled with sand. Simmons looked over at Elijah and asked, "So what name are you going by these days?"

The old man grinned. "Elijah Johnson."

Simmons smiled. "Elijah—very old-fashioned. I like it."

The crater engulfing the prison was now nearly full, and Alan managed to focus enough to ask, "You said The Fallen did this? Who are The Fallen?"

Elijah stood next to Alan and peered down at the fresh dirt that kept rising from below. "The Fallen are those elite warriors who turned from the Light—those who plummeted into the Darkness."

"Elite warriors," echoed Alan. "You're talking about angels. Elite warriors are what we call *angels*—you're talking about fallen angels."

"Yes," replied Elijah, "The Fallen have come back to the Realm of the Living. I've seen this happen once before."

"That's impossible," protested Simmons. "That's against the binding prophecies of the Light. That's—"

Elijah interrupted. "I know, I know. I can't explain it yet, but it's happening."

All three stared across the newly turned earth that was now level as Simmons asked Elijah, "You said you have seen this before?"

"Yes, a very long time ago." Elijah looked at Simmons, who appeared to be struggling with his recollections of the past. "Your memory has been clouded by battle, but I will take you to the place that may contain some answers. I will help you remember."

Alan interjected, "Did you say you two met five hundred years ago?"

Elijah smiled once again. "We *met* a long time before that, but I haven't *seen* Michael in five hundred years."

Alan was stunned. "How old are you, Michael?"

Simmons looked somber and stared at the ground. "I . . . I don't know."

"Yes," said Elijah. "You've forgotten many things—perhaps even who you are. But I'll try to fill in the void for you based on what I know."

Alan was still in shock from all that had happened. He turned to Elijah. "How old is he? When was he born?"

"Thousands of years ago. It's getting late now, so let's meet tomorrow morning, and I'll show both of you."

∼

"Where are we going?" Alan asked Elijah on Wednesday morning, when the three men met again at Alan's office.

"To the place where I once lived," Elijah intoned. "A land in which I was once a great king a very long time ago."

Alan was a bit skeptical and wondered if he could trust Elijah, so he pressed him further. "Exactly, where is that—like, on a map?"

Elijah ran his fingers through his short, curly, gray hair. "It's off the coast of Greece. It won't take us long to get there—just a few minutes' walk."

Alan would have rejected this concept, but he had traveled with Simmons enough to know that those who come from the realm beyond the living, be it heaven or hell, have an ability to manipulate time and distance. Many times he and Simmons would leave to walk someone through the long marble hallway, and what took hours had not taken more than a second of time in the living world, he had learned when they returned. He remembered traveling great distances that took only a few minutes, as though they had turned a corner in the car and magically appeared at a destination hundreds of miles away.

As the three began to walk, the sun beat down on Alan's face and felt somewhat comforting in this time of great confusion and anxiety. As he took his next step, he felt his foot sink into something soft and pliable. Glancing down, he found himself walking along a white sand–covered beach, and the aroma of the sea filled his senses.

"So, we're here—in Greece?" he asked incredulously.

Elijah nodded. "We're on the island of Skyros right now, in the Aegean Sea."

Alan and Simmons followed Elijah. Alan noticed that Simmons looked depressed, as though a great burden were weighing him down.

"Are you okay, Michael?" Alan inquired.

Simmons nodded. "I'll be okay. I need some answers. I need to know what we're up against."

"You will soon," Elijah predicted, as he stopped and turned toward the water. He walked forward. As the three of them came to a place where the sand was wet from the lapping waves hitting the shore, Alan asked, "Where are we going now?"

"It's this way," answered Elijah, as he continued walking into the ocean.

Alan followed until the water was at his knees, then stopped. "Wait a minute! Are you saying we need to swim? I don't think this is a good idea."

"No," replied Elijah. "We need to continue walking. Trust me."

"Yeah, well, that's the problem," Alan rebutted. "I don't know you. How do I know you're not working for the wrong side?"

"He's not," Simmons assured him. "I know him from other dealings —he's affiliated with the Light, but I'm sketchy on the details."

"Okay, Michael—if you say so." Alan shrugged and followed them into the sea. The three men were soon submerged. Alan held his breath and kept walking. For some strange reason, he was able to walk with ease along the bottom of the sea, just as though he were on land.

Elijah noticed him struggling to hold his breath and said, "No need to do that—breathe."

Alan was amazed that he could actually hear the words coming from Elijah's mouth, just as though they were standing on the shore. He was reluctant to suck in the water quickly, so he inhaled ever so slightly through his nose, and, to his sheer astonishment, he felt air flowing in instead of the cold seawater. Inhaling a bit more, he drew the breath down into his throat. Once he was sure that the water would not drown him, he breathed in deeply, filling his lungs completely. The sensation was overwhelming. He could feel the cold liquid all around him, but the oxygen was pumping through him with every breath.

"This is incredible," he commented, noticing that his voice also carried through the water.

Elijah turned and smiled, but Simmons kept moving forward, looking serious and concerned.

They walked for about an hour or so, and Alan marveled at the wonderful display of sea life that was all around them. His anxiety level increased rapidly when a twenty-foot shark swam very close to them, but it quickly vacated the area when Simmons pulled out the same long white marble rod that he had used to open the prison door. Now it illuminated the sandy bottom.

Another thirty minutes passed, and, as they continued walking, Alan noticed that he could no longer see the surface and that the surrounding sea was pitch-black, except for the light emitting from the rod in Simmons's hand. The eerie feeling of lightlessness was closing in, and, at one point, he was tempted to tell the others that they should stop and go back. Just as his mind started racing, he spotted a faint glow in the distance. They continued forward, and, as they did, the glow became bigger and brighter. Alan could vaguely make out some type of structure off in the distance, and soon he noticed a large crack in the sea floor.

"What is this?" he asked.

"This is where the land was broken off and fell into the sea," explained Elijah.

"This was once land?"

"Yes, all of this was once above water."

The three of them moved on, and, in an instant, Alan found himself walking on a sandy beach. They had passed through some type of barrier that divided the sea from the air, and they were no longer surrounded by water. There appeared to be a sky overhead and an illuminating glow that resembled faint sunlight. Beyond the beach was junglelike terrain, and, way off beyond that, Alan could see mountains. He stared in amazement at the wonderful surroundings that were buried far beneath the ocean and wondered how all of this could be possible.

Continuing down the beach, they came to a place where Alan observed what appeared to be remnants of several two-story buildings constructed of thick wood and all attached to one another. The buildings ran hundreds of feet down the beach and seemed to have been buried in the sand; they were apparently more than two stories, but only the top two levels were exposed.

"Who constructed these buildings?" he asked.

Elijah smiled. "Those aren't buildings."

"Then what are they?" Alan looked puzzled.

"It was a ship."

"A ship?" Alan shook his head in disbelief. "It would have been

enormous." As they approached the end of it, he could make out the
bow that was mostly buried in the sand. "What did this ship carry?"

"You'll see," replied Elijah. "Follow me."

Alan and Simmons followed Elijah as he turned away from the beach
and entered a narrow pathway into the jungle. After a few minutes, they
came upon a clearing that encircled a small picturesque lake. As they
were rounding the edge of the lake, Alan saw something that made him
freeze. Panic gripped his chest, and he whispered, "Nobody move."

Down by the lake was an enormous male lion. Its head was lowered,
and it was lapping up water. As Alan stood perfectly still, hoping that
the animal would not see them, Simmons and Elijah also stopped and
stood silently. Alan was about to make a run for it back to the beach
when he saw something that bewildered him even more. As the massive
cat stood at the edge of the water drinking, a small white-tailed deer
walked up beside it and stood inches from its massive shoulder. The
deer lowered its head and began drinking right next to the lion.

Simmons smiled and said, "It's okay, Alan—they won't hurt us."

Alan shook his head in complete disbelief. "This can't be—those two
animals would never tolerate being that close to each other. One is a
predator and the other is prey. And besides that, they don't exist in the
same geographical habitat. What's going on here?"

"Do you see that small grotto off to the other side of the lake?" Elijah
motioned to a mound of earth that was ornately decorated with a colorful display of wildflowers and other plants.

"Yeah, I see it."

"That is the grave of a man who was a shepherd of animals. He was
a great man whom they loved and respected, and here they pay him
tribute," Elijah explained.

"Sorry," replied Alan. "This is a bit hard to swallow. I still can't believe
it. Who was this man?" As Alan continued to look over at the tomb,
he noticed the variety of wildlife that was flocking to the area: birds,

squirrels, rabbits, and even a large hawk that stood on a branch of a tree overlooking the entrance.

"You know the story," said Simmons. "The storms came for forty days and forty nights and flooded the land. This man built a great ark that held one pair of each species of animal."

Alan's mouth was now agape. "Are you actually talking about the story of Noah? You mean to tell me that this is the grave of Noah, and that ship on the beach was the ark?"

"Yes," replied Elijah confidently. "This is where life began once again and branched out to all corners of your world. The animals here pay tribute to this great man—they go elsewhere to hunt and eat. Near this grave, they live in peace with one another."

"That's incredible—it's almost unbelievable."

"Indeed," said Elijah. "Let's keep moving. There's more to see."

They ventured forward, and Alan's mind was still racing over what he'd just encountered. As the mountains grew closer, Alan could see an enormous castle at the top. The men seemed to be approaching the edifice from the back. As they arrived at the bottom of a huge cliff that led up to the enormous palace, Alan could see a steep flight of narrow stairs cut into the rock that ascended all the way to the top.

They began the climb, and before long they reached the final step. They stood on the wall of what Alan could now see was an ancient fortress. The view went on for miles, and a huge garden below the castle led to a large valley encompassed by mountains. The three made their way around the wall until they reached an old wooden door that revealed a steep flight of stairs going down. They descended and found themselves in a huge open room that had an enormous ornate wooden table in the center and about forty chairs. Wood crackled and sparked from the large fireplace that was positioned at the far end of the room.

Alan stared up at a huge tapestry that hung from one of the thirty-foot walls. He noticed it was of some type of battle scene, with a tall bearded man standing on a cliff overlooking a huge field. The man held a huge lightning bolt in one hand, poised to throw it like a javelin. Down below there were four distorted-looking figures that resembled giant winged people. One of the figures held what looked like a ball of fire in one hand and was yelling up at the bearded man as though enraged.

"Oh, yes," Elijah commented. "Do you know Greek mythology?"

"A bit," replied Alan.

"Then you'll recognize this as one artist's rendering of Zeus defeating the Titans. The old gods, or Titans, as they were called, were dethroned by the new gods, or Olympians—Zeus was their leader."

"I am familiar with the story," Alan nodded.

"Walk with me, and I shall tell you my story and perhaps assist Michael in remembering more of his past."

Simmons nodded. "That would be very helpful."

The three continued through the castle and out the main gate, then traversed the huge garden. In the center of the garden was a large obelisk with strange writing on all sides. Elijah stopped in front of it and said somberly, "Michael, this is your mother's grave."

Simmons's eyes widened, and he scanned the markings, "I never knew her or my father. I've searched for both of them in our world, hoping that one day I would come across her, but I've never been able to find her. My worst fear is that she was captured and was being held captive in the Darkness. What was she like?"

"Oh, she was a wonderful, charming woman—always smiling and ready with a kind word. I do not know where she is, but I brought her back here when she was killed."

"She was killed?" asked Simmons sadly.

"Yes," replied Elijah, as his gazed dropped to the ground. "She was killed in the battle that ensued outside this castle. She was struck down by The Fallen—the very creatures I now believe we are dealing with. Follow me, and I will explain further."

As Elijah led them out of the garden and into the field beyond, Simmons asked, "Why can't I remember them?"

"You were killed as a baby—murdered," replied Elijah.

"Murdered?" Alan gasped. "Murdered as a baby? Who would do such a thing?"

"We never knew for sure, but most definitely it was someone affiliated with the Darkness. Whoever it was must have been threatened by you walking among the living, but, when they killed you, the Light gained a powerful ally. You were born thousands of years ago, as I mentioned before. Your mother was given the gift of youth and lived for many years, serving the Light and interacting among the living until she was killed in the battle that occurred just beyond the walls of this fortress."

As they entered the field, Alan noticed statues that were situated randomly. The workmanship on them was spectacular and very lifelike. He moved closer to one to observe it better and studied the pure white rock from which it was carved. As he ran his hand across an outstretched arm of the sculpture, it broke off and disintegrated into white powder. Withdrawing his hand quickly, he said, "I'm sorry—they must be very old and fragile."

"Yes, indeed," replied Elijah. "They are very old, but it's okay. They tend not to weather as well down here." A tear ran down his cheek. "They were all once my people."

"Your people?" Alan inquired, bewildered. His gaze scanned the grassy terrain, and, to his astonishment, he now realized how many statues there really were: hundreds, thousands, or more, perhaps—as far as the eye could see.

"Yes," said Elijah, as he dabbed his eyes. "I made many mistakes as a king. My thirst for knowledge led to the downfall of my people. I left for a long period, and I gained great knowledge, but I stole it—I took it in a manner that was not right."

"How was that?" asked Simmons.

"I ventured to a place I was not invited, in the world beyond this one—into your world, Michael. There I looked upon a throne, where the Light resided. I instantly gained a vast amount of knowledge, but the burden of guilt was consuming, and I regretted what I had done. I asked for forgiveness, and the Light granted me such. From that day on I swore allegiance to the Light and all that was right and good. That's why I'm here among the living: to try to make things better."

"You looked upon the throne of God?"

"Yes," Elijah said, hanging his head in shame, "but I was not invited to do so. After the Light had forgiven me, I returned here to my people to find that the Darkness had infiltrated the land. This grand castle you see once sat in the world above the sea and overlooked two large cities. Upon my return, those cities had been corrupted from within. The Darkness seeped through them and deteriorated the moral fiber of the society within. Only a handful of strong-willed citizens still possessed the values that our society had once held high: kindness, caring, and compassion. The rest were riddled with corruption, selfishness, and evil. Where good and honest people had once stood, there were now only hollow beings—empty and soulless."

Another tear streaked down his face. "There was a revolt. Those who followed the Darkness attempted to do away with the few who did not. The mob was closing in, and there were others coming toward us from in front. Angels, as you would call them, came down to help us as we fled farther into the field. We ran and never looked back. The angels flew down into the middle of the field, and, as a blinding light erupted behind us, the cities were leveled, and all those facing the Light were turned into these statues; they were turned into—"

Alan interrupted, whispering, "Salt."

"Yes, you know the story?"

"The cities of Sodom and Gomorrah. Those who looked back were turned into pillars of salt." Alan reached out and touched another statue, which also crumbled in his hands. "I know the story."

"Was my mother with you?" asked Simmons.

"Yes. She had made it out with us. We continued running until we ran into them."

"Who?" Simmons demanded with a touch of anger.

"The Fallen," Elijah answered. "Four of them descended upon us, and the two angels that had leveled the cities rushed to our aid. They collided with a terrible deafening crash. One of The Fallen transformed into a whirling cyclone but was felled quickly by the other two angels. Another Fallen caused the earth to crack and lift as the entire piece of land we now stand on was torn from the ground. The water then rose around us, caused by the third of The Fallen, who swept us out to sea. We sank quickly, and one of the angels surrounded the land with the bubble that now encases it. The battle continued as the three remaining Fallen eventually defeated the angels. They then turned on us as we began to flee back to the castle. Your mother stopped and turned to face them in order to distract them from striking us all down. I yelled to her, but . . . " he paused as he looked up, and tears streamed down his cheeks.

"Please," Simmons pleaded, as he put both hands on Elijah's shoulders. "Tell me what happened."

"One of them struck her down. It was the one who controls fire; her name is Ellestria."

Alan interjected. "Sodom and Gomorrah were supposedly located by the Dead Sea, yet we're off the coast of Greece."

"Yes. This is how far Manis carried us across the sea."

"Who?" Alan was confused.

"Manis," repeated Elijah. "Manis is The Fallen who controls water. Each of them controls a different element. The one who was defeated first was named Andora, and she controls wind. The last one was Archilus, who controls earth."

Alan saw Simmons gritting his teeth, obviously upset by the news of his mother. He placed his hand on Michael's shoulder, and Simmons nodded, grateful for his concern.

"How did you survive, then?" asked Simmons.

Elijah pointed to a high rocky cliff that overlooked the field. "On that overlook there appeared a figure draped in a brilliant light. The remaining three Fallen noticed it and closed in, but, as they did, the figure destroyed each of them with a gleaming streak of light. They were gone in an instant. We buried your mother back in the garden."

"And my father?" inquired Simmons. "Did you know my father?"

"No, I did not, and your mother never spoke of him, either."

"Elijah, you said that The Fallen who attacked you could manipulate the elements. Do you think these are the same ones who have committed the recent disasters we've been dealing with?" asked Alan.

"Yes, I do. You see, The Fallen were once elite warriors of the Light, or, as you would say, they were once angels. All angels are ranked according to their power—I believe the living refer to the ranks as *choirs* or *orders*. These particular angels had been in the order of virtues, which was known for its interaction with humanity and its manipulation of the elements."

Simmons interjected, "But that's impossible. You know there are rules, and the elite—or angels, rather—cannot interact among the living unless the Light grants permission. Also, I am familiar with the four Fallen you named. They fell in the battle here and were captured. When they fall in battle, they turn into piles of dust, which we collect and hold forever—rending them virtually powerless in the Light."

Alan knew that what Simmons was saying was true because he had rescued an angel that was held prisoner in the Darkness. The angel had been reduced to a mere vial of dust, but when Alan released it into the Realm of Light, it sprang to life once again.

Simmons continued to shake his head in protest of Elijah's theory. "Elijah, there's just no way these could be the same Fallen—we are holding them in one of our vaults as prisoners . . . unless . . . " Simmons's eyes grew wide as a horrible theory entered his mind. "Unless . . . oh, no! That can't be . . . we need to go." Simmons sounded a bit panicky, which was very unusual because of his typically cool-headed demeanor.

"Where are we going?" asked Alan.

"We need to go to my world—the world of the Light, or heaven. We need to get there fast—I fear the worst. Let's get moving."

~

The three men hurried back to the castle and up to a large wooden door that led to the library. Simmons opened the door, and everyone stepped through and found themselves in a lush green valley with tremendous cliffs on both sides.

"Oh, no," said Simmons, shaking his head, "it's starting to make sense now. Sister Lucille Franconi was the nun who was initially murdered in a ritualistic manner. Her mother was guarding the vault where we kept Andora, The Fallen who controls wind. Oh, I hope I'm not right."

Simmons moved quickly, and the others struggled to keep up. As they came to the other side of the valley, Alan could see a large building with tall Roman columns. They entered the building, and Simmons immediately started scanning the walls, which contained numerous shelves of clear glass bottles filled with dust. Simmons continued to scan the shelves until his eyes affixed on a particular glass jar.

"Ah, here it is," he said, carefully removing the jar from the shelf and holding it up to the light. It was empty. "Oh, no, it is as I had feared! Andora has been freed, and Sister Franconi's mother is nowhere to be found."

Simmons sat down for a moment and rubbed his temples. Then all at once he sprang to his feet and announced to the other two, "Quick! We must go check on the others." He opened the door, motioning for the other two to go through it. He led them to three other vaults and found the same results: all were unguarded. Ellestria, Manis, and Archilus were gone, and so were the people who were supposed to be guarding them: family members of Alexander Burnstein, the general store owner; of Eva Stevenson, the pediatric surgeon; and of Jimmy Howard, the twelve-year-old boy with cerebral palsy.

Simmons emerged from the last vault with a look of dread on his face. "All four of The Fallen are gone—freed—and now they walk among the living. You were right, Elijah."

"Unfortunately so," admitted the old man.

Simmons composed himself, then said in a confident voice, "Something has gone wrong. We need to find Mr. Burnstein, Dr. Stevenson, Jimmy Howard, and Sister Franconi."

"How are we going to do that?" asked Alan.

"I'm confident they have been captured and imprisoned among those who serve the Darkness. We need to venture into that realm and get them back. I can't go, nor can Elijah—you know that, Alan."

Alan nodded in acknowledgment of what Simmons was saying. From his previous ventures into the Realm of Darkness, Alan knew how weak and frail Simmons had become from being in that world. He guessed that Elijah would fare no better. The living, however, were not affected by the Realms of Darkness and Light—they could function fine in either place. "I'm not sure I can do it alone," Alan said apprehensively.

"Of course not," replied Simmons. "We need to activate the order and have you join them to become one of the Disciples of Light."

"Join the order?"

"Yes, we will gather them up at once," replied Simmons with determination.

"But that still leaves the problem of finding a way into the Realm of Darkness," said Alan.

"I think I can help you with that," replied Elijah. "There is a portal down in the field near my castle. It was left there by the four Fallen who invaded the realm of the living. You may be able to use it to go back."

"Excellent," replied Simmons. "We'll gather the order and leave at once. Let's make our way back under the sea—back to the Lost City."

Chapter 23

The Rising Sea

F BI SPECIAL AGENT IN CHARGE Amanda Gregory walked the sandy white beach wondering why the emergency meeting had been called. Typically, they would meet in a secured location, but she hadn't been back to the Lost City for some time. As she stopped for a moment to shake the sand from her shoes, she noticed three figures approaching her and recognized them at once as other members of the Disciples of Light. The tall man with the buzz-cut hair was General James Wiggins. Supreme Court Justice Richard Sumner walked to the right of the general, and to the general's left was Senator Linda Swanson. The four met, and Amanda asked, "Anyone know what this is about?"

"No," replied Justice Sumner, "I was hoping you knew." The others shook their heads to indicate that they, too, were unclear about the purpose of the meeting.

"I'm unaware," said Amanda. "Well, I guess we need to go."

The four walked out into the sea and slowly made their way downward.

~

Alan sat with Simmons and Elijah at the great table within the castle. As people started arriving, Alan recognized Amanda Gregory, who sat down next to him. When sixteen people were present and seated, Simmons spoke to the group. "Thank you for coming on such short notice. We have some pressing issues to deal with. Four of The Fallen are among the living."

Everyone looked concerned as he continued. "We have discovered that those Fallen have been released from where they were being held and that those who guarded the vaults are missing. Four people have been recently murdered, and all four are related to those who guarded The Fallen. I believe that the murders were done intentionally to somehow free The Fallen; this is evident in the fact that those murdered, along with their relatives who guarded the prisons where The Fallen had been contained, are missing and most likely prisoners among the Darkness. We must find those four and bring them back to the Light."

General Wiggins spoke. "Whoever did this had to gain access to the realm where the vaults are located in the Light. How were they able to enter?"

"We're unsure of that right now, but hopefully the ones we bring back will be able to tell us." Simmons placed his hand on Alan's shoulder, "This is Alan Crane, and he will be the newest member of this group. He has ventured into the Darkness before and performed exquisitely."

Alan half smiled and felt intimidated to be counted among a group that held such important positions in society. Simmons continued, "We'll need to divide into four teams, and we need to execute this quickly."

The groups quickly formed, and each group was assigned to find a different person. The first group was to look for Sister Franconi, the second group was assigned to find Mr. Burnstein, the third group was sent to find Dr. Stevenson, and the fourth group—to which Alan was assigned with Amanda, General Wiggins, and Senator Swanson—was to find Jimmy Howard.

As Alan's group walked toward the door, General Wiggins said, "Better make this quick—I'm not sure how long I can tolerate being with some self-serving politician."

Alan glanced over at Senator Swanson, who gritted her teeth and shot back, "Well, I don't plan on being in a foxhole with some egotistical cowboy—but then again, who am I kidding? Most of your combat experience was probably behind a desk." Alan's face turned pale as the general stopped and turned toward the senator.

The general then looked over at Alan and said, "Lighten up, son," and smiled at the senator, who started laughing. "Behind a desk," repeated the general. "Got to give you credit for that one, Linda—that was good," he chuckled. The senator grinned, then said to Alan, "Welcome to our group."

"Uh, thank you," replied Alan. "I have to admit I'm a bit intimidated."

"Why is that?" asked Amanda.

"There are so many important people here who hold so many important positions."

Senator Swanson stopped and turned toward Alan. She was an attractive woman in her early fifties with shoulder-length, auburn hair. She had a distinguished presence about her and a very articulate way of speaking. "You, Alan Crane, are the only Light Bringer who is among the living at this time. That position is extremely important. As for these positions that you perceive to be *so* important, like senator and general, how long do we actually hold them?"

Alan pondered what she was saying as she continued. "How long are we alive? Perhaps a hundred years, at best?" She smiled, as Alan stared at the ground, thinking of his own mortality. "And how long are we dead?" She waited a few seconds to allow this to sink in Alan's conscious mind, then answered her own question. "Forever—we go to the world beyond the living, or heaven, as you would call it, for eternity. So what's more important, the positions you keep while you are alive or what you do after you die?"

Alan nodded, indicating that he understood what she was saying. She placed a hand on his shoulder. "So many of my colleagues believe that they are *so* important because of the positions they hold or the perceived power that they wield, but in fact it's all a misperception on their part because in the end, after they pass on, none of it matters."

The color drained from Alan's face again, and his expression revealed that he had been given too much information to process all at once. Swanson must have picked up on this, for she said, "Let your heart not be troubled; we're honored to have you among us, Light Bringer. We need to attend to the task at hand." Alan nodded and smiled as the four made their way out of the castle.

Elijah, Simmons, and the four groups quickly walked through the garden and out to the field beyond. Elijah had explained that the doorway to the Darkness was on the far side of the field up on one of the mountains. As they reached the middle of the field, Alan felt something wet strike his face and roll down his cheek. He looked up, and another drop hit him on the ear. He wiped it off and looked at the clear liquid on his fingers. *Rain?* he thought. A steady downpour of rain fell on everyone. Alan looked around, confused, then asked Elijah, "Does it rain down here?"

Elijah looked concerned as he replied, "No."

Suddenly the rain stopped, and Alan heard a low rumbling sound emanating from the horizon. He strained to hear what is was and where it was coming from. It grew louder, and Alan could tell that it was coming from an area near the mountain that contained the portal to the Darkness, which was a great distance from where they were.

As the sound became louder, Elijah stopped, and so did the rest of the group. "This sounds bad," he said.

Alan moved to the front of the group, and, as he stared into the distance, an overwhelming feeling of fear gripped him because he could see what was in front of them. A huge wave of water rose up and was rapidly closing in on them.

"Run!" yelled Elijah, and, with that, the group scurried toward the higher ground surrounding the field.

Alan breathed hard as they finally made it to the rocky ground off to one side and up onto a gradual rise. The water filled the entire lower area and seemed to stop. Alan was about to breathe a sigh of relief, but then he saw something that made his heart pound even faster. In the center of the field, now covered in water, a figure rose up. It looked like a giant standing about thirteen feet tall with huge gray wings. Alan recognized what this was, since he had seen an angel before. This must be one of The Fallen.

Just then Elijah yelled out, "Manis!"

The huge figure looked over in Elijah's direction, threw its head back, and emitted a horrible, menacing laugh. In a deep beastlike voice it replied, "Good-bye, Solomon," then opened its massive arms. From each of its outstretched fingertips, torrents of water began to flow forth as though being forced through holes punched in a dam. Alan noticed the water level rising and knew that the ground they were standing on would not keep them dry for very long. Somehow he knew that the rising water here would drown them all, unlike the water that surrounded the Lost City that allowed them to breathe normally.

As Alan began moving back with the others, he noticed someone scrambling up the side of the mountain. The figure scaled the rock like a spider crawling up a wall, and, as he stared harder, he realized that it was Simmons. Alan continued to move upward to avoid the rising water and watched Simmons make his way to the edge of a cliff that overlooked the now sunken field.

Alan had heard the great angel call Elijah Solomon, and he wondered if this was perhaps who Elijah really was. Perhaps he was King Solomon, known for his wisdom and lore of how he battled demons, or maybe he was some type of descendent of the historically famous king. *Could this have been prior conflicts with The Fallen?* His thoughts were soon interrupted by Simmons.

"I remember now!" boomed Simmons.

The water from The Fallen's fingertips stopped at once, as it looked up to observe Simmons, then hissed, "You!"

"Yes, it's me, and I remember you . . . you!" Simmons accused and pointed his finger menacingly. "You! Manis, The Fallen angel of the water! You fell from the order of virtues—you and your brethren killed my mother!" Simmons raged.

Manis looked angry, as he stared at Simmons with cold, black, steely eyes. "You will not be victorious this time!" he screeched. He flapped his massive wings and hovered above the field for a moment, then his limbs and body seemed to liquefy, becoming a large sphere of water that shot toward Simmons like a cannonball. Simmons was holding his white marble rod as he braced himself for the collision. The explosion was tremendous and knocked everyone to the ground. Alan was dazed only for a moment, and, when he looked up, he saw Simmons standing on the ledge and Manis lying in the water below. The Fallen angel stood back up on the top of the water and shook his head as he steadied himself for yet another attack.

Simmons walked to the very edge of the cliff and yelled, "I remember how I defeated you before, and you shall fall once again!"

Manis reached down and lifted a massive ball of swirling water, then swung his arm back as though he were about to pitch a baseball. Simmons threw the rod like a javelin. It shot from his hand with a brilliant gleaming light that was nearly too bright to look at. The rod struck The Fallen angel in the center of the chest, and he let out a terrifying shriek that caused Alan to shudder. Manis fell back into the water and gripped the massive wound made by the rod.

The water rapidly drained as Alan watched Manis shrivel, then turn into a pile of fine black dust. As Alan stared up at Simmons, who was once again holding the marble rod, his memory flashed back to the tapestry in the castle of Zeus hurling the lightning bolt at the Titans. He now knew where the story had come from; he was confident that the Greeks who had written the myth of the fall of the Titans had actually witnessed Michael Simmons defeating The Fallen.

Simmons called down to the others. "You need to keep going and rescue those four from the Darkness. I will join you later."

"Where are you going?" Alan yelled back up to him.

"I'm going to do what I did many years ago. I'm going to hunt The Fallen."

"Be safe, my friend," Alan replied.

Simmons smiled as he leaned against the rod, which was once again in his hand. "I will see you soon."

CHAPTER 24

Into the Darkness

T HE WATER HAD NOW RECEDED FROM THE FIELD, and the four groups made their way to the very back, where they began climbing a long flight of stone stairs that zigzagged back and forth up the mountain. When they reached the top, Alan noticed that they were standing on a cliff, and the rock in front of them had a large old wooden door set in its side. The gap between the doorjamb and the door seemed to be absorbing the light from its surroundings, and Alan quickly remembered that this was an indicator that the passageway led to the Darkness.

"Once we pass through, how will we know where to go?" Alan asked.

"By these," Elijah said, holding up a cloth sack he'd been carrying.

"What's that?" Alan studied the old burlap bag that was tied at the top with an old rope.

"These are the Arnequians; in the language of the divine, *arnequian* means 'fondest memory'".

Alan was recalling many words from the language of the divine that he had learned from his previous travels to the Realm of Light. He did not recognize this word, so he requested a further explanation. "What do you mean by 'fondest memory'?"

Elijah elaborated, "When good people are captured and held among the Darkness, they still hold on to some of their fondest memories—not even the traumas of the Darkness can take that away from them. It's what the Disciples of Light use to locate people who have been taken prisoner."

Elijah set the bag down and untied the rope. He pulled out a small, tattered wooden cross that he handed to a member of the first group, who stepped forward to receive it. "This cross was made by a seven-year-old boy in a poverty-stricken land where Sister Franconi established her first mission," Elijah said. "The boy's parents were dead, and he was starving when Sister Franconi found him. She fed him and nursed him back to health. He carved this from a piece of old driftwood and gave it to her to show his gratitude. The boy went on to help with the mission and render aid to a great many people—his life saved hundreds of others."

A woman stepped forward from the second group as Elijah pulled out an old worn cloth the size of a handkerchief. "Alexander Burnstein was weak and near death in a German concentration camp during World War II," Elijah recalled. "A young American soldier approached him, pulled this cloth from his pack, and wiped the grime, sweat, and blood from Mr. Burnstein's face, then gave him a drink of water from his canteen. The soldier's words as he carried him out still echoed in Mr. Burnstein's mind: 'You're safe now. We won't let them hurt you anymore—rest easy . . . rest easy.' Mr. Burnstein carried this cloth in remembrance of that soldier—the hero who saved his life." Elijah handed the cloth to the woman.

Alan watched as a tall, young man with blond hair stepped forward from the third group. Alan strained to remember why he recognized the man, and, as the man smiled at Elijah, Alan noticed he was missing a bottom tooth on the left side of his mouth. *Slavic Macavey*, Alan thought, *the professional hockey player. He's one of the Disciples of Light?* Alan stared in astonishment as Slavic waited for Elijah to pull out the next Arnequian. This time it was a piece of paper.

"This was a picture drawn by a four-year-old girl who had been saved as a baby by a new procedure that Dr. Eva Stevenson had developed," Elijah explained. "The girl had very little chance of living, and even if she did live, there was a high probability of several debilitating disabilities. The critics told Dr. Stevenson that her procedure would not work, but she proved them wrong, and four years later the girl was living a normal life with no disabilities. She drew this picture of herself and the doctor." Elijah held up the paper that depicted stick figures of the doctor and her patient holding hands, then handed it to Slavic.

Alan stepped forward on behalf of the fourth group. Elijah pulled out a small medal attached to a thin silver neck chain. "This is a medal that Jimmy Howard received from his uncle, Joseph Howard, who was one of Jimmy's favorite people," Elijah stated. "Uncle Joe made Jimmy feel like all of the other kids, and in one particular instance he helped him to play with the others inside an inflatable bounce house at a friend's birthday party." Elijah handed the medal and chain to Alan, who studied it for a moment.

"I know this pendant," he said, recognizing the picture of Saint Camillus on one side and the star with the triangle on the other.

"Yes," confirmed Elijah. "That was a medal that Jimmy's uncle used to wear. It bears the symbol of the Disciples of Light on the back because he was once a member."

"So Jimmy Howard's uncle was one of the Disciples of Light?"

"Yes." Elijah nodded. "He was guarding one of The Fallen."

"But Michael and I gave that medal to Jimmy just before we walked him to the Light."

"Yes, and it was found just beyond the doorway that you escorted him through, which I find most disturbing."

Things were starting to fall into place for Alan as he realized that The Fallen, Jimmy Howard, and his uncle were all linked in some manner.

Perhaps he would get some more answers once they located Jimmy.

Each group stepped through the door, leaving Elijah behind. Alan's group went in last, and Alan could feel the anxiety mounting in his gut in anticipation of venturing into the Darkness again. He followed General Wiggins, and a cold chill came over his face. As the old rickety door shut behind them, Alan found himself in complete darkness, like that of a cave where you cannot see your own hand right in front of your face.

"Okay," he said, taking a deep, slow breath, "what now?"

Amanda's voice said calmly, "Take out the Arnequian. It works like a compass."

Alan had no idea what she was talking about, but as he removed the medal and held it in front of him, a narrow beam of light shot forth and spun around them for a moment, then became transfixed in a specific direction.

Senator Swanson's voice came from behind Alan. "You see, the memory draws us to our destination. It is the Light in the Darkness, like a speck of hope that glistens in a sea of despair."

The beam of light seemed to keep traveling forward into infinity, like a flashlight pointed at the night sky. Alan strained to make out a wall or an object nearby, but it seemed that wherever they went, the place was dark and wide open.

"Are we in the Darkness yet?" he asked the others.

"No," replied General Wiggins. "This is the place that leads us to that realm."

They continued walking a long way, and, after about two hours, Alan noticed that the surroundings were becoming a bit more illuminated. Although he could not see a ceiling or walls, he could perceive that they were on a narrow black marble pathway approximately twenty-five feet wide. Walking to the edge of the pathway, Alan peered over the side into the darkness and realized that they were actually on a bridge. The beam of light emitting from the medal shot forward and finally struck something hundreds of feet in the distance. The group members drew closer to where the light had landed, and, as they did, Alan could see it reflecting in all directions.

Finally, they arrived at what seemed to be a huge wall, and Alan looked on in astonishment at the sight before them. As far as the eye could see in all directions, there were black marble bridges that led to the massive wall in front of them. At the end of each bridge in the center of the wall was an old wooden door that Alan recognized as the pathway to the Darkness.

"There must be thousands or even millions of these bridges and doors," he said to the others.

"Yes," replied Amanda, "that's why it's so important to have the Arnequian, or else you could be lost in here forever."

The general put his hand on the door handle and looked back at everyone. "Ready?"

Alan's hand reached down and felt the hilt of the dagger he was wearing on his belt. It had been a gift from Simmons some time ago. The blade was made of white marble, and Simmons had told him that it was a weapon that was used in battle between the Light and the Darkness. Alan nodded to the general, who opened the door, and the four of them walked through.

CHAPTER 25

Battling the Wind

MEANWHILE, BACK IN THE FIELD OF THE LOST CITY, Simmons was trying to figure out how he could sense the location of The Fallen. Instinct had drawn him to a snow-covered mountain peak near Mount Everest. The sunlight illuminated the trees and glistened off the ice-covered branches, which made a beautiful picturesque scene as he scaled the icy rock. At the top, he found a large flat area that appeared to be a small frozen lake. Oxygen up here was nearly nonexistent, and the temperature was lethal. This would have concerned Simmons if he had been among the living, but being from the realm beyond life had its advantages.

As he made his way toward the center of the ice, he looked down to see a ghastly sight. A foot or so below the frozen surface, there were people suspended in the frozen lake, and, as Simmons continued to study them, he soon recognized one. "Johnny Bartel," he whispered, remembering the boy who had led the hate group to kill Mr. Burnstein.

"Yes," said a female voice from the other side of the lake. Simmons looked in that direction and saw one of The Fallen sitting on a large stone table. She was about thirteen feet tall, like the others, with huge gray wings and clad in obsidian armor. "Welcome, Illissia Alontis," she said, as her great wings slowly flapped, allowing her to hover just above the table. Simmons recognized the strange phrase: it was his rank in the army of the Light. An Illissia Alontis was a Light Guardian, one who commanded twelve army units known as a seristrum.

Readying himself for a fight, Simmons pulled the foot-long marble rod from his belt, extended it to the length of a walking stick, and waved it in front of him. In an instant he was clad in the white polished stone armor worn by the soldiers of the Light in their battles with the soldiers of the Darkness. "So tell me, Andora, have we met in battle?"

Andora smiled as her jet-black eyes became transfixed on Simmons. "I see that your memory still has some gaps in it. Our last battle must have taken its toll on you."

"You and your brethren killed my mother!" There was rage in Simmons's eyes that The Fallen angel certainly recognized. She raised her arms and muttered some words, and Simmons braced himself into a defensive stance with his rod. As she finished the incantation, Simmons saw black smoke rising from the lake, and within seconds, people who had been suspended under the surface were standing all around him, clad in black armor and wielding a multitude of weapons.

Andora let out a horrible sinister laugh as Simmons surveyed his potential attackers. There were twelve in all, and a large man wielding an enormous sword lunged at him from behind. Simmons quickly turned and parried the attack, then struck the figure with the rod, which passed through the man's midsection and turned him into a pile of black dust.

Johnny Bartel stood in front of Simmons and yelled to the others, "We must all attack at once. On my command—go!" The group closed in simultaneously, and Simmons knew that he could not strike everyone down at the same time, so he raised the rod above his head and plunged it down hard into the ice beneath his feet. A tremendous light from the impact ignited the ground with a brilliant explosion that shattered the lake and melted most of the ice in the surrounding area. Simmons found himself falling into a seemingly endless chasm, and he realized that there was no water below the ice on the surface. His enemies were falling, too, and one by one he was able to strike them down with the rod, turning them into dust that scattered in the wind. The top of the chasm was getting farther away, yet the bottom was nowhere in sight.

Andora's voice rang out and echoed from above, "Do you feel the wind, Michael? Do you feel its power?"

He could see her closing in on him. She was spinning like a cyclone, sucking up everything she passed. Simmons angled his arms and legs to propel himself toward one of the rocky walls, and when he was very close to the wall, he forced the rod into it. The rod cut quickly into the stone wall and slowed his fall so he could gain footing on a small ledge off to one side. The sharp rock cut a chunk of flesh from his forearm, which would have caused unbearable pain to anyone among the living. He stood up and looked at the wound while the muscle, tendons, and skin rapidly re-formed like new.

Andora was hovering in front of him, a whirlwind surrounding her. In a low, demonic voice, she said, "You feel the power now, Michael?" She reached out an enormous hand, which quickly grasped Simmons's throat and formed into a clawed talon.

"Save your intimidation for the living," he replied. "Your depiction of the demonic is merely a scare tactic to inflame the imaginations of men—I know better, Andora." He spun the rod with two hands and brought it down hard on the angel's massive forearm. It passed completely through and turned her arm and hand to dust. Andora howled in pain and fell backward, then regained control and plunged down in an attempt to flee.

Simmons walked to the edge of the tiny shelf he was standing on, and in one fluid motion he lifted the rod above his head and plunged headfirst over the side like a world-class diver. His body was perfectly straight as the rod cut through the wind. Andora was just up ahead, and as Simmons drew within ten feet of her, she turned in an attempt to fend him off. The end of the rod pierced the black breastplate of her armor, and, just as they struck the ground, she exploded into dust, which settled on the rocky bottom of the deep gorge.

Within seconds, Simmons's wounds had healed, and he gathered up the black-dust remnants of The Fallen angel. These remains would be taken to the Realm of Light, and Andora would once again be imprisoned.

CHAPTER 26

The Tower

ALAN AND HIS GROUP WALKED OUT OF a musty brick alley onto a roadway. The scene looked very similar to the last one that Alan had ventured into in the Realm of Darkness. Familiar wrought-iron gas lamps lined each side of an old brick street. As Alan scanned the surrounding area, he spotted a castlelike stone tower off in the distance. All four members of his group began making their way to the tower, which sat high on a hill that could be reached by a small winding dirt path.

He noticed that the street was vacant of people, as it had been during the last rescue mission he'd undertaken. Just before the group turned onto the path, a figure appeared up the road. The others slowed in order not to arouse suspicion. The figure drew near, and Alan could see that it was very tall and wore a hooded cloak that prevented anyone from seeing its face. It walked at a quick pace, and, when it was within five feet of Alan, it whispered, "You're on the right path, Light Bringer. I was sent here to tell you the way. Go to the tower; the one you seek is being held there."

"Who are you?" Alan asked skeptically.

The figure stepped closer, and Alan could make out a portion of the face underneath the hood. It was a distinguished-looking old man with a long gaunt face and thin nose. "That's not important. You need to get into that tower, and do not use the front entrance—it's a trap. Once you pull the handle of the door, the jaws will spring, and you will be killed. There's another way in. Around the back of the tower, there's a hidden trapdoor in the ground near the old withered oak tree. Follow the catacombs below the tower to reach the main floor, but be wary of the guards." The figure turned and continued walking down the street.

"Do you trust him?" Alan asked the others.

"No," replied the general. "No one here can be trusted, but we'll be cautious when we approach."

They continued up the path, and, as they drew nearer, Alan noticed that the tower was much larger than it had first appeared. The diameter must have been at least 150 feet, and it was twice as high as it was wide. Its walls were covered with thick vines that snaked their way upward, and Alan observed that the only windows were at the very top. He and the others walked around until they came to an old wooden door with a heavy brass handle. The door was recessed into the tower about ten feet, and, as they stepped closer, Alan noticed that there was no ceiling, only a tall dark shaft.

"Wait," Alan said to the others as he scanned the walls and floor, where he noticed a fine ground powder and reddish-brown stains spread about.

"What do you make of this?" asked Senator Swanson.

Amanda stepped up to examine the powder and stains with Alan.

"It's blood," replied Alan, as he continued to survey the reddish-brown streaks.

"Indeed," agreed Amanda. "And this powder appears to be ground bones."

"Everyone back up," directed General Wiggins, as he slowly stepped away from the tower entrance. The others quickly followed as the general drew forth a knife and cut a large vine from the tower wall. He returned to the door and carefully tied one end of the vine to the handle, then backed out of the entryway. Everyone stood behind him as he yanked hard on the vine, which tugged on the door handle. A thunderous roar could be heard overhead, and a tremendous crash knocked everyone to the ground as a huge stone block smashed down from the hollow shaft above into the entryway.

"Maybe the old man was telling the truth," said Alan.

"Perhaps he was," replied the general, as his eyes became transfixed on the huge stone, which was now being slowly lifted back up the shaft in order to reset the trap.

"Let's walk around the back and see if we can find the alternate entrance," Alan suggested. He led the group around to the other side of the tower, and, sure enough, an old dead oak tree stood twenty feet from the back wall. They circled around it until Amanda called out, "Found something over here." She stomped her foot on what sounded like a piece of metal, which was covered with dirt and grass.

As Alan was clearing away the foliage, his hand struck something that felt like a handle. He gripped it tightly and pulled upward, which caused the outline of a door to come into view though the dark soil. The others joined in and helped him pull up on the handle until the door creaked open, and a cold musty stairwell could be seen descending into the darkness.

Alan pulled a badge from his pocket, unraveled the chain that it was attached to, and hung it around his neck. The badge was another gift from Simmons that they used when walking people to the Light. He noticed that the others did the same, hanging similar objects around their necks that resembled pendants with a symbol in the middle of each. Alan studied the symbol on his for a moment, then realized where he'd seen it before: it was the same symbol that was displayed on the back of the medal that Jimmy Howard had worn—the medal that was given to him by his uncle who had once been a Disciple of Light.

As the group started down the narrow stairwell, the pendants and the badge glowed to illuminate a short distance in front of them. After about twenty minutes of walking, Alan looked back and could barely see the trapdoor. Finally they came to a small landing, where another door stood in front of them. Alan reached up and touched the low ceiling above their heads just to make sure they weren't standing underneath another shaft. He jerked the handle, and the door opened. Everyone stepped through to the room beyond, which was lit by torches that lined the walls.

The room appeared to be a very large storage area; there were boxes and crates scattered about. The group members quickly made their way to the other side and up a short flight of wooden stairs to another doorway. The room beyond that was similar to the one below, and they repeated this process about ten times, until they eventually reached what appeared to be the main level of the tower. Alan could see the front door, where the trap had claimed many victims.

A large circular room on this level contained a grand display of multiple suits of obsidian armor. A stairwell that wound around the exterior of the tower led to the next level, and as the four quietly climbed to the next room, Alan spotted two figures clad in black armor on the far side of the room. The four descended back to the main room without detection so Alan could devise a plan to get past the two guards.

He and Amanda each put on a suit of obsidian armor. General Wiggins and Senator Swanson posed as prisoners, clasping their hands behind their backs and pretending to be bound. Alan took the lead, and Amanda walked behind the group as they approached the guards.

Both guards drew long curved swords as the taller of the two spoke. "What the hell are you doing in here?"

"I have prisoners to deposit," answered Alan in an annoyed tone of voice.

"We weren't notified of any more prisoners being brought in," the shorter guard piped up, keeping his weapon ready.

Alan pulled out the sheathed sword that had accompanied the armor, knocked the shorter man's sword to one side, and grabbed him by the tunic. He pulled the guard's face close to his own as he yelled, "Look, jackass, perhaps you don't understand the seriousness of this matter! One of The Fallen is gone, and these prisoners are from the Disciples of Light. Things are not going well, and we had direct orders to bring these two in to hold with the others. Now, if you want me to take them back and tell our superiors that I had two idiots who refused to cooperate, I will, but it's your funeral."

The taller man sheathed his sword and put both of his hands up as he said, "No, no . . . it's fine. We weren't aware of the circumstances. Go ahead up. I'll notify the others that you're coming."

Alan shoved the shorter man back and released his grip. The four turned and headed up the stairs to the next level. The next set of guards they came to said nothing but merely nodded, and the group ascended several other floors similar to the main one.

As they rounded the outside stairwell to one of the top floors, they noticed that this room appeared to be a large dining hall with a huge wooden table in the center that held twenty place settings. There was one figure seated at the table, a short man with a scraggly beard. He rose from the chair and made his way over to where the four stood. As he came close, Alan could smell the whiskey on his breath. He staggered a bit, obviously drunk, then said, with a Hispanic accent, "Hmm . . . what do we have here?"

Alan repeated his scheme. "Prisoners to be kept with the others. They are members of the Disciples of Light, and we have word that one of The Fallen has been defeated." He continued to study the man's face, and, as he did, Alan realized that he recognized him but could not recall from where.

"The Disciples of Light." The man laughed and drew a curved dark-bladed dagger from his belt. Alan recognized it as one of the distinct weapons that the soldiers of Darkness used in battle.

"Well," continued the man, "I see that we have met our counterparts —our mirror images." He had to stretch very far in order to press the dagger against General Wiggins's neck because the general was so tall and he was so short. In a flash, the general brought both of his hands from behind his back, using one to fend off the knife and the other to grab the man by the throat. Alan punched the man in the jaw, knocking him to the floor unconscious.

"What was he saying about meeting his counterpart, or mirror image?" Alan continued to study his face, trying to figure out where he'd seen him before.

Amanda took off her helmet and stood beside Alan. "I don't know what he meant by that, but do you recognize him?"

"Yes, I do, but I can't recall from where."

"You most likely know him from an intelligence alert that the FBI put out. His name is Sergio Espanuega, and he's a drug lord from South America." Amanda smiled. "And how fitting—he's in hell and not even dead yet. Who says there's no justice in the world?"

The comment made Alan chuckle as Amanda put the helmet on her head once more, and they walked up the final stairwell to the room above.

Upon reaching the landing at the top, Alan peered down a long hallway where prison cells lined both sides. High above the cages, he could see the coned roof of the tower and the tiny windows that allowed minimal light to enter. The four quickly made their way to the end of the hall and found two of the cells occupied. The first contained an old withered man who was cowering in a corner. Amanda used a key she had grabbed from the coat pocket of Sergio as he lay unconscious on the floor. She swung the door open and ran to where the old man was lying on the dirt floor.

Alan grabbed the key from her and opened the second cell, where he saw Jimmy Howard curled into a ball and seated in a wheelchair. Although Alan had witnessed Jimmy walking freely in the Realm of the Light without his wheelchair, Alan knew that in the Darkness, he would be even weaker than when he was alive.

Jimmy screamed when he saw Alan coming toward him in the black armor, but Senator Swanson ran to him and took his hand, which was clasped so tightly against his body that it took great effort to pry it away. Her touch seemed to calm the boy, and as Alan took the medal from his pocket and placed it around Jimmy's neck, he smiled and blurted out the words, "Uncle Joe . . . get Uncle Joe."

Alan realized that the man in the other cell was Joseph Howard, Jimmy's uncle. He heaved the twelve-year-old onto his back, and they began the trip back down the stairs. General Wiggins was close behind, helping Joe Howard walk by propping him up under one arm. The room below, where Sergio had been knocked out, was now vacant, which meant that they had to hurry.

As Alan made his way across the room, he noticed the blood on the floor from the injury he had inflicted on the drug lord. Walking forward toward the stairs, he stepped on something hard, and as he moved his foot he saw that it was a ring that must have fallen off Sergio's hand during their altercation. He quickly grabbed it and placed it in his pocket.

To Alan's surprise, they did not encounter any guards on the way down as they hurried back to the basement and out through the trapdoor by the tree. Alan was exhausted by that time, and he switched places with General Wiggins, who picked up Jimmy while Alan helped Uncle Joe along. It was a short distance to the alley that led back out to the catacombs and the doors connecting them to the Realm of Darkness.

As they entered the alley, Alan could see the door, and he thought, *There's something wrong—this is too easy.* Just as the thought crossed his mind, he heard the sound of people behind him, and when he glanced over his shoulder, he saw an assembly of figures clad in black armor rushing toward them.

"Run!" he yelled to the others, who were in front of him.

Alan's badge hung around his neck and illuminated the way across the long black bridge that led them back to the place where they had started their journey. The soldiers were not far behind and were closing in quickly. Alan looked back over his shoulder and saw that the closest figure was a huge man who carried an enormous hammer. The soldiers stopped as the big man raised the hammer above his head and smashed it down on the bridge in front of him. This seemed to cause a shock wave that emanated forward, starting a chain reaction that began collapsing the black marble walkway that was the only way out.

The deteriorating bridge was falling in sections hundreds of feet below to the next level. Alan lost his footing and lurched forward. He yelled to Amanda and Senator Swanson, "Grab Joe," as he quickly passed the old man forward and tried to regain his balance. The edge of the collapse was nearly on him when he realized that his ankle was twisted, making it difficult to stand. He felt the first portions of marble slip away under his feet as he grabbed for the broken ledge, trying to pull himself back up. The horrible sensation of falling was overwhelming him, when suddenly he felt the strong grip of a hand on each of his arms, hoisting him up onto the bridge. Looking up, he saw the general struggling to pull him upright and stay ahead of the falling walkway.

"Get out of here, General!"

"Nobody gets left behind, soldier! You know that! Now on your feet and move it!"

Alan gritted his teeth and pushed forward through the pain piercing his ankle. The doorway was now in sight, and the others had already passed through. He and the general were the only ones left on the bridge, which was falling fast. Alan hurled his body into the opening, and both of the men fell to the ground on the other side. As he lay on the soft grass and looked up to see sunlight warming his face, he realized that he was not back in the Lost City near the mountain range where they'd started from. He rubbed his ankle and got to his feet; the air was quickly restoring his energy.

His ankle seemed to hurt less, and as he stumbled a bit, two people stopped him from falling: one was Jimmy Howard, and the other was Uncle Joe. Both of them were standing strong and refreshed as Alan realized that they were in the Realm of the Light. The general was standing next to him, and so were Amanda and Senator Swanson. They all began walking down a familiar cobblestone roadway that led to a place Alan had seen before, that he had visited years ago. The city was an exact depiction of ancient Rome—actually, Alan had been told, ancient Rome had been copied from *this* place. He was still confused about how the doorway opened here instead of onto the mountain where they'd started from, but, as he thought about it further, he concluded that Jimmy Howard and Uncle Joe could not return to the realm of the living once they were freed.

They passed through the huge entryway, and Alan took in the sight of the Colosseum looming in the distance.

"They used Jimmy to get to me," said Uncle Joe.

"How so?" asked Alan.

"They murdered Jimmy, and that opened a doorway for them to get to me, a vault guard. Once they subdued me, they freed The Fallen."

Alan nodded as the last piece of the puzzle fell into place. Whoever murdered Sister Franconi, Eva Stevenson, Alexander Burnstein, and Jimmy Howard did so to gain access to the Realm of Light and to the vaults that imprisoned The Fallen. Each of the four murder victims had relatives who had previously been charged with guarding the vaults. That's why these four were chosen to be killed. The murdered were to follow in the footsteps of their relatives and help guard the vaults of The Fallen. The murders ensured that the doorways the four victims walked through to get to the Light would also connect direct pathways to the vaults. The ritualistic techniques used in the killings must have given the murderers the ability to locate these doors.

"We need to meet Elijah in the great hall to sort this all out," said General Wiggins.

As Alan continued to walk, his thoughts wandered to his family. He knew that time was of no essence in these realms, so his wife and his daughter would not notice that he had been gone any longer than usual on a workday, but he did miss them so.

CHAPTER 27

The Mystery of the Sphinx

T HE CHASM WAS DEEP, and it took Simmons a long time to scale the slick stone walls back to the mountaintop. An inner sense or instinct drew him to the locations of The Fallen, and this time he found himself in Egypt. His armor gleamed in the sunlight as the heat of the desert beat down upon him. He traversed the massive dunes and battled fierce sandstorms until finally, from a distance, the vision of ancient structures came into view. One of them was a distinctive landmark with the face of a human and the body of a cat. As he drew very close, he could make out the great statue that was supposedly built by the Egyptian pharaoh Khafra.

"Beautiful, isn't it?" asked a voice behind him.

Simmons turned to see Archilus, The Fallen angel of earth, standing fifteen feet from him. Archilus walked forward and spoke again. "Humanity believes that this great statue was built by one of its own," he laughed, as he shook his head.

"Oh, how the living are so conceited and arrogant. The pharaoh Khafra did not build this. I did, many years ago in another world. It was weathering from exposure to the rain day after day, so I moved it here. The people of this world study it and can't figure out why there are no references to Khafra engraved on it. They marvel at the fact that it was built centuries ago and cannot figure out how the ancient Egyptians moved the heavy blocks used in its construction. All of their attempts to determine its age come up unfounded, because it is much older than it should be for this area. I used to fly in at night and visit the pharaoh, who worshiped me as a god."

"I'll bet you liked that," Simmons said snidely. "And you call the living arrogant?"

The Fallen angel smiled as he came a few steps closer, his massive feet leaving enormous impressions in the sand. Simmons took out his rod.

"Oh, Michael," said Archilus. "So righteous you are—just like your father."

"You didn't know my father!" Simmons shouted as he gripped the rod with both hands.

"Oh, but I did," said the angel, folding his arms and stretching his huge gray wings.

Simmons drew a deep breath and regained control of his emotions, then said, "You and your friends killed my mother, and I'm here to send you back where you belong."

"I was imprisoned a very long time, Michael, and I have no intention of going back. The other two you have defeated were not as strong as I and Ellestria. You will lose if you fight either of us, and then you will be imprisoned in the Darkness. I'll let you live if you walk away now."

"You forget I'm not alive, Archilus, and I think that once again you're acting arrogant if you believe you wield more power than the others."

"No, it's true, Michael. I do hold more power. Do you know where power is derived from?"

Simmons stood his ground silently as he waited for the first attack.

"Humanity has different theories about power. Some people think it comes from money. Some think it comes from control. But the truth is that power is based on knowing. The more you know, the more power you wield. Those among the living who know a great many things have the most power, and, as such, all of those other perceived aspects of power, such as money or control, fall into place from knowing. It yields great influence and manipulation."

"Just as you're trying to manipulate me now?"

"Very well," replied Archilus. "If you want a fight, then a fight you shall get."

"Take a good look around," Simmons said as he pointed at the massive figure. "When we're finished, you will join the other pieces of sand that you stand upon."

Archilus folded his wings around him and began spinning rapidly, burrowing under the sand until he couldn't be seen any longer. Simmons twirled the rod and scanned all directions. Suddenly the ground near him erupted, and a huge hand, formed from the desert sand, rose up in the air and smashed down on him. He raised the rod above his head, and it radiated a great white light that was blistering hot. The sand that was crashing down on him solidified into a massive mound of glass that he shattered with one stroke of the rod.

Taking a few steps forward, he felt a hand wrap around one of his ankles and pull him under the earth. He was traveling downward through sand, soil, and rock at a rapid pace. The hole above him was filling in as he continued, so he tucked his knees and rolled, swinging the rod under his feet and severing the grip of the hand. Burrowing his way upward, he found himself standing at the base of one of the great pyramids. He quickly climbed to the top, scaling the large blocks, but as he did, the enormous structure began to sink rapidly as though the earth was swallowing it up. The top of the pyramid descended into the desert just as he leaped off and ran to one side.

There was now a vortex of sand on the ground that was expanding rapidly. Simmons scaled the sphinx, ran to the very top of the head, and threw his rod into the sky. It raced upward and struck the upper atmosphere with a tremendous eruption of thunder and lightning. A huge black storm cloud instantly formed overhead and quickly poured down torrents of water that filled the vortex to the brim. The rod fell back into Simmons's hands, and he watched as Archilus shot up from under the water gasping and coughing.

"Like an earthworm during a downpour, don't you think?" Simmons said cynically.

The Fallen angel rose to his feet and jumped into the air. He leveled out, then dove at an incredible pace toward Simmons, like an eagle descending on its prey. Just before impact, Simmons jumped into the air and swung his rod, which severed Archilus's head from his body and instantly turned him into the familiar black dust.

As Simmons gathered up the dust, he looked up and said, "One more to go, Mother—one more to go."

CHAPTER 28

An Ancient Cult

THE GREAT HALL WAS NOT ACTUALLY IN THE CITY that resembled ancient Rome; rather, it required a fairly long walk up a huge mountain that led to a bridge that linked to a massive castle. Inside the main entrance of the castle, there was an enormous room with massive doors on each of the walls. Scattered around the room were stone tables and chairs, each table set with a wonderful display of delicious food. Alan's group quickly walked across the room and through one of the doors that led to a secluded area with a large table and chairs placed in the center. Seated around the table were the other three groups of the Disciples of Light, Elijah, and the people they had rescued.

Elijah spoke to everyone. "We have now concluded, from all of those we have here, that beings from the Darkness murdered four people in order to gain access to the Realm of Light and to free The Fallen, whom Michael now hunts. Those four victims were picked because their doorways led to the vaults where The Fallen were being held. Relatives of the four murder victims had been assigned to guard the vaults, and it is now apparent that an organized group of people among the living orchestrated this plan to free The Fallen. Our next step is to determine who these people are and what this group is."

"I can tell you one of them," Alan offered. "Sergio Espanuega, a drug lord from Colombia. We met him on our journey. I found this on our way out—I think he dropped it." Alan pulled the ring from his pocket and placed it on the table. Elijah grabbed it and studied the markings, then handed it back to Alan.

"I've seen that symbol before, Alan. It's that of an ancient cult."

Alan studied the symbol on the top flat portion of the ring. It consisted of three ovals that intersected one another. He placed the ring back into his pocket and pondered what significance this had to the murder suspects.

"We need to further identify the people in this group," Elijah instructed. "Does anyone have any other information that may help?"

Alan offered, "Based on the number of stab wounds in the victims, I would guess that there are twelve of them, and I'm confident that at least one is a woman, since I found a specific brand of high-heeled shoes imprinted in blood at some of the crime scenes."

A man from the first group, which had rescued Sister Franconi, spoke up. "Yes, we encountered a man we recognized as Jack Stone, the famous billionaire record producer."

Alan interjected, "Wait a minute. Jack Stone was recently affiliated with a group called Aviance Inc. that may have had some ties to our murders. I'll need to check on it further."

A woman from the group that had rescued Mr. Burnstein said, "And we encountered this man, whom we had to subdue." She held up a cell phone that displayed a picture of an unconscious man, then passed the phone around to the others. Alan glanced at it but didn't recognize the person.

When the phone came around to Amanda, she said, "This man's name is Smith Donnavan. He's a black-market arms dealer with heavy connections, and we've been tracking him for years. Not only does he have easy access to a multitude of weapons, it also seems he must have good military connections, because he has been able to get military-grade explosives and such."

The wheels were spinning in Alan's mind as he asked, "Would this also include a substance called napalm-B?" Alan distinctly recalled Nigel from the lab telling him that the flesh on the burned body had been crystallized, as though it had been exposed to this new form of napalm, which had been developed from Greek fire.

"Absolutely," replied Amanda. "In fact, we have had cases where Mr. Donnavan used that exact substance to destroy evidence at some crime scenes we discovered."

"Okay, anyone else?" asked Elijah. Nobody spoke for a moment, so he concluded, "We will need to check further into the identities of these people and attempt to discover what their plans are. We'll need to consult with Michael soon and see what else needs to be done."

The meeting concluded, and they all made their way out. Alan followed the others back out of the Realm of Light and found himself right back in the town of Riverston, where it was still Wednesday. He made his way home just in time for dinner and spent the evening relaxing with his wife and his daughter, trying to put the haunting memories of the last week out of his mind.

Right before he lay down in bed, he placed the contents of his pockets on his dresser. He stared at the ancient symbol on the ring from Sergio Espanuega and wondered what secrets it would soon reveal.

CHAPTER 29

The Temptation of Evil

S IMMONS MADE HIS WAY UP the old volcano called Mount Mazama. The Native Americans who had once inhabited the area believed that their god Llao lived inside the great mountain. They told of the legendary battle between Llao and his archrival, the sky god Skell. As Simmons reached the top and looked out over the lake that had formed from the enormous crater, he knew that the battle that had taken place was not between Llao and Skell but rather between himself and The Fallen angel Ellestria. Simmons spotted her sitting on a large rock on the island in the middle of the lake. He made his way over and walked up behind her.

"I know you're there, Michael." Her voice was somber. "Come over here so I can speak to you."

Simmons cautiously moved in front of her but kept his distance, awaiting an attack. She sat staring down at the huge lake.

"Do you remember this lake?" she asked.

"Vaguely, but let's get down to the real reason I'm here."

She ignored his remark. "It was once a huge volcanic crater that erupted with fury and passion—don't you remember?"

"No, but I do remember that you killed my mother."

"Oh, Michael," she said as a tear ran down her face. "You really can't remember why your mother died?"

"Don't play your games with me, you abomination! I'm here to send you back."

She sighed heavily and disappeared. Simmons ran to the rock she had been sitting on, then jumped as he felt a hand on his back. When he turned around, he saw her, but she wasn't a huge armor-clad warrior any longer. Instead she was a bit shorter than he, with jet-black hair and steely blue eyes. She was beyond beautiful, and she drew very close and ran her hand across his chest. He took an apprehensive step back, but she gently closed the gap once more as she placed her arms around him and said, "So quickly you have forgotten about us. We were together. I was your wife. Don't you remember?"

He pushed her back. "You lie! You killed my mother."

She once again stepped forward as another tear ran down her face. "Yes, it's true, I did kill your mother, but only because you commanded me to do so. You had been taken by the Darkness, and I followed the Light. Your mother tried to pull you back, and you ordered me to kill her—that's when I fell into the Darkness, so I could be with you."

Doubt was now filling Simmons's mind. "That cannot be true," he blurted out unconvincingly, as he tried hard to remember.

She caressed his hair with her slender hand. "It's true—I did it all for you. I loved you more than anyone ever loved you. After your mother died, the Disciples of Light pulled you back into their realm. They did something to you, Michael, and made you forget your past. And as they did it, they pulled you away from the Darkness but left me here to live in grief and despair—forever alone, without you."

"No." Simmons shook his head in disbelief. "I wouldn't have killed my own mother."

"You were consumed by the Darkness—it wasn't your fault," she cooed, pulling him closer. Her eyes were hypnotic, and, as she drew her lips very close to his, he could feel her warm breath, which smelled like wild orchids. The sensation was intoxicating, and she continued to speak softly. "I've come back to you. Now we can be together forever. We used to come to this place when you were alive—before you passed over to the world beyond the living. We walked hand in hand with our children and—"

Shaking his head vigorously, he pushed her away quickly and regained his senses. "I was murdered as a baby. We couldn't have walked hand in hand or had children."

She drew a deep breath, and a look of hatred came over her face. She transformed into a thirteen-foot winged warrior that stood glaring down at him with jet-black eyes. "Can't blame me for trying." She flashed a sinister smile. "It's too bad—we would have made a perfect couple, even though your father wouldn't have approved."

Simmons stared back at her with contempt, loathing his own naiveté. "Who is my father?" he shouted, as he reached under his cloak for his rod. Anxiety gripped him when he could not locate it. Peering upward, he saw that Ellestria had the rod hovering just above her outstretched hands.

"Oh, your father is nobody special—in my opinion, anyway." She smiled and changed the subject. "Did you know that this rod was forged in the center of a star? Its creator poured the power of the Light into it, imbuing it with all that is good and right. That's why it's so powerful, but its craftsmanship is so unique that only one person can wield it. It's such a pity that the one person is you." She hurled the rod into the center of the lake, then flew up a few feet and hovered.

Simmons quickly plunged into the lake after the rod. Out of the corner of his eye he saw Ellestria reach her hand into the water. As he swam with incredible speed toward the gleaming marble rod, he could now sense that the water temperature was rising rapidly. At nearly 1,000 feet down he regained the rod and swam speedily toward the side of the lake. The water was now bubbling with heat, and his skin was slowly melting away. Reaching the side of the lake, he speared the rod into the ground and began burrowing through the volcanic rock.

About 100 feet into the rock, he turned and began moving upward quickly. It took him only a few minutes to break the surface, and he found himself a great distance from where he had started. He could still see Ellestria boiling the water with her hand and smiling with great satisfaction. His skin was starting to re-form, and he carefully made his way around the lake and behind the small island, where she was now standing. The water was still boiling, so he leaped from the shore to the island in one jump but remained perfectly silent while doing so, a feat that no living man could have accomplished.

Sneaking around the small island, he readied the rod to attack. He jumped to the spot where Ellestria had been kneeling by the water, but she was no longer there. Looking up to the horizon, he saw her massive wings carrying her higher into the sky. She spoke softly to herself, but Simmons's keen senses could hear her words. "The end of Michael, and now the end of the Light Bringer."

"Alan," Simmons whispered. "She's going after Alan."

The sun beat down on the cemetery where Alan often came to visit the grave of his brother, who had died many years ago. As he sat on a small marble bench, eating his lunch, he looked around at all of the headstones and wondered how each of them had died.

"Alan," said a voice, startling him.

He saw a woman approaching him. She was very beautiful, with long black hair and blue eyes. "Quickly," she said urgently. "We must go back to the Lost City under the sea. The others are gathering."

"Who are you?"

"I'm a friend of Michael's, but there's no time to explain. We need to meet him and the others quickly."

Alan nodded, and they made their way to his car.

~

Simmons's instincts pulled him to the Lost City. He climbed the stairs up the back of the castle and quickly made his way out into the garden, where he paused briefly to look at his mother's grave. Halfway out into the field beyond the castle, he spotted Alan walking with Ellestria. As Simmons approached swiftly, the angel spotted him and looked shocked.

"What!" she exclaimed. "This can't be! You were dead."

"Who are you?" Alan demanded, backing away from her.

"My name is Ellestria," she replied calmly. "Michael has not been completely truthful with you, Alan."

"Yeah, right," Alan muttered.

"Don't listen to her, Alan—it's a trap. She's trying to manipulate you," Simmons warned.

"No, it's the truth," Ellestria interjected. "Michael doesn't want you to know of our relationship. He doesn't want you to know that he orchestrated some of the killings."

"It's a lie!" yelled Simmons. He readied the white marble rod in his hand.

"I don't believe you for a minute," Alan told Ellestria.

"It's true," she insisted persuasively. "Michael set the wheels in motion for us to kill those people. Think about the people who have died, Alan."

"I have! You killed a twelve-year-old kid."

"Not true," she replied. "Sister Franconi, Dr. Stevenson, Mr. Burnstein, and Jimmy Howard were not killed by me or the other Fallen—they were killed by the living. Michael coordinated that with the other members of the Order of Darkness. He set the whole thing up. The people we killed were evil souls who haunted your society—think about it."

She paused for a few seconds, then continued. "Think about it, Alan—a hate group, a gang of drug dealers, a state prison, and a violent bunch of corrupt Mob murderers. Michael wanted to rid this world of those people, and, if he had to sacrifice a few innocent people in the process, then such was the cost for the greater good."

"Michael wouldn't do that," Alan objected. "He wouldn't kill anyone."

Her expression remained serious and sincere. "Michael can't even remember who he is. Michael"—she pointed an accusing finger at him—"can't remember the Darkness that lurks inside his soul. You want to know who Michael really is?"

Alan and Simmons were both stunned for a brief moment, awaiting her answer. "Michael is one of us—he's one of The Fallen. He was taken and manipulated by the Light; however, his corrupt instincts are taking over." She sighed. "Michael used me and the other three angels, and now he means to do away with us. Alan, he will kill you, too, when he's done with you."

"Don't listen to her, Alan. You know me—I would never betray you," Simmons gazed at Ellestria with contempt.

She spoke quickly, rebutting Michael's attempt to convince Alan of his innocence. "Those are the same words he used with me and the other three. But it doesn't have to be like this, Alan. You could join me, and we could rid this world of the most evil people in society. You have access to names and locations of many evil people. Join me, and we can actually do some good."

Simmons had toyed with the idea of attacking her, but Alan was too close, and he knew that she could snuff out his life in an instant, which is why he allowed the accusations to continue. He was about to yell to Alan once again, but then something happened that made his heart sink deep in his chest.

Alan nodded and said to Ellestria, "I think you're right."

"What!" exclaimed Simmons. "You surely don't believe—"

Alan cut him off. "Michael, you said you didn't remember your past, and what she is saying makes sense. You're always talking about the 'bigger picture,' and let's face it—you're not exactly human. You must be one of The Fallen."

"Alan, what are you saying? I would never . . . "

"You already have, Michael. You planned those murders, and you led me to those bodies! All so you can fulfill a greater good and rid the world of evil. I'll bet you are justifying your actions in your mind even as we speak." Alan pointed his finger at Simmons contemptuously.

Simmons's shoulders slouched forward as a feeling of despair overwhelmed him. "No, Alan . . . no . . . that's not the truth."

Ellestria looked absolutely gleeful. She knew that she had stabbed Simmons through the heart without lifting a finger.

"Kill him," said Alan. "Kill him, and I'll join you to rid the world of more evil."

She nodded and made her way over to Simmons, who threw his rod to one side, appearing to surrender.

Ellestria grabbed him up by the neck and hurled him into the air with tremendous force. His body struck the ground, and the impact made a huge hole in the earth. She pounced on him like a lion subduing its prey, pinning him to the ground. Her hands became as hot as branding irons, and Simmons howled in pain as they seared his shoulders.

"Now you will fall, Michael, and be captured in the Darkness." Her head and torso began to glow and form into a fiery vortex. Simmons knew this was the end as she drew closer to him, and his flesh began to burn away. Suddenly her body and head started to re-form, and Simmons could see her eyes grow wide. She let out a horrible scream, and her hands released their grip on his shoulders. Her body fell onto his and twitched uncontrollably for a few seconds just before she exploded into fine black dust. As the dust settled, Simmons saw Alan standing over him, holding a dagger with a white marble blade. Alan reached out his hand and helped Simmons to his feet.

"Thank you, my friend." Simmons extended his hand, and Alan shook it.

"Michael," Alan explained, "you know that everything I said back there was just so—"

Simmons interrupted him. "I know—no need to say it. I know." He smiled and retrieved his rod as the two made their way out of the Lost City.

CHAPTER 30

The Order of Darkness

HAVING RETURNED TO THE Riverston Police Department, Alan was sitting at his desk when Simmons entered, looking depressed. He was no longer dressed in the traditional white armor; instead, he once again wore the typical business attire in which Alan was used to seeing him. After emitting a long sigh, Simmons plopped down in a chair. "What's wrong?" asked Alan.

Simmons shook his head. "I can't remember my past, Alan. What if Ellestria was right? What if I *am* one of The Fallen, and I just don't remember?"

"Michael, you know that's not so. You're a good person . . . or whatever you really are." Alan searched for the right word and tried to make a joke of it. "You know what I mean. You've helped a great number of people. What does your heart tell you?"

Simmons nodded slowly. "Perhaps you're right, but the mystery remains of who I am and where I came from."

Alan had been thumbing through the crime scene photos of the Burnstein murder. "We'll find the answer in time, Michael—you have to have faith."

"I do have faith," Simmons affirmed. "The Light guides me. But how I wish there was some direction I could take to know more—some sign or symbol or code that would make sense of all this."

"Symbol," repeated Alan, sounding distracted.

"What?" asked Simmons.

Alan grabbed a photo from Mr. Burnstein's autopsy. "Look at this symbol." Alan pointed to the picture of Mr. Burstein's forearm, where a small tattoo was located.

"Yes, that's a tattoo from a Nazi concentration camp. Mr. Burnstein must have been a prisoner there."

"That's from a concentration camp?"

"Yes," replied Simmons. "They tattooed the prisoners. True evil at work; it was a time when the Darkness thrived. There were so many who suffered and died. I remember how terrible it was just before I walked many of them to the Light."

"But look closely below the tattoo. There's a very tiny symbol barely visible near the base. I've seen it before—three oval-shaped marks that intersect." Alan reached in his pocket and pulled out the ring that had fallen off Sergio Espanuega. The symbol on the ring matched the symbol on the tattoo. "Elijah said that it was a symbol from an ancient cult. Ellestria alleged that you were part of the Order of Darkness. I wonder if that's what the murderers call their group. What does this all mean?"

Alan took a deep breath, then recapped what he knew to try to put it in perspective, "Twelve people in a group that's called the Order of Darkness and that uses an ancient symbol. The twelve from the Order of Darkness murdered four people to gain access to the vaults that contained The Fallen angels. Once The Fallen were freed, they infiltrated our world and started killing evil people," he said, referring to the murders at the McCallister farm, the meatpacking plant, and the Mendello docks.

"It doesn't make sense, why would they kill evil people?"

"That's easy," replied Simmons. "They're recruiting."

Alan hadn't considered that possibility, but now it made sense. The more evil people The Fallen killed, the more warriors they would have on the other side for the battles between the Darkness and the Light. "So they were recruiting to increase their numbers?"

"That's a definite possibility." Simmons stood up and began looking through the case file. "Wait, you missed something."

Alan looked over at the flyer from the Optimist's Corner organization as Simmons pointed to the two *i*'s in the word *Optimist's*. Instead of a dot above each letter, there was the tiny symbol of three interlocking ovals. Alan's eyes grew wide as he saw it. He accessed the Internet and pulled up the Aviance Inc. website. There, above the *i* in the word *Aviance*, was the same symbol.

"Aviance Inc. is the Order of Darkness," Alan declared. "Patrick Kent's fingerprints were on this flyer. He's one of them—he's in the Order of Darkness. But he died in the prison collapse."

They were both silent for a moment, then Simmons said, "Perhaps he didn't die. Maybe he made it out."

The wheels in Alan's head were spinning once again. He held the flyer and read out loud the same information he'd seen on the website: "'If you are feeling rejected, down-and-out, and want to join a real team with people who care, call us at the toll-free number listed below.' You were right, Michael; they prey on the outcasts. They're recruiting them for the Darkness."

Alan stood up and walked over to a dry-erase board that hung on his wall. He uncapped the marker and wrote down the following notes to decipher the possibilities:

Order of Darkness (Aviance Inc.)

12 members—possibilities—committed four ritualistic murders—to access vaults/prisons where The Fallen are held—freed The Fallen, who recruit those for the Darkness.

1. Sergio Espanuega—drug lord—found his ring and holding Jimmy Howard prisoner.
2. Jack Stone—found holding/guarding Sister Franconi.
3. Smith Donnavan—black-market arms dealer found guarding Mr. Burnstein.
4. Patrick Kent—former CFO for Aviance Inc.—prints on flyer.
5. Unknown member—possibly female—high-heeled shoe prints at crime scenes.
6. Unknown member
7. Unknown member
8. Unknown member
9. Unknown member
10. Unknown member
11. Unknown member
12. Captain Paul Lee?—murdered Ross Woler and Emily Austin. Is he a member?

Alan turned to Simmons. "Do you think Lee is one of them?"

Simmons was about to say something, then a serious look came over his face as he held up his index finger to indicate that his thought had been interrupted by something urgent.

"What is it?" asked Alan with concern.

"Someone has died, and we need to walk them to where they need to go."

At that instant, the phone on Alan's desk rang. It was Detective Clint Rogers. "Hey, boss, just thought you'd want to know that there's been a prisoner killed down at the county jail."

"Okay," replied Alan. "Do we know them, or do we have any cases that they were involved in?"

"It was Captain Lee . . . Captain Paul Lee."

Alan's face paled as he nodded slowly and said in a stunned voice, "Thanks, Clint. I'll head down there and check it out."

Alan looked over at Simmons. "Let me guess—the person we need to help is at the county jail."

Simmons said nothing but just nodded, and the two walked quickly out the door.

CHAPTER 31

Falsely Accused

A LAN AND SIMMONS ENTERED THE COUNTY JAIL and made their
way past the in-house officer back to the holding area. The cell door
was open, and Captain Paul Lee's body was sprawled on the floor. A
large bloodstain soaked the chest area of the orange jumpsuit he was
wearing, and protruding from the wound was a shank crafted from a
piece of wood that had been sharpened to a point. A forensic team had
arrived and was taking photos and gathering evidence.

Alan asked the county jailer who stood near the cell entrance, "Any
idea who did this?"

The jailer shook his head. "No idea—we found him like this. We suspect that it was one of the prisoners who had access to the carpentry
area of the jail, based on the improvised wooden knife that was used to
kill him. He just arrived here tonight, less than two hours ago. Someone
must have really had it in for him."

"What do you mean he just arrived here?" Alan inquired suspiciously.

"He just came in from a medium security state facility about two
hours ago."

Alan shook his head. "I'm confused. Why would they transfer him from a medium security facility back to this jail? Is that common?"

"No, it isn't. I'm not sure why they transferred him here. It's very strange."

"Is there any chance I can get a look at the paperwork?" asked Alan.

"Sure, I'll grab it," replied the guard, and he disappeared down the hall. He returned a moment later, and Alan scanned the paperwork. His eyes fixed on the signature of the person who had ordered the transfer: Chief Justice Annette Anderson.

"Michael, this order is signed by Judge Anderson, the same judge who transferred Curtis Norman. We need to pay her a visit once we're done."

"Agreed." Simmons turned to the jailer. "Could you give us a few minutes to take a look around the scene?"

The man nodded and walked back down the hall. Captain Paul Lee's spirit stood up and said, "Alan, I need to tell you something before we depart."

"You want to confess?" said Alan with contempt. "I don't know why we're here. There's very little chance you'll make it to the Realm of Light."

"Alan, I didn't kill anyone. I was framed."

"Yeah, right," replied Alan. "I've heard that one before."

"No, Alan, it's true. I didn't kill anyone. I was on to something with those cases you were working. I'm confident that someone set me up. I think I was getting too close."

"Tell me what you know," directed Alan.

"I was on to a possible suspect in the four murders you were look- ing into. I got a tip from an informant off the street that there was a guy who paid big money for some items that were stolen from the New York Museum of Natural History."

"That's not making any sense to me. What does that have to do with the murders?"

"It was twelve ceremonial daggers—that was the stolen property."

"Very interesting," Alan commented. "Do you have any further information on these daggers?"

"Not much other than that they were ancient knives used in some twisted ceremonial crap by an ancient cult—whatever that means," said Lee.

"Ancient cult?" Alan repeated, remembering the symbol from the Order of Darkness ring, from the logo of Aviance Inc. and the Optimist's Corner, and from Mr. Burnstein's autopsy photos.

"Yeah, something like that," replied Lee.

The three walked down the hallway and through a door that led to a booking area. As they entered, they found themselves standing in the long dark marble hallway that Alan knew was the beginning of their journey.

Alan asked, as they began walking, "So who was the guy who was buying these daggers?"

"It was Randy Mantle, the millionaire who owns a professional football team and a professional basketball team. I set up some surveillance on him and caught him eating lunch with Smith Donnavan—a black-market arms dealer."

"Yes, I'm familiar with Smith," replied Alan, as he recalled that Donnavan was guarding Mr. Burnstein when he was captured in the Darkness. "Why didn't you tell me any of this before?"

Lee let out a long sigh and said in disappointment, "Well, I guess because of my ego. I was self-centered and arrogant and wanted all of the glory for myself. I was wrong, and I apologize for being that way."

"It's all in the past now. I'll check out Mantle when I get back."

"Wait, there's more," said Lee. "I put a wiretap and a trace on Mantle's phone."

Alan rolled his eyes, then said sarcastically, "Oh, I bet that was real legal, right?"

"No, no," Lee protested. "I got a court order from a judge to do the tap."

"Don't tell me—let me guess. It was signed by Chief Justice Annette Anderson from the appellate court," Alan joked.

"How did you know that?" asked Lee in astonishment, and Alan immediately stopped laughing.

Alan looked concerned as he confirmed, "You're sure that the order was signed by Judge Anderson?"

"Yep, one hundred percent sure."

"What did you find from the wiretap?"

"Mantle had been communicating with a guy in the state pen—a guy named Patrick Kent," Lee informed him.

Alan gasped. "Kent?"

"Yeah, you know him?"

"Oh, yeah." Alan was now convinced that Randy Mantle was another member of the Order of Darkness.

They continued walking the long dark hallway for another forty-five minutes, until they finally came to a doorway leading to a large, long room. About thirty feet into the room was a huge statue. Just beyond the statue there was no floor; instead, there was a huge wall-to-wall pit that stretched about fifty feet to the other side of the room. Alan peered at the opposite side of the room and could see an old wooden door that emitted faint light from the door frame. There was a stone ledge that jutted out from the door about twenty feet or so—just big enough for two or three people to stand on.

"There," said Alan, pointing at the door. "That's where we need to go."

Simmons nodded in agreement. Alan looked down into the seemingly bottomless pit and said, "I know what's down there—I can feel it. The Darkness rises from below. We'll have to figure out a way to traverse this pit without falling. Michael, can you scale these walls and make it across?"

"Perhaps," replied Simmons. "But that won't do us any good with getting you two across, and remember, I can't go first."

Alan nodded in acknowledgment, then said, "What's this statue doing here?"

All three of them looked up and studied the statue. After a few seconds, Lee walked to one corner of the room and returned holding a sledgehammer. "I know what this statue is."

"Really?" asked Alan. "What is it?"

Lee continued to stare at the face of the massive stone figure, which wasn't well lit. "It's me," he told them. "It's my ego, my arrogance. Look how big it is." He paused for a moment, then continued, "And I know what we must do."

"And what would that be?" Alan queried.

"We need to knock it down—something I should have done a long time ago. The statue is about sixty feet tall, and it's only about fifty feet to the other side of the room, where that ledge hangs out. If we can knock the statue over, then we could use it as a bridge and walk across it to the ledge."

Alan found two more sledgehammers in the same corner of the room and handed one to Simmons. As Lee was about to take the first swing at the enormous base of the huge figure, Alan said, "Wait a second. Michael, hit this with your rod and see if you can knock it down." Simmons drew forth his rod and struck the base of the statue, but it did not chip or budge from its original location.

"Okay," said Alan, a bit disappointed. "I guess we'll have to do this the hard way."

The three men slowly chipped away at the bottom of the gigantic figure. Alan shielded his eyes as tiny stone fragments flew off and hit his face. After hours of hammering, the huge monument finally gave way and fell over, creating a bridge to the other side. The three quickly walked across, and Alan was exhausted. Before Lee opened the door, he turned and said, "Alan, there's one more thing I need to tell you before I leave. I did not die from that makeshift knife in my gut. I was shot. Before you arrived, someone appeared and drew a gun, then began firing. I was hit three or four times in the chest before I went down."

"Did you get a look at his face?" asked Alan.

"No, he looked like all the other jailers in that place. He had his hat pulled down low, so I couldn't really see who he was. Obviously, he was law enforcement—I could tell by the way he pulled the gun and by the shooting stance he took right before he fired. The wooden knife was put there after I was dead in an attempt to cover up what really happened."

"I'll check it out when we get back," said Alan, as he extended his hand.

Lee shook it. "I'm sorry I was arrogant and self-absorbed."

"It's okay," replied Alan. "I'll make sure you're vindicated and that the real offenders are caught. Take care, Captain."

"Farewell, Alan," said Lee, as he stepped through the door.

CHAPTER 32

The Dead Man's Gun

A LAN AND SIMMONS CAME BACK OUT TO THE CELL AREA, where Lee's body was lying on the floor. They had not missed a moment of time since they left, for once again the realm beyond the living had manipulated time and distance.

Two men in dark suits showed up in the hallway outside the cell. They were pushing a stretcher that had an open body bag on top. One of the two men appeared very nervous and seemed to be avoiding contact with Alan and Simmons.

"Who are you two?" asked Alan.

The nervous man said nothing, but the other replied, "We're with the mortuary transport service for the medical examiner. We have orders to take the body down to the morgue."

Alan continued to stare at the nervous man and soon realized that he recognized him from the public defender's office.

"Jeremy Switzenger—is that you?" asked Alan. "Aren't you from the public defender's office?"

"Uh . . . yeah . . . oh, hi, Alan. I didn't recognize you."

"Yeah, whatever. What the hell are you doing picking up bodies for the medical examiner?"

"Well, you know, I needed some extra money, and— "

"Yeah, right." Alan cut him off. "And you're making extra money by picking up bodies for the medical examiner. I don't buy it, Jeremy—and I'll bet you're going to tell me that Judge Anderson ordered you to move the body."

Switzenger turned pale and looked as though he were going to pass out. He dashed off down the hall, followed by the other man, and they quickly made it back through the doors that led to booking. Alan tried to pursue them but lost them after they ran through the door, which had closed and locked behind them.

"Let them go," said Simmons. "But you may want to add Mr. Switzenger to the list of possible members of the Order of Darkness."

Simmons and Alan placed Lee's body in the body bag and loaded it onto the stretcher.

"We better escort this corpse down to the medical examiner's office personally so we know it gets there," Alan stated. He called a mortician who owed him a favor and asked him to come and transport the body.

When they arrived at the morgue, Alan and Simmons kept their eyes on Lee's body. Andrea Catanick, the same medical examiner whom Alan had dealt with at the meatpacking-plant crime scene, met them inside and said, "Good to see you, Alan, but what are you doing here?"

"We're escorting this body. I have reason to believe that someone tried to steal it to destroy evidence."

Dr. Catanick motioned to the men who had wheeled the body in place to put it on the examining table. She unzipped the body bag, and the two men helped her remove the body.

"Someone wanted to make this look like a stabbing," said Alan. "But I have reason to believe he was shot. His name is Paul Lee, and he was a police captain from the Evansville Police Department."

"Oh, yes," replied Dr. Catanick. "I heard of this case. Wasn't he up for murder charges?"

"Yes, but now I have a suspicion that he may have been set up."

"Well, let's do this now so we don't have anyone else try to break in and tamper with the evidence. By the way, who tried to make off with Captain Lee?"

Alan was reluctant to give too many details, so he said, "It was a couple of people posing as members of the transport service that brings the corpses here to the morgue. We're still checking into the other details."

"Really! That's quite disturbing," she said, as she began to do preliminary documentation for the autopsy. Dr. Catanick was meticulous in her analysis. She examined the wound, then started to wipe off the caked blood, which revealed a small hole just to the right of where the shank had penetrated the body.

"You may be right, Alan; these do look like bullet wounds." The autopsy continued, and after much examination and documentation, Dr. Catanick removed three hollow-point bullets from the chest cavity and placed them in an evidence bag. "The knife was placed in the body postmortem. It appears that Captain Lee was shot to death and then stabbed." She handed him the paperwork and the bullets.

"You may want to keep this quiet, Dr. Catanick. It seems that people who are involved in this incident are turning up dead, and someone is trying very hard to cover something up."

She nodded. "I understand. If anybody shows up here, I'll send them to you."

"Okay. Well, watch your back," warned Alan, then he and Simmons slipped out the door.

They got into Alan's car, and Alan said, "I need to get a ballistics run on these bullets ASAP to see if they match any other shootings we've had recently."

"Head over to the FBI lab, and we'll run it through our database," Simmons offered, as they sped away from the morgue.

Within a few minutes, they pulled up in front of a fairly new gray building with no windows and only one door. They entered a small lobby, and Simmons used a pass card to get through a door that opened into a long hallway. Near the end, two double doors opened to reveal an extensive laboratory, where Simmons exchanged pleasantries with the lab technician and explained the situation.

The technician removed a bullet from the bag and examined it under a microscope that also took a photo of the markings and striations. The photo was then run through the database of all the different bullets that had been recovered in shootings from the area. Within fifteen minutes, the technician said, "Got a match on one. It says that the owner of the gun is the Evansville Police Department, which issued it to Captain Paul Lee."

"What!" Alan exclaimed. "That's impossible. Are you sure?"

"Yep," replied the technician. "That's what it says. Evansville PD is one of the departments that test-fires its weapons and submits the ballistic results to our database. We can tell which officer is linked to every bullet fired in a police shooting incident if that department is involved."

Alan shook his head and looked at Simmons questioningly. "This can't be Lee's gun. I have it in evidence—I seized it for the Major Case Squad after the Ross Woler murder."

"Could it have been a different gun?" offered Simmons.

Alan looked at the screen where the technician had read the information. "Not likely. It's the same make and model as his issued duty weapon."

"Perhaps someone stole it out of evidence?"

Alan shook his head. "Doubt that, but I guess it wouldn't hurt to check." He called the dispatcher and requested to talk to an evidence officer. After a brief conversation, he turned to Simmons and said, "Our evidence officer says that the gun is still in evidence and has not left. We need to take a look at it once we get back to the office."

Simmons turned to the technician. "How exactly do we log these ballistic tests into the database?"

"We get the photographs from the rounds recovered from the victim or the scene and the rounds from the gun when it was test-fired. We do have ballistic results from the fire investigator Ross Woler's murder. Let me pull those up." The technician accessed some additional results and brought them up on the screen. "Yep, it's a match. The gun registered to Captain Paul Lee was the murder weapon for Ross Woler, and it appears that this gun also killed Captain Lee himself."

"Are you sure the gun you have in evidence was properly test-fired, Alan? If not, then perhaps the results were mixed up with another gun."

Alan nodded. "Yeah, Rich told me it was, but let me check with him again." He pulled out his phone and called Rich. "Rich, it's Alan."

Detective Rich Blane replied, "Hey, Alan, guess you heard about Lee?"

"Yeah, in fact, that's why I'm calling."

"Oh, why's that?"

Alan tried to summarize. "Special Agent Simmons and I went to the county jail to take a look at the scene, and we discovered through the medical examiner that Lee was shot and not stabbed, which means that whoever did it was most likely not another prisoner—it must be somebody from the outside."

"What!" exclaimed Rich, with almost the same reaction that Alan had had to the ballistics results.

"It gets worse than that. We ran tests through the FBI lab, and its database shows that the gun that killed Lee was, in fact, *his* gun issued by your department."

"That's impossible," Rich replied. "Don't you have that gun locked up in evidence?"

"Yes, but that's why I'm calling you. Did you ever test-fire that gun to get the ballistics?"

"Of course, I had the lab do it—and it matched the murder of Ross Woler."

"Yeah, I know, that's what the FBI just told me also. I figured that I would double-check with you just to be sure."

"What the hell does all this mean, Alan?" Alan could sense the fear and apprehension in Rich's voice.

"I'm not sure, Rich, but it's big—very big. I have reason to believe that there are several powerful people involved here and that some may have ties to our legal system. Keep your head down, and we'll talk soon."

"Will do, and let me know what else you discover. I don't want to be anywhere around when this thing blows up."

"I will," said Alan.

Simmons asked, "What now?"

"I need to talk to the evidence officer back at the station who is guarding Lee's gun."

"I probably need to touch base with Elijah and update him on all we've found," Simmons noted.

"Sounds good," replied Alan as the two departed together.

∽

Back at the station, Alan opened the ziplock evidence bag and, using a handkerchief, carefully removed the gun. He picked up the empty bag and examined it to see if it had been tampered with. The chain of custody listed on the front of the bag clearly indicated that it was he who had submitted it into evidence, and, up to this point, nothing indicated that this weapon had ever left the evidence room.

Shaking his head in frustration, he examined the gun again by pulling back the action and releasing it. Once more his eyes went back to the evidence bag, but this time something caught his attention. The information on the bag included the make, model, and serial number of the weapon, but the serial number on the bag did not match the serial number on the barrel of the gun. Alan disassembled the gun and discovered that the serial number on the barrel was different from the serial number on the frame of the gun. The gun frame was indeed Captain Paul Lee's duty weapon, but the barrel was not

Alan quickly called Rich. "Rich, it's Alan. Someone switched barrels."

"I don't understand. What do you mean?"

"Someone switched the barrel of Lee's gun. The serial number on Lee's gun frame doesn't match the one on the barrel—someone switched it."

"Are you sure?"

"I'm looking at it right now. You need to find out who this serial number is registered to."

"Okay, let me have it, and I'll check."

Alan relayed the serial number on the gun barrel. When he was finished, Rich added, "Listen, Alan, something has come up, and I have some information that points to involvement of an appellate court judge named Annette Anderson. I don't want to jump to any conclusions yet, but—"

"Judge Anderson?" Alan interrupted. "I have information also. She's the one who put in the transfers for Curtis Norman and Captain Lee. I suspect she has something to do with this whole mess."

"I'm on my way down to speak with her. Do you want to meet me there?" asked Rich.

"Sure, I'm on my way." As he made his way back out to his car, he decided that he should give Simmons a call to let him know that he was going down to see Judge Anderson. If she was part of the Order of Darkness, then he'd feel much more comfortable with Simmons there, in case anything went wrong.

CHAPTER 33

Betrayal

I T WAS 4:30 PM AS ALAN MADE HIS WAY UP the long set of steps that led into the federal courthouse. It took him a few minutes to clear security, then he took the elevator to the fifth floor to Judge Annette Anderson's office. As he approached the door, a voice behind him said, "Alan, wait up." He paused and turned to see Detective Rich Blane hurrying down the hall.

"I can't believe all of this is happening," Rich said, shaking his head.

"Yeah, I agree. It just keeps getting worse."

The two entered the judge's office, and a secretary sitting at a desk stopped them. "Can I help you, officers?"

"Yes, we need to see the judge right away. It's about a murder case," Rich asserted.

"Uh, okay—one moment. I'll let her know," the secretary replied, then disappeared through a door behind her.

"Let's not give her too long," Alan suggested. "If she gets suspicious, she may run."

"Yeah, I agree," said Rich. He walked to the door and turned the handle.

The door opened, and the secretary appeared in the door frame. "The judge will see you two now."

They walked through the door into a huge office ornately decorated with cherrywood molding and trim. In the center of the office sat a large oak desk. As they entered, a middle-aged woman with blond hair and hazel eyes rose from a burgundy leather chair and walked around to meet them.

"Good afternoon, gentleman. I'm Judge Anderson. What can I do for you?"

"I'm Lieutenant Alan Crane, and this is Detective Rich Blane. We're investigating a series of murders, and we need to ask you some questions."

"Of course," replied the judge coolly. "Ask away."

"There was a transfer order signed by you for a young man named Curtis Norman. He was transferred from the county jail to a minimum security state facility to a maximum security state prison. We just want to know why you signed those orders."

She smiled, as though she had known that Alan was going to ask her that question. "Does it really matter why I signed the papers?" She walked back to her chair and pulled open a drawer. Drawing forth a document, she placed it on the desk. "Is this the document you're referring to?"

Alan scanned the transfer forms for Curtis Norman, then said, "You also transferred Captain Paul Lee from a state facility back to the county jail. I'm wondering what an appellate court judge is doing transferring prisoners for cases that have no relevance to you."

She drew out another form from the drawer. "Here's the one for Captain Lee's transfer."

"That really doesn't answer my question, Judge," reiterated Alan.

Brushing her hair back from her face, Judge Anderson began to laugh.

Alan raised an eyebrow and cocked his head to one side as his hand rested on his gun. Rich must have had the same elevated anxiety, because he drew his gun and pointed it at her.

Alan put his hands up in the air. "Okay, everyone calm down! There's no need to escalate this situation. Judge Anderson, can you come back over here by us? You've obviously got my partner a bit spooked at the moment."

Rich gripped his gun tightly as he directed the judge, "Keep your hands up and walk around the desk slowly." She held her position and smiled as Rich continued to talk. "Alan, I didn't tell you that I ran that serial number you gave me and found out whose gun it was registered to."

"Whose was it?"

Rich pivoted the barrel of his gun and pointed it at Alan's chest. "It's mine."

Alan was stunned. He stood looking over at Rich, who now was holding him at gunpoint.

"You!" Alan could barely get the words out, he was so utterly shocked.

"Yeah, it was me. I switched the barrels. I killed fire investigator Woler. I was the one who took the car to the junkyard to grind it up. It was me who spelled my own name wrong on the salvage receipt so you would think that Lee did it to set me up. I was the one who wore Lee's shoes to the crime scenes so you would think he committed the murders. I shot Emily Austin, Dr. Eva Stevenson's secretary, and it was me who killed Johnny Bartel and planted the knife in Lee's house."

"And you shot Captain Lee in the jail? He said that the person who killed him took a shooting stance just like a police officer would."

"Yes."

Alan stared at him for a moment, then declared, "You are a member of the Order of Darkness."

Rich nodded. "Yes, you're correct."

Alan was feeling the effects of ultimate betrayal, so he asked in near disbelief, "Why? Why would you do this, Rich?"

Rich answered cynically, "Because, Alan, I want to be on the winning side. The end is near, and war is—"

He never finished the sentence. Alan heard three loud cracks and saw the flash from the muzzle of a small revolver that Judge Anderson was holding in her outstretched hand. Three distinct holes in Rich's chest oozed blood that spread over his white button-down shirt as his body fell to the floor and Alan watched his life expire. He looked back at the judge, who was now pointing the gun at him.

"He always had a big mouth," she said, smiling.

Alan looked down and noticed her designer Jessie Allen spiked high-heeled shoes. "Nice shoes. I'll bet you've killed a lot of people in those."

She pursed her lips and scrunched her nose up, then grinned. "Killer high heels, Lieutenant Crane?" She laughed at her own joke then quickly became serious. "Good-bye, Lieutenant Crane." Her finger began squeezing the trigger, and Alan thought about trying to dive one way or another.

Suddenly an object flew by his head with incredible velocity and struck her in the face. The impact pushed her back into the bookshelf behind the desk. Her nose exploded with blood, which shot everywhere. Alan watched as her body slowly slid down the wall, leaving a long, dark trail of blood where the back of her head had been smashed in by the force of the object. He looked down to see a large book lying by her feet and concluded that this was the object that had been thrown. Looking over his right shoulder, he saw Simmons standing behind him.

"You killed her with a book?" Alan was incredulous, as he continued to gaze at the gruesome scene.

"I'm not proud of it. But she would have shot you."

"I'm not complaining, just in awe of how hard you threw that book!"

A cold air penetrated the room, and Simmons quickly drew forth the white marble rod from under his jacket. The light in the room dimmed, and the door to the left of the desk opened slowly to reveal a tall, gaunt man with a thin bony nose, who stepped into the center of the room. He was dressed in a long, hooded black cape, and Alan recognized him as the man he had met when he was trying to rescue Jimmy Howard from the Realm of Darkness.

An evil smile came over the man's face as he spoke in a low snake-like hiss that caused a chill to run up the back of Alan's neck. "Ah, my cousin," he said, looking at Simmons, "you're a true killer." He motioned to the judge's bloody corpse lying on the floor. Simmons gripped the rod in a defensive stance as the man stepped forward to reveal a black stone rod identical to the white one Simmons held. The spirits of Rich Blane and Judge Anderson stood up as the tall cloaked man motioned for them to walk through the door behind him. They did so without speaking a word.

"Still have that birthmark on your chest?" The man pointed a long finger on his skeletal hand at Simmons.

Simmons ran his hand over the deep raised scar located directly over his heart, then once again gripped his rod, preparing to strike.

The cloaked man must have sensed Simmons's intent to swing, for he stepped back toward the open door that was now consuming all of the light in the room. "Not yet, but we'll meet soon. The lamb is close to the slaughter, and soon the One will be free," he said cryptically, revealing several decayed teeth as he smiled sinisterly. He then turned and walked through the door, which slammed behind him.

"Who was that?" asked Alan, his voice quivering as the adrenaline coursed through his veins.

"I don't know."

"He called you 'cousin,'" said Alan, rubbing his temples. "Is he related to you?"

"No idea. I don't recall seeing him before."

"What's the birthmark on your chest he mentioned?" Alan inquired curiously.

"It's not a birthmark," replied Simmons, as he unbuttoned his shirt to reveal a long purple scar over his heart. "Someone stabbed me when I was a baby. It's how I died. That's where the mark came from."

"He said something about 'the lamb' being 'close to the slaughter' and 'the One' being 'free.' Do you have any idea what that means?"

Simmons shook his head. "No, I don't."

The two of them quickly searched the room for any other information that might serve as clues about their recent encounter. Nothing of interest or value was found. Simmons removed a small metal ring of keys from Rich's pocket and threw them to Alan.

"So what now?" asked Alan.

"Go home and spend time with your family. I'll pick you up tomorrow. We need to go search Rich Blane's house to see if we can find anything else relating to the Order of Darkness. After we're done, we'll consult with Elijah to see if he can make sense of any of this."

Simmons bowed his head low, as though something were wearing on him. Alan noticed his inner struggle. "Michael, you're not a killer."

Simmons shook his head slowly. "I took her life without giving it much thought. I did it so quickly and completely, like it was an instinct."

"No," rebutted Alan, "you gave life."

"What are you talking about?" asked Simmons skeptically.

Alan repeated, "You gave life—to me. My wife and daughter will be able to see me tonight because of you. You've done a great deed here tonight. You're not a killer, you're a hero."

Simmons smiled as Alan extended his hand. The two men shook hands, then departed the courthouse.

CHAPTER 34

The Hidden Evil

ALAN RETURNED HOME AND ATE DINNER WITH HIS FAMILY. His wife, Alison, noticed his grim expression. "Work getting to you again?"

"Yeah, it's been a bit overwhelming."

Alan had never told his wife or his daughter about his interactions with the Light and the Darkness. Alison had met Simmons but didn't know his true identity or background. Alan constantly struggled with telling her, since she was his best friend and confidante. His reservations stemmed from concern for her safety and the well-being of his daughter, Missy. No matter how bad things got at work or through his journeys, Missy always made him smile and laugh.

She sat at the table with her bright blue eyes gleaming. "Daddy, I had a lemonade stand today."

"You did?" Alan asked enthusiastically.

Alison nodded. "Yes, she did. She and her friend Peter sat out front and sold lemonade."

"Wow, that's great!" said Alan. "How many glasses did you sell?"

Missy looked up as she was searching for the answer to his question. "Well, just two. One was to Mrs. Green next door, and the other was to Little Red Riding Hood."

Alan laughed, "So you sold a cup of lemonade to Little Red Riding Hood? What did she look like?"

"It was a he," she corrected.

Missy always had a knack for concocting stories because she had a vivid imagination. Alan smiled. "So Little Red Riding Hood was a boy?"

"Well, he was old. Not a boy like Peter. And his riding hood wasn't red."

The smiled quickly disappeared from Alan's face. "So there was a man you sold some to who had a hood that wasn't red?"

"Yeah," she replied. "But I could see his face."

Alan's anxiety rose slightly. "So what did the man look like?"

"He was a little scary, because his hand was like a skeleton, but he was nice and bought some lemonade."

"Did the man say anything to you?"

"Oh, yes, he asked me and Peter if we wanted to come with him, but I told him no, and Peter told him that he would tell his mommy. So then he left."

"What!" exclaimed Alison. "I hadn't heard any of this, and I was watching from the front porch. I didn't see anyone but Mrs. Green speaking to the children. Are you sure you saw this man, Missy?"

"Oh yes, I saw him," she insisted.

"Did the man give you anything?" asked Alan.

"Well, he gave us some money for the lemonade. Mommy has it in the money box." She pointed her finger to the counter where a shoe box colored with markers sat closed.

Alan looked inside and noticed two quarters, a $100 bill, and a familiar-looking ring. "Did Mrs. Green give you two quarters?" Alan held up the quarters, and Missy nodded. "And the man gave you this?" He then held up the bill, and once again Missy nodded. Glancing at the ring, he saw the familiar symbol that connected it to the Order of Darkness. He slipped it into his pocket before his wife noticed it.

Alison had a horrified look on her face. "I never checked the box. I had no idea. . . ."

Alan nodded and held up his hands as he saw Missy starting to get scared. "It's okay. Not a big deal."

Missy asked, frightened, "Is Mommy okay?"

Alison composed herself and smiled. "Everything is fine, sweetheart."

Alan whispered to Alison, "I'm going to have someone make a report of a suspicious person on this, possibly an attempted abduction. Let's not do any more lemonade stands until I can figure out who this was. Call me right away if you see anyone around the house."

Alison nodded. "Okay, I'll keep an eye out and let the neighbors know."

Alan finished his dinner and went into the bedroom to call Simmons. He filled him in on what had happened, and Simmons said he'd have a security expert come over and set up an alarm system.

Later that night, after Alan had checked on Missy, who was fast asleep, he lay awake in bed next to his wife, who was looking at a magazine.

"Alison, it really concerns me that this guy came by today. Abductions happen all the time. It seems that society is falling apart."

She closed the magazine and placed it on the nightstand, and a concerned look came over her face. "There are evil people out there, Alan."

"Believe me, I know that for sure," he replied.

"But there are more good people in the world than bad—and that's why we need to stick together. If the good people become divided, then the others will take over. Those bad people are working hard to corrupt all of us. They are really working hard to strip away our values. They are vile, evil individuals who abduct, molest, and murder kids. They cheat, steal, and lie. I wonder how much more the world can take before it all blows up."

She grabbed a Bible that was sitting on the nightstand and opened it to the place where a bookmark was sticking out. "It's so ironic that we're having this discussion, because this past week my Bible study group was reading the story of Sodom and Gomorrah."

Alan's face looked blank as he slowly asked, "You were reading the story of Sodom and Gomorrah?"

"Yeah. Well, we were supposed to read something else this week, but we had one member who was insistent on reading Sodom and Gomorrah. Anyway—"

Alan cut her off. "What was this member's name?" he asked very slowly, raising one eyebrow.

Alison scrunched her lips and looked up, trying to recall the name, "Uh, it was Jerry . . . Swizen—"

Alan interrupted again. "Jeremy Switzenger from the public defender's office?" His heart rate sped up as he recalled that just recently Jeremy had tried to steal Lee's body from the county jail and Simmons had suggested that he might be a member of the Order of Darkness.

"Yeah, that's him—oh, I wasn't aware he was from the public defender's office."

"I may want to go with you next time you have this Bible study," said Alan, trying to calm himself.

"Oh, sure, honey, we'll just need to get a sitter." Alan nodded, and Alison continued, "Anyway, as I was saying about the Sodom and Gomorrah story, everyone was corrupt and God sent two angels to destroy the cities. The angels appeared as regular men and stayed with a man named Lot. The rest of the citizens wanted to seize the men who were staying with Lot, but he refused to cooperate, so the crowd attempted to take them by force. The angels helped Lot and his family escape the city and told them to flee but not to look back. Lot's wife looked back as the cities were being destroyed by fire and brimstone, and as a result she turned into a pillar of salt."

Alan nodded his head as his thoughts flashed back to the field just beyond the castle in the Lost City. He could still feel the statue of salt crumbling in his hand and falling to the ground. "Yes, I remember the story," he said to Alison, as he stared blankly at the ceiling.

"Well, it happened before, and it can happen again—and the way society is going these days, who knows?"

There must be more to all of this than I'm seeing, thought Alan. *A piece of the puzzle must be missing, and I must find it.* Alison's words echoed in his head as he tried to fall asleep: "It happened before, and it can happen again."

Chapter 35

Saving the Lamb

A LAN GOT UP LATE the next morning, since he had lain awake most of the night thinking of everything that was going on. He was reluctant to leave the house, fearing for his family's safety. Alison convinced him that everything would be fine; she'd call him if anything out of the ordinary occurred. After kissing both of them good-bye, he left for the office. As he arrived at work, he met with the on-duty patrol sergeant and explained what had happened with his daughter. He felt a little bit better knowing that the patrol division would keep an eye on his house and his family.

Simmons met him at the office, and the two left together to continue their investigation involving Rich Blane. He was glad to be away from the station, because the media was all over the administrations of both the Riverston and Evansville Police Departments. Someone must have leaked information on the deaths of Rich Blane and Judge Annette Anderson.

They arrived at Blane's house, and Simmons asked, "Is he married?"

"Nope," replied Alan. "He's divorced, so the place should be empty."

Alan unlocked the door with Rich's keys, which they had taken yesterday. He looked over at Simmons to see whether there was any need to search the home at gunpoint. Simmons shook his head to indicate that they would be safe. Alan made his way into a small office that was just off the living room on the first floor. He searched through an old rolltop desk and found something peculiar written on a torn piece of paper. It appeared to be a poem, and it seemed to be familiar:

> *Honor the Light of the day*
> *When the fires loom in the distance*
> *When the waters rise*
> *When the winds blow strong*
> *And the earth shakes underfoot*
> *A kind word from a friend*
> *A helping hand from a stranger*
> *Gives us the strength to weather the storm*
> *And guard that which is right*
> *From those who do wrong*
> *To walk the path of victory*

After studying it for a moment, he recognized that it was the poem that Curtis Norman's father used to keep in his wallet—the poem that Mr. Norman must have lived by, since he'd taken a line from it and inscribed it on the back of his watch.

"Michael, look at this."

Simmons glanced at the piece of paper. "It seems to make more sense now, doesn't it? The fire, water, wind, and earth refer to The Fallen that we defeated. Then the lines that say 'gives us the strength to weather the storm and guard that which is right' refer to watching over the prisons that held The Fallen."

"What does Curtis Norman's father have to do with all of this?"

"Good question. Let's keep looking." Simmons sat down in front of a computer.

Alan pulled open a long file-cabinet drawer and started looking through folders. As he thumbed through a folder labeled Business Meetings, he came across a meeting agenda for Aviance Inc. He pulled it out and scanned it:

Aviance Inc.
Quarterly Business Meeting
Board of Directors

Patrick Kent—absent
Mason Monahan—present
Annette Anderson—present
Jonathan McWilliam—present
Monte Lundy—present
Adam Feldon—present
Smith Donnavan—present
Sergio Espanuega—present
Jeremy Switzenger—present
Carmen Andola—present
Jack Stone—present
Randy Mantle—present
Sergeant at Arms Rich Blane—present
CFO Matthew Russ—present
   Call meeting to order
   Old business
   New business
   Discussion
   Reports
      Financial
      Productivity
      Recruitment
         Adjournment

"I got something here," Alan said excitedly, as he pulled the agenda from the folder. "It looks like a business meeting for Aviance Inc., and it has their board of directors listed. Many of them are those we've dealt with from the Order of Darkness."

Simmons stood up and glanced at the paper Alan was holding, "That *is* the Order of Darkness. Looks like they also have people in important positions of authority—a governor, congressmen, high-ranking judicial members—it's all here."

"What's it all mean?" asked Alan. "And how does Curtis Norman or his father fit into it?"

Simmons shook his head. Then Alan's face lit up as though a match had been struck in his mind. "Curtis Norman and his father—a father and son. Just like the four others who were killed who had relatives who guarded the vaults. But all of The Fallen are once again captured, and Curtis Norman's father wasn't guarding any of The Fallen. Curtis died in the prison earthquake; I wonder if he made it to where he needed to go?"

Simmons had a look of revelation on his face. "We didn't walk him to where he needed to go."

"What does that mean?"

"It means he's not dead. Patrick Kent escaped, and he took Curtis Norman with him. We need to find Curtis!"

Alan shook his head in confusion. "But Curtis isn't related to a guard of the vaults of The Fallen."

"Curtis's father may not be responsible for guarding any of the vaults of The Fallen we recently defeated, but that doesn't mean anything. There were over a hundred and thirty million angels who fell the day the Darkness came to be. Mr. Norman may be guarding another one of The Fallen—one who's much worse than the four we encountered. We need to find . . . " Simmons's voice trailed off as he turned back to the computer, which was now displaying bank records for Rich Blane. "He recently purchased an airline ticket to London."

Simmons quickly called Special Agent Amanda Gregory. Alan listened to Simmons's half of the conversation.

"Amanda, it's Michael. I have reason to believe that Detective Rich Blane was one of the Order of Darkness. I'm looking at a piece of paper that I believe contains the names of the other members, and I need to know if they've reserved any airline tickets recently." Simmons quickly relayed the names and listened for a few minutes. He hung up and turned to Alan. "They're all going to London, and I'll bet that's where Curtis Norman is going."

"Why would they go there?"

"I don't know, but I think they're going to kill him in order to access the place where his father is—Curtis is the lamb being led to the slaughter."

The words pierced Alan's mind as he remembered the old bony man saying it to him and Simmons during their confrontation at the courthouse.

"Quick!" Simmons cried. "We need to find Elijah and stop this!"

~

Alan found himself sitting once again at the large table inside the castle of the Lost City. Elijah sat across from Alan as Simmons filled him in on their recent discovery of the Order of Darkness and the theory about Curtis Norman.

"I will visit Curtis's father in the Realm of Light and see where he is located," Elijah offered. "You two need to get to London and figure out why the Order of Darkness is meeting there."

"Is there anything significant about London that would attract them to that particular location?" asked Alan.

Simmons shook his head, and Elijah replied, "I can't think of anything."

"Have you discovered the identity of this mysterious cloaked man who keeps showing up?" Alan asked, thinking of his daughter and her lemonade stand.

"No, unfortunately not," replied Elijah. "What was it that he said?"

Simmons quoted the cloaked man: "The lamb is close to the slaughter, and soon the One will be free."

Elijah ran his fingers through his coarse gray hair. "Describe to me again what this man looked like."

"He was tall and very thin, with a bony nose and fingers," Alan recalled. "He wore a long cloak with a hood that covered the sides of his face."

Simmons added, "The robe had long sleeves that hung down to his wrists, and he carried a rod identical to the one I have, but it was crafted of some type of black stone."

"You are describing a type of ceremonial clothing. Perhaps something used in a ritual," Elijah commented.

"Like a human sacrifice where twelve people stab an innocent person," Alan stated cynically.

"Exactly." Elijah nodded. "That's exactly it. The Order of Darkness is tied to this man dressed in ancient ritualistic garb, and they stabbed four people with knives."

"Actually," interjected Alan. "I think they stabbed their victims with ceremonial daggers."

"Why would you think that?" Elijah inquired.

"Because Captain Lee told me after his death that he had information that someone was paying lots of money on the black market to buy stolen ceremonial daggers that were used in some ancient rituals. I also associated that with the logo I found that was linked to Aviance Inc. and the tattoos."

Elijah's face lit up, as an overwhelming sense of understanding consumed him. "That's it!" he exclaimed.

Alan shook his head. "*What* is it?"

"What you just said. All of this is tied to ancient cult practices and rituals. Stonehenge is approximately ninety miles from London."

"So?" Alan was still confused.

"Stonehenge was rumored to be a place that is tied to ancient cult practices. It's actually an altar, and one of the pieces located within it is called the Slaughter Stone."

Alan's face turned pale as he repeated the words of the cloaked man once again, "The lamb is close to the slaughter, and soon the One will be free."

"Yes," replied Elijah. "They're not going to London for a meeting. They're going to kill Curtis Norman at Stonehenge."

Simmons looked at Alan. "We need to go quickly."

"I will go check on Curtis's father, Howard Norman, and see what he guards."

"Be careful, Elijah," cautioned Alan, as he and Simmons hastily made their way out of the castle.

"Godspeed, my friends, Godspeed," Elijah yelled to them as they departed.

∾

It was very early morning, and the sun wasn't up yet as Alan and Simmons traveled down the A344 road approximately two miles west of Amesbury, England. As they drew near Stonehenge, Alan could see the large stone structure forming in the darkness. One particular stone set off to one side caught his attention, and he remembered the details from his college world history class many years ago.

"There's the Heel Stone," he said, pointing to the enormous rock that seemed to protrude from the ground. "I remember the tale surrounding the stone. It was also called the Friar's Heel because the legend told of a friar who claimed to have witnessed the devil placing the massive stones. The devil laughed and commented that nobody would ever be able to tell who placed the stones, but the friar yelled at him, saying that he would tell everyone. In a fit of anger, the devil threw a stone at the friar and struck him on the heel." Alan motioned toward the massive rock. "The stone then stuck in the ground."

Simmons nodded as Alan stopped the car. "Yes, but it wasn't exactly the devil, and the person the stone was tossed at was not a friar."

Alan was silent for a few seconds as his face contorted with confusion. "What do you mean? It was only a legend, or folklore."

"Glimpses of my memory are returning to me slowly. I was here the day that you speak of, battling one of The Fallen. She did throw the stone at me, and it did stick in the ground after it knocked over one of the Slaughter Stones. I defeated her up near the Altar Stone in the middle of the circle."

Alan sat stunned for a moment. "Which of The Fallen was it? Ellestria?"

"No, it was none of The Fallen that we've fought. She was much more powerful but of the same order as the others."

"Do you remember her name?"

"Arielle," said Simmons. "Let's go—we need to find Curtis."

The two exited the car and made their way up near the massive stones. Alan scanned the area as they walked, and within minutes they saw a figure lying on a massive stone slab on the ground in front of them. The sun slowly rose behind them and was starting to illuminate the ground.

"That is the Slaughter Stone," commented Simmons, pointing to the stone slab that was lying flat on the ground.

"Yes, and that's Curtis Norman." They ran to where Curtis was lying motionless. Alan looked him over and did not notice any stab wounds or other injuries. He checked for a pulse but found none. Tilting Curtis's head back, he blew two breaths into his mouth and administered CPR.

"He's dead, Alan."

"I'm not giving up on him yet," Alan insisted, as he continued to feverishly compress Curtis's chest with his hands. A bead of sweat ran down his face, dripped off his chin, and splashed onto the reddish stone block below. He felt the warmth of the sun creeping up his back, and, as a beam passed over his shoulder, he saw it illuminate the middle of the structure, striking the central stone that Simmons had called the Altar Stone.

"He's dead, Alan. Look, I can see the door!"

Alan glanced up at Simmons and saw that a door was now visible at ground level, set within the Altar Stone. Alan continued to give two more breaths.

"Come on, Alan, we need to get Curtis's soul through this door to where he needs to go. Then we can see if the others from the Order of Darkness fled into the Realm of Light."

Alan pushed down hard on Curtis's chest as Simmons reached for the door handle. All at once the door disappeared. "It's gone," Simmons said, astonished.

Alan wiped the sweat from his forehead and glanced up at Simmons. He, too, noticed that the door was no longer there. Placing two fingers on Curtis's neck, he yelled, "I think I've got a weak pulse!"

Simmons ran back to where Alan was huddled over Curtis and placed his hand on the young man's chest. "You did it, Alan! You brought him back!" Simmons's hand illuminated a faint radiant glow, and Curtis Norman sat up, coughing.

"I'm . . . I'm . . . alive," he said with disbelief, taking long, deep breaths. "I saw you guys coming up and was waiting to go through the door."

"Curtis, where did the others go who brought you here?"

Curtis pointed toward the center of the stone structure, where the Altar Stone was located. "There was a door in that stone block. They went through there."

"Quickly, then," urged Simmons, "we need to get back to the Realm of Light and locate them before it's too late."

CHAPTER 36

A Father's Duty

PATRICK KENT AND THE OTHER MEMBERS of the Order of Darkness quickly made their way to the place Howard Norman was guarding. They hurried through the narrow stone chasm and beyond a long field, where they saw the stone prison vault off in the distance.

"There it is," said Patrick, pointing toward the horizon. He was frustrated and upset because they had been delayed in accessing the Realm of Light and finding their target quickly. They had captured Curtis Norman and moved him around to avoid detection, but he couldn't understand why they had been told not to kill him like the others. For some reason, they had to poison him so he would die slowly, unlike the other victims, whose throats had been cut and their bodies stabbed with the ceremonial daggers.

"We should have already been here and gone by now," he grumbled to the others.

"I'm sure there was a good reason to poison the boy instead of stabbing him," replied Jack Stone, the billionaire record producer.

"Yeah, well, because of that poisoning crap, we were delayed in getting to the door that led us here. It would have been much easier to kill him quickly and get to where we needed to go. I hope nobody was tipped off. Alan and Michael were close on our trail."

"Stop your whining already, Kent. You're worse than my first four ex-wives combined," replied Stone.

Patrick whirled around and put his face very close to Stone's. "If anyone knows we're here and there's a welcoming party waiting for us, then you can kiss your rich ass good-bye, Stone."

"Both of you need to shut up," said Senator Jonathan McWilliam. "Let's get to where we need to go and follow the plan."

They continued walking along a high ridge that ran across the back side of the prison. Peering down, Patrick could see a tall, husky man with a white beard. "There he is—there's Howard Norman. I'll destroy him and get the key; everyone else wait here." He took out a long curved dagger with a jet-black blade.

Crawling on his belly down the ridge, Patrick hid behind the huge stone prison vault and wormed his way up to a large oak tree about ten feet away from where Norman was standing. Gripping the dagger tightly in his hand, he broke cover and ran toward his target, intent on burying the blade deep into his back. He was inches away from success when a gleaming light streaked toward him and knocked him back several feet, and he felt his chest explode. He looked down to see the gaping hole burned through the center of him, and then he fell to the ground, dead.

∾

Alan stood beside Simmons and noticed the rod reappear in his hand, then he saw Patrick Kent fall to the ground. Black smoke arose from Patrick's arm, where the tattoo that he possessed began to pulsate. Suddenly, a huge void appeared under his body and spread out into the ground like a spider web.

"Into the Darkness," said Alan, as he watched the soil under the body turn black from the void. He remembered the first time he had seen the tattoo on Kent's arm. It was during his battle with the forces of Darkness that Patrick had once led. An advisor had told Alan that Patrick had apparently struck a deal with a high-ranking member of the Darkness, who gave him the tattoo, which upon death would transport him to hell. He watched as the last remnants of the body were consumed by the black dirt, and he wondered what demon Patrick had bargained with for his perceived gift.

"Indeed," added Simmons. "Into the Darkness, where he belongs."

Curtis spotted his father and ran to him. The two embraced, and Curtis said, "I love you, Dad, and miss you."

"Oh, Curtis, I love you, too, and you'll be seeing more of me now. I'm glad to see that you've become the man I've always wanted you to be."

"What do you mean?" Curtis looked confused.

"You need to join Mr. Crane here to walk those in need to the Light. He'll show you what to do."

"Drop the rod," said a voice behind him. As Alan looked over, he saw Simmons drop his rod to the ground and noticed that there was a man standing behind him with a dagger held to Simmons's throat. Nine more people emerged from the ridge that ran behind the prison and surrounded them. They all drew black-bladed knives and held them ready.

"Hurry and get it," yelled the man who was holding Simmons at knifepoint.

Another man grabbed a large key from Howard Norman's belt and ran into the vault. A moment later he returned, holding a medium-size urn. "Got it," he yelled, as he held it up to show everyone.

"No!" yelled Mr. Norman.

"Yes, old man," replied the man holding the knife on Simmons. "These are the remains of Arielle The Fallen. Once we release this one into the world of the living, our victory will be swift." He then turned his attention to the others present. "We need to kill these four and return to the Realm of—"

The man was interrupted by a low rumbling sound that could be heard in the distance. It grew louder, and Alan could see the approach of soldiers dressed in white marble armor carrying an array of weapons. In the sky, there were streaks of gray that shot down and struck the ground like thunderbolts. When the dust settled, Alan stared at the massive elite warriors wearing their battle armor and wielding enormous hammers and swords.

Angels, he whispered. In an instant, there was an explosion, and one of the angels landed close to Alan and Simmons, knocking everyone to the ground—including the man who had been holding Simmons hostage, whom Alan now recognized as Jack Stone. Simmons quickly stood up and recovered his rod. The remaining members of the Order of Darkness threw down their weapons and surrendered.

From the back of the crowd, Elijah appeared. He snatched the urn of Arielle from the arms of the man holding it and disappeared back into the vault. Returning quickly, he said to Alan and Simmons, "You have done a great service today, by not only saving Curtis and Howard Norman, but also preventing Arielle from escaping into the world of the living. She was the leader of the other four and would have done great damage to those who still live. Thank you for your efforts."

Alan smiled. "Just glad to see all is well."

"Yes," replied Elijah, "all is—" His words were interrupted by another angel landing with an enormous crack and rumble. The huge figure walked up to Elijah and spoke in his ear.

"What?" said Elijah, looking shocked. "That can't be."

The huge angel nodded and spoke to him again.

"This is terrible! This is catastrophic! We must go—to Hollistrom!"

Alan yelled back to Curtis Norman, "Stay here with your father! We'll be back to get you soon!"

CHAPTER 37

The Fallen Throne

A S EVERYONE DEPARTED QUICKLY, Alan asked Simmons, "What is Hollistrom?"

"Hollistrom is our central vault, where we secure numerous members of The Fallen. It is the biggest one in the entire Realm of Light."

"So it's like a huge prison?"

"Exactly," replied Simmons.

"And which of The Fallen are held there?"

"All of them except for Arielle and the other four we recently defeated."

Alan shook his head in disbelief. "All of them? How many is *all* of them?"

Simmons looked pale as he quietly answered, "There are millions of them."

They followed Elijah and the others down a long cobblestone road. After ten minutes or so, Alan spotted what looked like a huge fortress. It was composed of large white marble blocks and rose hundreds of feet into the air, making it difficult to see the top. Hordes of warriors clad in white stone armor converged on this fortress, some on foot and some on horseback. Five angels plummeted from above and stopped about 100 yards from the main entrance. As they pushed forward, Alan could see why they were not rushing into Hollistrom.

Posted in front of the massive main gates were about 150 warriors clad in obsidian armor. This, in and of itself, would not have kept the forces of Light from advancing; however, in the very center of the group was a large figure with dark gray wings standing nearly fourteen feet tall. Alan was bewildered how this fallen angel could exist in the Realm of Light. In previous battles, he had fought with warriors of Darkness who channeled their power through man-sized voids in the ground that led to the Darkness, but he'd never seen a fallen angel in the Realm of Light.

The energy it would take to sustain such a thing would be tremendous, and, as powerful as The Fallen angels are in their own realm, the Darkness, they are equally weak in the Light. A soldier of Darkness who fell in battle would become old, weak, and crippled, but a fallen angel who ventured into the Realm of Light would become mere dust.

"Michael, do you see it?"

"Yes, and I recognize him."

"Who is he?"

"It is Gressil, who was once in the Order of Thrones before becoming one of The Fallen. He's more powerful than the other elite here, for they are what you would call 'regular angels.'"

"Is Gressil more powerful than the other Fallen we've encountered?"

"Yes, the others were from the Order of Virtues, which is the fifth rank of angels from the top. The Order of Thrones is third from the top. Gressil hasn't attacked yet and appears to be holding his ground."

"How is it possible that he can sustain himself here?"

Simmons shook his head. "I don't know; it would take an incredible source of power streamed from the Darkness. Stay here."

Simmons walked forward and made his way through the crowd. He gripped the white marble rod in his hands as he approached the front. The huge angel spotted him. "Michael, have you come to challenge me?"

"I'm curious why you're here," Simmons replied calmly.

"No, you're not, Michael, you're curious *how* I'm here." Gressil let out a booming laugh that caused the front lines of the forces of Light to back up a few steps.

Simmons held his ground. "So why are you here?"

"It's long overdue that we take control, Michael. The Day of Darkness is near."

"I don't think so," replied Simmons. "You cannot beat us, and you know that."

Anger surged through the jet-black eyes of Gressil as he roared like a beast. "You will fall, you arrogant gnat." His wings opened wide, and he drew a huge battle-ax from his back. More of the soldiers backed up, but Simmons readied his rod. Five angels clad in white armor walked up and stood beside Simmons as a show of solidarity. Gressil laughed an evil, horrifying laugh. "So I will kill you all, then."

Simmons hurled the rod at Gressil, and it streaked through the air like a thunderbolt. The huge dark figure brought the ax up, and the rod hit it, shooting a brilliant array of sparks in all directions and burning a superficial scar across the ax blade. Gressil brought the ax down near Simmons, who jumped out of the way.

The ground opened beneath the massive strike, and a huge chasm formed that swallowed up those who could not flee in time. The five angels flew up into the air and attempted to strike at Gressil's head with huge hammers and swords. As big as The Fallen angel was, he was nevertheless very agile and dodged all of the blows, except one that landed on the side of his head. The impact didn't seem to injure him, but it did daze him for a moment.

Simmons saw the opportunity to strike, and, as Gressil flew up into the air, Simmons hurled the rod, which penetrated one of his massive wings. It burned a large hole through the gray feathers, and Gressil howled in pain. The Fallen angel then landed and turned back toward the other hovering angels, who were now circling overhead trying to land other blows. His massive ax twirled in his hand and shot forth black streaks of light that struck two of the angels, causing them to plummet to the ground and explode into piles of fine white dust, which were consumed by a black void that formed underneath.

Gressil faced Simmons once again and brought the ax down hard for another strike. Simmons jumped backward, but it wasn't far enough. The very top of the ax struck downward toward his head, but he brought the rod upward, and it shaved off the top portion of the blade. He spun and brought the rod down hard on the angel's huge hand, burning a deep wound across the knuckles. Gressil roared with pain and anger as he jumped back and hurled the ax into the air toward the remaining three angels, who were still trying to land blows. The great ax moved with incredible speed and seemed to track two of them, swirling around and sending them hurling downward.

Gressil then brought a massive fist down in an attempt to crush Simmons, who sidestepped the blow, but this caused him to lose his balance and fall to one side. The huge angel quickly scooped him up with the other hand and gripped him tightly. The white marble rod fell to the ground, and Alan watched as Gressil tightened his grip, attempting to crush Simmons.

Alan sprinted down through the crowd toward the rod. He was unsure what it would do to him if he touched it, but there was no time to think about it. Simmons would soon be destroyed. Grabbing the rod in his hands, he felt a surge of power that coursed through his entire body. Strength surged in all of his muscles. Gritting his teeth, he swung the rod with every ounce of energy he possessed. It cut through the massive armored boot of Gressil's right leg and through the tissue just above his heel.

The Fallen angel shrieked as he fell to one knee and released Simmons, who rolled out of his massive hand. Gressil then turned in a fit of rage and brought his palm down hard in an attempt to pulverize Alan. Placing the end of the rod on the ground, Alan crouched as low as he could. The rod passed through The Fallen angel's palm, and Gressil withdrew his hand, which continued to burn from within. Fine black dust fell from the wound as The Fallen angel pulled the burning rod out with great effort and dropped it.

The warriors clad in obsidian armor advanced on Alan, who scrambled backward in an attempt to distance himself. Instantly, a soldier with a huge black-bladed sword closed in on him and raised his weapon to strike. Three gleaming streaks of light hit the soldier's chest before he could finish the attack, and Alan knew that the warriors of Light were beginning to engage the enemy.

A massive battle was now underway, and Alan watched as the soldiers on both sides fought intensely. He ducked behind a tree and saw flurries of arrows in both directions as streaks of black and white crossed in midair. Simmons had regained his footing and scrambled to retrieve his rod. Gressil was slowly making his way back to his feet, trying to keep his balance despite the injury to his ankle.

A group of warriors clad in black armor advanced on Simmons while two of their archers shot their arrows toward his chest. He spun the rod and quickly shattered the incoming projectiles, then turned to engage the others, dispersing them quickly. Gressil gripped the handle of the massive ax once more and pulled it from the ground. He held it high overhead and dropped another blow down toward Simmons, who jumped backward as the blade buried itself deep in the earth.

As Gressil was trying to free the ax from the ground once again, Simmons jumped onto the blade and ran up the angel's outstretched arm, like a cat scaling a tree. When he reached Gressil's shoulder, he leaped off, then plunged the rod deep into The Fallen angel's chest. The gigantic figure threw his head back and shrieked so loud it shook the ground. Simmons fell as Gressil exploded into black dust.

The battle raged on, and the last of the angels landed, smashing dozens of black-armored warriors who were now retreating into the prison. Alan made his way up to Simmons, and the two of them fought alongside the warriors of Light, pushing the enemy back into Hollistrom. The tide of the battle seemed to have completely turned in their favor as they breached the main gate and entered the huge marble fortress.

Alan scanned the surroundings, noting that the entire structure was lined with countless shelves that rose higher than the eye could see. His observation of the massive prison was interrupted by a terrifying sight: a huge black and purple vortex that spun deep into the floor like water circling a drain. Far above on the shelves were soldiers clad in black armor who were throwing urns into the spinning pool of darkness. As the urns hit and shattered, the black dust inside them formed into The Fallen, and Alan watched their dark gray wings glide downward into the maelstrom.

The soldiers of Light quickly scaled the sides of the tower, climbing the winding staircases that circled the outer edges. Their foes were quickly defeated, and Alan watched the dozens of black-armored figures plummet downward into the vortex.

Alan shouted, "What the hell is that, Michael?"

"I don't know. I've never seen a source of power like that before, but that explains how Gressil was able to exist in the Realm of Light."

As the last of the forces of Darkness fell, Elijah entered the room and scanned the walls. "So many were freed. So many of the captured Fallen are now back in their own realm—in the Darkness."

"So how do we fix this?" asked Alan.

"I don't know," replied Simmons, "but this is bad—really bad."

CHAPTER 38

A Father's Love

ALAN, SIMMONS, AND ELIJAH CONTINUED to stare at the whirling blackness piercing the floor. More warriors clad in white stone armor began arriving, along with other angels. They were all transfixed, gazing into the vortex until a voice from near the main entrance announced, "The Illissia Seritus has arrived."

"What's that mean?" Alan whispered to Simmons.

"The Illissia Seritus is the leader of the Order of the Seraphim, the highest rank among the elite warriors."

Alan noticed all of the soldiers and angels gettiing down on one knee. He followed suit and watched as an enormous figure glided through the threshold of the main entrance. It was the biggest angel he had ever seen. It stood eighteen feet tall with massive legs like large oak trees and two enormous white wings that ran the entire length of his body. His skin emitted a golden glow that rose like smoke.

Alan glanced at Simmons and Elijah, both of whom were awestruck by the giant's presence. The angel said nothing but simply walked to the center of the room and plunged his massive hand into the middle of the vortex. Alan watched as shards of light shot from the angel's fingertips and devoured the black whirlpool. The angel looked upward and seemed to be surveying the walls, then he turned back toward Alan, Simmons, and Elijah.

Alan gazed up at his eyes, which were crystal clear and hypnotic. The angel spoke in a soothing peaceful tone. "Elijah, how have you been?"

Elijah bowed. "Good, very good. However, today is a dark day."

"No need for the formalities," the angel said, smiling. "Everyone may stand up, and I would like to speak to you three for a moment." Alan, Simmons, and Elijah followed the angel as he walked to the very end of the room and peered upward. "It seems that only a few now remain. All the others have been freed."

Alan looked up at the shelves above and noticed there were large cabinet-like boxes standing open with damaged locks, which the soldiers of Darkness had cut their way through.

"Who was held in those?" asked Alan.

The angel answered, "Those were the leaders of the Darkness. You know some of their names: Asmodeus, Mephistopheles, Beelzebub, Arioch, and many others."

"Was Satan, or Lucifer, one of them?"

"He is their leader, but he was not among them. He was in the Darkness and now he has his army back."

Alan nodded, then asked, "May I humbly ask your name?"

"Oh, you know who I am, Light Bringer. I am the leader of the highest order of the elite—the Order of the Seraphim."

A look of recognition came over Alan's face. "You are Michael, the great archangel."

"Indeed," replied the archangel, "and I named my son after myself." He looked over at Simmons, who was in shock. "I see you still carry the rod I forged for you many years ago. How I've missed you, my son. Come, let us all walk. I've much to talk about."

The four of them left the prison and made their way out onto the countryside. As they walked, Simmons said, "Father, I don't remember most of my past. I was told that I had not been among the living for very long."

The archangel replied, "That is true. You were murdered as an infant, but I sent you back to walk among the living and help those in need. Your purpose is very important, because you will have to face great evil among the living and lead those who follow the Light to victory. You have been given great skill in battle, and that is why you were able to defeat The Fallen."

"How did all of this come about? How did the Darkness invade the prison and free The Fallen?"

The angel looked down as though a heavy burden had been placed upon him. "It seems that an elaborate scheme was put in place. The forces of Darkness led you to believe that they were out to free Arielle and the other four Fallen you encountered. But that was actually a distraction. They wanted you to find them attempting to free those five so they could make their way into Hollistrom as our forces were called to stop the assault on Arielle's vault."

"You mean everything surrounding the Order of Darkness, the murders, and the abduction of Curtis Norman was a hoax—a mere setup?"

"Yes, that's why they poisoned Curtis Norman instead of killing him. They wanted to delay the Order of Darkness from actually freeing Arielle so they would draw all of our nearby forces to aid in the defense."

Alan shook his head and felt guilty for being tricked.

The angel perceived his disappointment, "Do not burden your heart with such guilt, Light Bringer—for all things have an order, and that path is forged for a reason. We shall walk it together and find the meaning in the end when the Light reveals what is right and just."

Alan nodded his head and swept the guilt from his mind.

"Father," said Simmons. "We encountered a man among the living who seemed to have led the Order of Darkness. He knew me and seemed to know my past."

"Yes," replied the angel. "He is the leader of evil among the living, and your purpose is to face him again one day. Within two years, war will be upon us, and we must all prepare."

"But war is already upon us, right?" asked Alan. "I have seen many battles up here, and, as I have been told by Michael and another Light Bringer, battles are won or lost, but the war never ends." Alan's memory traveled back to the time he took the place of a fallen Light Bringer named Darion in order to defeat the forces of Darkness.

"The skirmishes you have seen are small and quick. The real war has not yet begun, and in the end, there will be a victor."

They continued to follow the archangel, who led them down a narrow cobblestone walkway. They came to a small wooden bridge that traversed a running stream.

"Go across the bridge and into the meadow, Michael; further answers await you there. I must take my leave now." The archangel spread his great white wings, and the gold smoke rising from his skin intensified. He shot from the ground with ease and disappeared in a stream of light.

Alan, Simmons, and Elijah crossed the bridge, and Simmons could now see a large meadow with a single huge oak tree off to the right. Below the tree was a small stone bench where a woman was seated. Her dark-brown hair blew gently in the breeze as she sat with a small blanket in her arms. As they drew closer, she stood, and Simmons saw that she was slim and petite with grayish-blue eyes. He looked into her face and a realization engulfed him. "Mother?"

The woman embraced him, and he returned the embrace. She smiled brightly. "I've missed you so much. You were only a baby the last time I held you. This was the blanket I had you wrapped in before you were stolen from me. I'm so proud of you, Michael."

Simmons was stunned and could find no words except "I love you."

She looked around and noticed Elijah, whom she hugged, "Good to see you again."

"Good to see you, Marissa. I had feared the worst after you died. We fled and thought that maybe we would have to walk you to the Realm of Light, but we couldn't find you. We feared that you had been captured and taken to the Realm of Darkness."

Marissa nodded. "I was taken there and held for thousands of years. Then recently there was a commotion outside the cell area where I was imprisoned, and three people showed up to free me. One was a missionary named Sister Lucille Franconi. They carried me out of the Darkness, since I was too weak to leave on my own, and returned me to the Realm of Light."

"Sister Franconi?" Alan looked confused. "She was just killed this year."

"Yes, and her missionary work was actually rescuing those from the Darkness. She is a wonderful person."

"So you've been in the Darkness all these years?" asked Simmons, as pity enveloped his face.

"Yes, but I'm free now, so don't despair—but there is more I must tell you. Michael, you have a brother and a sister who were born at the same time you were."

"Triplets?" Alan inquired.

"Yes," nodded Marissa. "You were abducted and killed when you were a baby. Your brother and sister were taken and hidden among the living to protect them. Your sister's birth name is Alona and your brother is Artonis. I'm unsure what they go by now, but they are not aware of who they are. Neither of them can be killed by the living, since they've been alive for thousands of years—the living call them immortal."

"But how was I killed if we were immortal?" asked Simmons.

"You were killed by an agent of the Darkness using a weapon forged in their realm. That will end the life of an immortal."

"Do you know where they are?" Simmons was now very curious about his siblings.

"No, I lost track of them; I was in the Darkness for so long. Most likely they are not aware of who they really are or where they came from—only that they cannot die. You must seek them out and convince them to join you in the coming war."

"But how will I know who they are or how to find them, for that matter?"

"You must look for signs of their immortality. Alan and Elijah can help, and so can the Disciples of Light. When you find them, you will know." Simmons nodded, and his mother smiled at him, then glanced over at the rod that he was leaning on. "Your father crafted that rod for you after you died. He said he wanted you to have a weapon that would protect you from the Darkness. It was forged in the heart of a star called Manacopia. The process consumed the star, condensing and harnessing all of its energy and brilliance into the rod. It contains all that is right and just. Keep it close; it is very powerful, and you will need it when you battle the evil that will soon rise."

She hugged Alan and Elijah first, then embraced Simmons and kissed him on the cheek. "Dark paths lie before us, but the light of dawn will always shatter the night. Seek out the other two and bring light to those dark places."

CHAPTER 39

The New Apprentice

S WEAT DRIPPED DOWN CURTIS NORMAN'S FACE as he made his way to the police academy locker room, where he quickly showered and changed, along with the other recruits in his class. As he put on his standard-issue gray academy uniform, his hand brushed over the scar that ran around his throat, and he briefly reflected on how close he had come to death on several occasions. It was the end of the day, and he was dead tired, ready to go home and rest. He loaded his books into a huge duffel bag and made his way out to the parking lot.

As he was walking through the lot, a gray Ford Crown Victoria pulled up in front of him, and the passenger-side window rolled down.

"Hey, Lieutenant Crane," Curtis greeted the driver.

"How was your day, Curtis?"

"Not bad, but extremely exhausting."

"Good," replied Alan. "Get in; we have some work to do."

Curtis looked slightly confused, but he threw his bag into the backseat and then buckled himself into the front seat.

"Where are we going, Lieutenant?"

"We have to help some people. You have a good future ahead of you, Curtis, but you have to learn the ropes, and we don't have much time to teach you."

"Oh, uh—okay."

"So what did you learn today, Curtis?"

"We did some defensive tactics, and we had some training on emergency childbirthing—had to watch a video on that one."

"Ah, yes, I remember that video—very graphic. Did anyone get nauseous?"

Curtis chuckled. "Well, there were a few people who looked a bit pale."

"And how about you—was the childbirthing video too much for you?" Alan was teasing him a bit.

"Shoot, no," Curtis replied in his southern accent. "I'm a country boy, Lieutenant. I've seen cows and horses born—ain't no big deal to me."

Alan laughed. "Well, that's good—guess you'll have a handle on that part of the job."

"You bet," Curtis agreed. "By the way, sir, where are we going again?"

"Like I said, we have to help some people. You'll see."

They continued traveling down the road for a few minutes, then turned into an old subdivision, where Alan stopped the car in front of a vintage brick house. There were two police cars parked in the driveway and a uniformed officer standing on the front porch. Curtis followed Alan into the house and down a short hallway to a bedroom. Crime scene technicians were photographing the body of an elderly man who was sprawled on the floor in a large pool of blood. Alan noticed the familiar wounds: the man's neck was slashed on each side, and there were multiple stab wounds on his torso. This was the third murder in two months, and Alan could tell by the stab wounds that a new Order of Darkness had formed since the battles he had been involved in three months ago.

Alan said to the crime scene technicians, "Can we have a moment to survey the scene?"

The techs nodded and made their way out of the room. Alan closed the door behind them, then bent down close to the corpse and examined the puncture marks, which appeared to all have been made by the same weapon—except for the wound in the very center of the chest. He drew out a small penlight and pointed the beam down into the central wound.

"Come closer, Curtis. You need to see this."

Curtis bent down and watched Alan move the beam of light near the opening in the victim's chest, which looked like a deep black hole. The light was sucked into the hole and absorbed. Curtis's eyes grew wide. "The light is being sucked into that wound. I've hunted all my life and killed lots of animals but have never seen anything like that. What is that, Lieutenant?"

"It's the Darkness, Curtis. This wound was made by one of its soldiers' weapons. The light is absorbed into it. I wanted you to see this and remember it so you recognize it in the future. This is the third victim we've had in two months, and although none of the victims were of similar age, race, background, or location, they all had something in common."

"What's that?" inquired Curtis.

"Aside from their current or former careers, all of them did some type of volunteer work to help people."

"I'm not quite following you, Lieutenant."

Alan explained. "The first murder victim was a teenage girl who organized a movement to discourage teen drinking and drug abuse. She had seen her best friend die in a car accident where they had been struck by a driver who was drunk and high. The second victim was a very wealthy businessman who owned a shoe company. He made millions of dollars per year, but for every pair of shoes that his company sold, he gave a pair away to children in poverty-stricken areas who would never have owned a pair of shoes otherwise."

"And who is this man?" asked Curtis, staring down at the corpse.

"This man was Ben Wilds. He retired many years ago and became a motivational speaker. In his early years, Ben had been in a great deal of trouble with the law. On one occasion, he had broken into a steel mill. As he was running across an overhead catwalk, he lost his footing and fell directly over a large vat of molten metal. He continued to fall closer and closer to the red-hot liquid—so close that it began to sear his flesh.

"Blinded by the extreme heat, the last thing he saw was a large figure with great wings who grabbed him just before he hit and pulled him to safety. The being healed all of Ben's wounds except for his eyes and told him that although he was now blind, he would be able to see the truth more clearly than most other people do. That lesson was engrained in his heart, and he went forth to fulfill the message of hope that his rescuer had bestowed upon him. Turning over a new leaf, he became a great motivational speaker. His speaking engagements included not only businesses, schools, and youth groups but also prisons and jails, where he was very successful at teaching the importance of values and the fact that it's never too late to change."

"Wow," said Curtis, with a blank look.

"You see, Curtis, all of these people were trying to encourage others to take the right path. They were bringing people to the Light."

"Who killed him?"

"If I had to guess, I would say that it's those that are working for the Darkness. I'm not sure who committed the murders, but perhaps we can ask Ben himself and find out."

At that moment, the old man's spirit stood up, and Curtis jumped back in shock.

"Hey, I can see again," Ben said with a grin.

"Sorry," said Curtis. "I've seen my father, who died years ago, and I know about the place people go after they die, but I just didn't expect a dead man to get up."

"No problem," replied Alan. "It's always shocking the first time you experience it. Well, let's get moving," he added, opening the closet door, and the three of them stepped into a dark marble hallway.

After Alan and Curtis had escorted Ben Wilds to the Realm of Light, they returned to Alan's car and left the scene. They had not missed a moment of time. Alan drove Curtis back to his mother's house and stopped in to visit.

Mrs. Norman was very pleased to see Alan and thanked him once again for not only finding and saving Curtis but also helping him to get into the police academy. Alan hugged her as he left and told Curtis that he would be back soon with other assignments. Curtis removed his father's watch from his wrist and flipped it over, rubbing his thumb across the inscription as he read it aloud: "Honor the Light."

Alan nodded. "Indeed, honor the Light." Then he stepped out the door and headed back home.

～

As Alan walked into his house and entered his kitchen, he noticed that dinner was already on the table, and Missy must have convinced his wife to allow her friend Peter to come over and eat. The two children sat near each other on one side of the table, and Alison smiled at Alan as he sat down. "You're a bit late. Did something happen at work?"

Alan nodded and whispered in her ear so the kids could not hear him. "Another man was murdered."

"Oh, no, that's terrible," she said aloud.

"What's wrong, Mommy?" asked Missy.

Alison hesitated for a moment. "Uh, nothing, honey. Daddy just had a bad day at work."

"Oh, I'm sorry, Daddy," Missy said, looking sad.

"Thank you, but I'll be okay," replied Alan, smiling at her.

Everyone bowed their heads, and Alan said a prayer before they ate. Alison was a great cook. She and her father had run a family-owned French bakery. The meal was delicious, and, as they ate, Alan asked Missy and Peter, "What did you two learn in preschool today?"

"We learned how to make a heart from red paper," said Missy proudly.

Alan smiled. "And what about you, Peter?"

"Our teacher read us a book."

"Ah, and what was the book about?"

"Well, it wasn't a very good book, but it was about stars."

Alan grinned at Alison, who also seemed amused by Peter's comments. "So why wasn't the book very good?"

"It said that stars are made from gas, but that's so silly. Everyone knows that stars are made from God, and gas is what my mommy puts in her car."

Alan laughed, then said, "You know, I believe you're right, Peter. You are a very smart kid—just like Missy."

Missy giggled and smiled at Alan.

As they finished eating, Alison brought out a large plate of fruit-filled crepes covered in chocolate syrup. Alan split one in half, placed the halves on two small plates, and gave one to each of the children. "So have you guys seen that old scary man who talked to you when you had the lemonade stand?"

"No," said Missy, shaking her head.

"He's not a nice man," replied Peter. "And he's a stranger. I don't talk to strangers."

Alan nodded. "That's very smart to do, Peter. Never talk to strangers, and if they try to talk to you, tell your mommy or daddy or someone you trust."

"Well, I scared him away," said Peter confidently. "He won't come back."

Alan politely disagreed. "Sometimes strangers do come back, so you have to be careful."

Peter shook his head. "No, he won't come back. He'll leave us alone. I'm sure."

Alan was somewhat curious about Peter's confidence, so he asked, "Peter, how do you know that the man won't come back?"

Peter's green eyes gleamed as he smiled at Alan. "Oh, I just know."

CHAPTER 40

The Champion
of the Light

MICHAEL SIMMONS BENT DOWN AND PLACED the wreath on his mother's grave. He walked out into the field beyond the garden and up onto the mountainside where he had defeated The Fallen many years ago. His strength had increased tenfold since he had learned more about his past, because the knowledge made him more powerful. Heaving an enormous stone block onto his back, he carried it back to the garden and placed it behind his mother's grave. The white marble rod burned into the stone as he began carving a huge sculpture. When he had finished, a giant statue of his father stood majestically above his mother's grave. He whispered the words to both of them. "I will not fail you—I promise." With that, he made his way out of the castle and back up to the shore off the island of Skyros.

His journey was long. He walked for many miles across land and sea until he finally arrived at a place where four rivers came together. A great waterfall stood before him that fed the four rivers, and he climbed to the top, then plunged into the huge body of water beneath him. Some instinct was pulling him toward the bottom, calling out to him. He continued downward, his rod illuminating the way.

Finally he came to a great barrier that separated the water and the air like a huge dome, similar to that of the Lost City. The area was too big to see the other side, and, as Simmons began to walk, he marveled at the intense beauty of his surroundings. The lush green grass blew gently in the breeze, and the soft illumination overhead appeared to be sunlight. There were trees of every kind growing on all sides and bearing fruit and colorful leaves. Breathing deeply, he took in the sensational aroma of blooming flowers and plants, which was almost intoxicating. He had seen many places, but this was perhaps one of the most stunning in all of his travels.

As he crossed a huge orchard, the terrain seemed to gradually rise into a rolling hill, and eventually he came to a path made of tiny polished stones that let into an enormous grove of massive trees. Just beyond the trees stood a small lake of crystal-clear water. Dipping his hand into the cool liquid, he drank. As the water ran down his throat, it filled him with energy and cleared his mind. He waded through the water, since it was not very deep and there was no way around it. He came out on the other side and followed the stone path, which continued there.

Walking along, he sensed that he was nearing the source that was drawing him. As the path led into a great clearing, he saw something that made him hesitate for a moment. A huge ornate iron gate stood in the background, and a giant winged figure stood in front of it.

"Do not fear, Michael, come closer," the angel said in a deep booming voice.

Simmons walked a bit closer and clutched his rod as a safety measure, as he focused on the huge flaming sword that the angel held in his hand. "Who are you?" asked Simmons.

"I am the archangel Uriel, the guardian of this place."

"And what is this place?"

"It has been called many things, but it is the place where it all began—

where life and humanity grew from the dust."

Simmons kept hold of his rod as he spoke. "I don't know why, but I felt drawn to this place for some reason. Have you summoned me here?"

"Not I," replied the angel. "The Light has guided you to this place. As you know, war will soon be upon us, and it's time to fulfill the prophecy and ready ourselves."

"Tell me of the prophecy, Uriel," requested Simmons.

Flames danced off the angel's great blade as he said in his thunderous voice, "War will be at hand, and the Light shall bestow the power upon a champion to lead the living into battle. The power is of clarity, and the clarity is of knowing."

"Am I that champion?"

"You are, indeed," declared Uriel.

"What must I do?"

"Beyond this gate lies a tree. It has been forever forbidden to eat of its fruit until such time as the Light sees fit to ready humanity for war. Pick only one piece of fruit, and take but one bite. Follow these instructions implicitly."

"I will do as you have directed," replied Simmons.

"Go, now, and fulfill what needs to be done."

The angel swung open the massive gates, which were lined with ivy. Simmons made his way through, and the small path led him to a tree whose trunk must have measured at least thirty feet in diameter. It was too tall for Simmons to see the top, and it emitted a silver smoke that wafted upward—similar to the gold dust that had risen from his father's skin.

As he drew nearer to the branches, he saw gleaming golden apples hanging down. They were perfect in size and shape, with absolutely no blemishes or marks on them anywhere. Carefully, he plucked one and held it in both hands as though it were a fragile piece of art. He drew it close to his mouth and bit into the crisp golden skin. The taste was an overwhelming sweet sensation of juice that appealed to all of his senses.

After that first bite, he was so very tempted to take another; instead, he carefully placed the apple on the ground and turned back toward the pathway out. His mind was spinning as energy surged through his body, and a keen sense of clarity filled his consciousness.

As he began to walk out, another winged figure stood in front of him blocking his way. Simmons clutched his rod, uncertain of her intentions.

"You need to take another bite," the angel said, as she landed behind him and picked up the fruit he had bitten.

"No, I was instructed to take only one bite."

"Your power will not be enough to claim victory if you do not eat the entire fruit."

"I know this story, and I know this game," replied Simmons. "I am not of the living, and temptations such as this will not entice me."

Still clutching the apple, she circled him, blocking the way to the path that led out.

"Move out of my way," Simmons commanded. "I know you are one of The Fallen—now move!"

"I am subservient to no man," she hissed as she lunged at him.

He quickly parried her attack and struck her down with his rod, reducing her to a pile of black dust.

As he made his way back to where Uriel stood, the gate closed behind him and the angel said, "Good, you have passed the test and have been loyal to the Light. You have my honor and respect. May you be swift in victory, and may the Light shine upon you."

CHAPTER 41

A Call to Arms

I T WAS EARLY SUNDAY MORNING, and Alan stared out the window as the sun glistened off the dew that dripped from an ash tree in his front yard. Alison and Missy walked out into the living room, and Alan smiled at both of them.

"Dad, do you like my dress?" Missy asked, twirling around so he could see all the multicolored butterflies around the middle.

"Oh, it's just beautiful," replied Alan.

"Okay, let's get going," said Alison, holding the door open for everyone to leave.

They arrived at their church early, and Alan admired the old eighteenth-century stone and brick. The large wooden doors in the front led into a room with a high vaulted ceiling with two sections of pews and a center aisle. At the very front of the church was a raised section that contained the altar. The distinct sound of an old-fashioned pipe organ bellowed familiar hymns as Alan, Missy, and Alison found seats near the middle.

More people made their way in, and within minutes the church was filled. Alan wasn't paying much attention as a procession made its way down the center aisle. He was absorbed in his usual routine of prayer as he thanked God for all of the things that made his life so great. As he finished praying, the service started and a familiar voice was reciting the Mass. Alan strained hard to see who the familiar voice was, and, as they came to the scripture reading, he saw Elijah step to a podium off to one side.

"Elijah," he whispered. "Who?" Alison whispered back.

"The priest—I know the priest."

He felt a hand on his left shoulder and turned to see Simmons standing behind him, smiling.

"Michael," he whispered as he returned the smile.

Elijah started reading from the book of Revelation: "When he opened the fourth seal, I heard the voice of the fourth living creature saying, 'Come and see.' So I looked, and behold, a pale horse. And the name of him who sat on it was Death, and Hell followed with him. And power was given to them over a fourth of the earth, to kill with a sword, with hunger, with death, and by the beasts of the earth."

The church was silent, and Elijah paused for ten seconds or so and then spoke. "Brothers and sisters, we are all called to serve, and someday we will all be called to fight for God. We will fight for all that is right and good. But over the years, we have become complacent and lazy. We have become vulnerable to attack and to the temptation of the Darkness. If we do not unite all of those who are good, all of those who want to walk in the Light, then we will be doomed. As I look around, I can see inside one's soul, and now is the time to cleanse it for the sake of humanity. "

He stepped off the podium and made his way down the aisle. Glancing around the church, he noticed that there were many who were not paying much attention. Alan noticed him nod to Simmons, who flashed him a smile. Elijah continued to speak. "God enlightens us all, and when we become distracted, He shines His everlasting light down upon us to illuminate the way."

Simmons stretched his neck upward, and, as he did, the once overcast sky above the church gave way to the sun as radiant beams of light streamed down through the old stained-glass windows. A marvelous display of color filled the church, and those who were not paying attention suddenly turned to hear what Elijah was going to proclaim next.

"The war between good and evil will come, and you can make a difference. Go out and be that person who shows kindness and compassion to others. The will of man will prevail . . . the will of man will prevail."

All eyes were now on Elijah as he made his way back to the altar and continued with the service. The Mass came to an end, and all of the congregants made their way out of the church. Elijah met Simmons and Alan and his family in the back vestibule, and they walked out the main doors together and down the stone stairs. Alison and Missy made their way to the car as Alan continued to walk with the other two. The beautiful sky was gleaming brightly overhead, and Alan asked, "Michael, did you have something to do with this weather?"

"Perhaps," replied Simmons. "I've learned many things lately that have allowed me access to newfound abilities."

"Abilities that we will need for the future fight," added Elijah.

"We will conquer it together, just as we've done so in the past," said Alan, which brought a smile to all of their faces. The church bells tolled as they made their way to the parking lot. A dark-gray storm cloud moved in and covered up the sun, threatening rain.

Elijah looked up. "See, Michael, one can only control the weather for so long. After that, it's unpredictable."

Simmons nodded. "So right you are, Elijah . . . so right you are."

The church was now empty except for the organ player, who had just finished the last hymn. He stretched his bony skeleton-like fingers and raised his dark hood over his head; he knew that it would be raining outside very soon because of the storm he had just summoned. His face broke into an evil grin as he hissed, "The will of man will fail, and Darkness will prevail." His fingers danced over the keys of the old pipe organ as he played Bach's *Toccata and Fugue in D minor* and laughed sinisterly. "The will of man is dead."

ACKNOWLEDGMENTS

OUR SINCERE APPRECIATION GOES OUT TO the special people in our lives who made this second book possible. To Tom and Betty Hill, who continue to inspire us by being Light Bringers in our lives. To Janet Bettag and Nikole Behlmann, who helped with our initial edits, and a special thanks to Patty Force, who spent countless hours preparing and formatting the final manuscript for submission. A special thanks to our literary agent Linda Langton for all her support.

Thanks to the great people at HCI Books who helped us mold this into a fantastic adventure. To our early readers, Roberta Van Haag and Terri and Mickey Olsen, who aided us with encouragement and support. Thanks to Jim Modglin for our book trailer.

Once again we need to thank our wives, Patty and Nicole, who keep us walking in the Light!

Thanks to all of the other people who read the drafts at different stages and gave us the needed compliments, criticisms, and endorsements that enabled us to continue this story.

A very special thanks to all of our Light Bringer fans, who have followed us through this amazing adventure with the first book in this series.

This acknowledgment page would not be complete or honest if we didn't put credit where it was truly deserved and thank God for His wisdom, guidance, and clarity. Without His love we would be nothing.

From us to all of you: Thank you, God bless, and stay safe.

In great moments of despair, there comes great clarity.

ABOUT THE AUTHORS

Lisa Hohenshell

CHRIS DIGIUSEPPI is an award-winning coauthor of *The Light Bringer*—his first novel, which made the St. Louis bestseller list in 2011. He has over twenty years experience in law enforcement at various levels, up to and including assistant chief of police. He is a graduate of the FBI National Academy and Northwestern University School of Police Staff Command. He is trained in various aspects of law enforcement and holds degrees in both human resources and business administration. Chris lives with his wife and children in Missouri. Visit the author at www.thelightbringerbook.com.

Lisa Hohenshell

MIKE FORCE is an award-winning coauthor of *The Light Bringer*, which made the St. Louis bestseller list in 2011. Mike has spent over thirty years in law enforcement and over twenty years as a police chief. He has numerous certifications in various areas of law, forensics, investigations, and criminology. He is a graduate of the FBI National Academy and served twenty-two years in the US Marines where he oversaw operations for twenty-seven military installations worldwide and ultimately retired as a captain. He holds degrees in political science and human resources. Mike lives with his wife in Missouri and has three grown children and a granddaughter. *The Fallen* is his second novel. Visit the author at www.thelightbringerbook.com.